"You're wearing a disguise, Addy McConnell.

"You wrap yourself up in plain-Jane clothes and pretend you're an iceberg."

"It . . . it isn't a disguise." Her words came out choppily, on quick, heated little breaths. Nick had kissed her more thoroughly than she'd ever been kissed in her life, and she was still reeling from the aftereffects. "I *am* a plain Jane who dislikes chest-beating Neanderthal men. And I *am* an iceberg. Just ask my ex-husband."

Nick walked away from her, then turned when he reached the door. "Why should I ask that bastard anything, when I got all the proof I needed, firsthand, that you're hot as a firecracker?"

"I am not!"

Nick grinned. "That was a compliment, Red. I like my women hot."

"I am not one of your women."

Nick looked back at Addy. "But you will be. . . ."

Dear Reader,

It's another great month for Silhouette Intimate Moments! If you don't believe me, just take a look at our American Hero title, *Dragonslayer*, by Emilie Richards. This compelling and emotionally riveting tale could have been torn from today's headlines, with a minister hero whose church is in one of the inner city's worst neighborhoods and whose chosen flock includes the down and out of the world. In this place, where gang violence touches everyone's lives—and will continue to touch them throughout the book in ways you won't be able to predict—our hero meets a woman whose paradoxical innocence will force him to confront his own demons, his own inner emptiness, and once more embrace life—and love. *Dragonslayer* is a *tour de force*, not to be missed by any reader.

The rest of the month is terrific, too. Marilyn Pappano, Doreen Roberts, Marion Smith Collins, Beverly Barton and new author Leann Harris offer stories that range from "down-home" emotional to suspenseful and dramatic. You'll want to read them all.

And in months to come look for more irresistible reading from such favorite authors as Justine Davis, Linda Turner, Paula Detmer Riggs, *New York Times* bestsellers Heather Graham Pozzessere and Nora Roberts, and more—all coming your way from Silhouette Intimate Moments, where romantic excitement is always the rule.

Yours,

Leslie J. Wainger
Senior Editor and Editorial Coordinator

PALADIN'S WOMAN

Beverly Barton

Silhouette™

INTIMATE MOMENTS®

Published by Silhouette Books New York

America's Publisher of Contemporary Romance

SILHOUETTE BOOKS
300 East 42nd St., New York, N.Y. 10017

PALADIN'S WOMAN

Copyright © 1993 by Beverly Beaver

All rights reserved. Except for use in any review, the reproduction
or utilization of this work in whole or in part in any form by any
electronic, mechanical or other means, now known or hereafter
invented, including xerography, photocopying and recording, or in
any information storage or retrieval system, is forbidden without
the permission of the publisher, Silhouette Books, 300 E. 42nd St.,
New York, N.Y. 10017

ISBN: 0-373-07515-4

First Silhouette Books printing August 1993

All the characters in this book have no existence outside the
imagination of the author and have no relation whatsoever to
anyone bearing the same name or names. They are not even
distantly inspired by any individual known or unknown to the
author, and all incidents are pure invention.

®: Trademark used under license and registered in the United States
Patent and Trademark Office and in other countries.

Printed in the U.S.A.

Books by Beverly Barton

Silhouette Intimate Moments

This Side of Heaven #453
Paladin's Woman #515

Silhouette Desire

Yankee Lover #580
Lucky in Love #628
Out of Danger #662
Sugar Hill #687
Talk of the Town #711
The Wanderer #766
Cameron #796

BEVERLY BARTON

has been in love with romance since her grandfather gave her an illustrated book of *Beauty and the Beast*. An avid reader since childhood, she began writing at the age of nine, and wrote short stories, poetry, plays and novels throughout high school and college. After marriage to her own ''hero'' and the births of her daughter and son, she chose to be a full-time home-maker, a.k.a. wife, mother, friend and volunteer.

Six years ago, she began substitute teaching and returned to writing as a hobby. In 1987, she joined Romance Writers of America and soon afterward helped found the Heart of Dixie chapter in Alabama. Her hobby became an obsession as she devoted more and more time to improving her skills as a writer. Now, her lifelong dream of being published has come true.

Special thanks to several good friends:
Gail Froelich, my Huntsville tour guide;
Edna Waits, for all the research material;
Willie Wood, for being a good listener and
giving great advice; and Linda Howington, for
reasons too numerous to list, but especially for
giving me a great title.

Prologue

Hoisting the beer bottle toward the woman sitting on the edge of the bed, he saluted her, his mouth widening into a smirk. "Tonight's the night."

"Are you sure?" Leaning down, she picked up the black silk robe from the floor. "If everything doesn't work perfectly and your man botches things, her daddy will call in a bodyguard like that." She snapped her fingers, her sharp mauve nails clicking together.

Reaching out, he circled her neck, caressing her naked flesh. "Don't you have any confidence in me?"

"Of course." She glared at him, a mixture of desire and fear in her eyes. "I just don't want anything to go wrong. We've worked very hard and been planning for a long time. There's so much at stake."

Gliding his hand downward, he cupped her breast, flicking his nail across the tight nipple. "Millions and millions."

She sighed when his caress roughened. "If anything goes wrong—"

He laughed. "Nothing will."

"Kidnapping is a federal offense. We could both wind up in prison. I just wish there were some other way. I hate the thought of—"

"Don't think about anything except all that beautiful money Rusty McConnell's going to lose to keep his precious Addy safe." He shoved her down on the bed, straddling her hips.

"You won't hurt Addy. You promise?"

"She won't be hurt. My guy said he'd use chloroform, then keep her bound and blindfolded until Big Daddy gives us what we want." He touched his lips to hers, whispering into her mouth. "You know I wouldn't lie to you."

All the while he took his pleasure with one woman, he thought of another. Addy McConnell. Sweet, sweet Addy. He had no intention of harming her—not until he'd taken what he wanted from her—not until her father had followed instructions and the authorities were off on a wild-goose chase. He really didn't want to kill Addy, but he didn't have any choice. Once his plan went into action and he'd accomplished everything he set out to do, Addy would have to die.

Chapter 1

Who was he? Addy McConnell wondered. He didn't belong here. She was certain of that. Despite the fact that he wore a black tuxedo similar to the ones worn by most of the men in the room, he didn't blend into the crowd. For one thing, he was taller than the average man, at least six foot three, and his big, muscular body appeared constrained by the confines of his well-fitting clothes. His black hair, though cut conservatively short, was slicked back away from his dark face, and a band of thick waves curled about his neck. His cheekbones were broad and high, his chin square with a slight cleft. A pair of deep-set brown eyes surveyed the gathering of Huntsville's social elite.

And a small diamond stud glittered in his left ear.

No, Addy thought, whoever he is, neither she nor her father had invited him to the party. That meant he was either a friend of Dina's, or he had crashed the engagement celebration of the year.

She'd been watching him for at least ten minutes, but the

man hadn't glanced her way. He appeared to be either distracted or bored. Perhaps both.

Addy hadn't missed the way most of the women in the room kept looking at him. Several had made advances. When he'd smiled and spoken to those women, they'd practically melted at his feet. A charmer. A Latin lover. A very dangerous man. All those expressions flashed through Addy's mind.

When a waiter offered him a drink, he declined. Using the black cane he held in his right hand, he limped away from the young brunette who'd been trying, in vain, to attract his attention.

Addy wondered what had caused his limp. He leaned heavily on the gold-tipped cane. Bracing himself against the wall near the French doors, he closed his eyes. She noticed a sudden tremor in his hand that clutched the walking stick, and knew he was in pain. Some irrational emotion stirred within her. She wanted to ease his pain.

With a disgusted grunt, Addy looked away, scanning the room for sight of a familiar face, anyone who would take her mind off the mysterious dark stranger. She really didn't know what was wrong with her. Men, as a general rule, didn't interest her much. Her ex-husband had cured her of any desire she'd ever had to experience the joys of a sexual relationship. So, why did this man, this dangerous-looking interloper, fascinate her so much?

"He's gorgeous, isn't he?" Janice Dixon said. "Can you imagine what he looks like without his clothes?"

Addy tried not to laugh at her cousin's comment. Petite and bosomy, Janice Ann Dixon issued an invitation to the male sex without even trying. But being a highly sensual creature, Janice took every advantage of what Mother Nature had given her.

"I'm sure he'd be willing to oblige, if you asked him," Addy said.

"You think he's easy, huh?"

"No." Addy suspected that despite the fact the handsome stranger emitted an easy charm, a dark and perhaps even troubled soul existed beneath his captivatingly smooth exterior. "But he most definitely is a man, and I've yet to see a man you couldn't seduce."

Janice snorted, the sound mingled with laughter. "I don't know if I should be flattered or offended."

"Be flattered."

"You seem unduly interested in our mysterious *señor*." Janice glanced across the room, then nudged Addy in the side. "He's going out onto the patio. Why don't we follow him?"

"Go right ahead." Addy had never chased a man, never followed one, never pursued one in any way, shape, form or fashion, and she certainly had no intention of starting now. Thirty-five was definitely too old to change the habits of a lifetime.

Long-legged and elegant in her purple silk jumpsuit, Ginger Kimbrew slipped her arm around Addy's shoulder. "Every woman in the room is in heat, and I see that includes both of you."

"Go away, Ginger," Janice said. "If three women follow him outside, it'll be a bit obvious, don't you think?"

"I don't have to follow him. We've already been introduced." Smiling, Ginger eyed Addy. "You have no idea who he is, do you?"

"No," Addy said. "Should I?" She turned to face her father's private secretary.

"I take it that dear step-mommy-to-be hasn't introduced you."

Addy was well aware of the animosity between her father's fiancée Dina Lunden and his most valued employee of ten years. Dina resented any attractive woman in Rusty's life, and Ginger, who had hoped her position as mistress would one day be elevated to wife, hated the woman who'd finally trapped the man she wanted. "Dina invited him?" Addy asked.

"She most certainly did." Ginger's smile widened, her lavender-shadowed eyelids almost closing.

"How do you know?" Janice turned her head quickly, looking up at the taller woman.

"I asked him," Ginger said, grinning, her wide red mouth exposing a set of perfect white teeth. "I introduced myself and asked if he'd crashed the party or if he had an invitation."

"You did what?" Addy stared at Ginger, amazed anew at the woman's lack of manners. But then, Addy admitted that many of the new breed of Southern women didn't worry overly much about manners. Her grandmother, mother and aunt would have been appalled.

"He's Dina's brother-in-law." Ginger seemed delighted to be the one with so much information on the most interesting man at Dina Lunden and D.B. "Rusty" McConnell's engagement celebration. "Well, actually, ex-brother-in-law is more accurate. He's Dina's first husband's brother."

"Dina seems to stay on friendly terms with all her former husbands' relatives," Janice said. "Just look how close she and her stepson are."

"Brett Windsor is very attractive," Ginger said. "If you like the Ivy League type. He's Dina's third husband's son, right?"

"That's right." Addy glanced toward the French doors, wondering what Dina's former brother-in-law was doing out on the patio. Had one of the female guests propositioned him? Was he meeting her outside? A shiver of unexplainable excitement rippled through her. A vision of herself standing on the patio appeared in her mind. The dark stranger held her in his arms, his wide, full-lipped mouth moving downward.

"I knew he was a Latin lover boy," Janice said, again elbowing Addy in the side. "Hey, didn't you hear what Ginger said?"

"What?" Half dazed by the vividness of her daydream, Addy stared at her cousin in confusion.

"His name is Nick Romero. Oh, God, don't you just love the sound of it?" Janice was practically writhing.

"I think the proper term is Hispanic." Ginger looked at Addy, seeking her agreement. "Anyway, you're right about one thing, the term 'Latin lover' does come to mind the minute you see him."

Addy wondered how much of Ginger and Janice's conversation she'd missed while indulging in a fantasy about the man they were discussing. It was quite apparent that the man had a mesmerizing effect on women, and she absolutely refused to allow any man, not even this one, to arouse any long-dead dreams of passion. No, she'd happily settle for the nice, warm feelings she shared with her friend Jim Hester. Though neither wealthy nor sophisticated, Jim was a dear man, and he possessed something that Addy desperately wanted, had wanted for as long as she could remember, had mourned the fact, after two miscarriages, that she might never have one of her own. Jim Hester had a child.

Addy didn't want or expect passion. As a Plain Jane, she'd long ago learned that despite the fact she had no problem attracting men, it was always her father's millions that attracted them and not her beauty or charm. Dina's stepson, Brett Windsor, definitely saw dollar signs whenever he was around her, so she didn't encourage him.

"I think you and I should give Addy a shot at Nick Romero," Janice said, and laughed when she saw the stricken look on her cousin's face.

"You're right. After all, a man like that just might find Addy's sweetness and innocence a real turn-on." Ginger stopped a waiter, retrieved a canapé from a silver dish, then popped it into her mouth.

"I'm hardly innocent," Addy said. "I'm a thirty-five-year-old divorcée, not an eighteen-year-old virgin."

"Regardless of that fact, you could write everything you know about sex on the head of a straight pin." Janice stopped a waiter for a fresh glass of champagne.

"Would you look at that?" Ginger nodded toward the French doors where a stunningly beautiful Dina Lunden was slipping outside.

Addy watched. Dina's black satin gown shimmered, every inch adhering to her slender body in a way that accentuated her round hips, her small waist and her voluptuous bosom. Even at forty-six, the woman reeked of sex appeal and looked at least ten years younger. It didn't hurt that she was classically beautiful, with a kittenish type of sexuality. The kind that had made Marilyn Monroe a legend.

"Looks like step-mommy-to-be has beaten us all to the punch," Ginger said. "I wonder what she wants to talk to Nick about in private?"

"Are you implying that there's something going on between Dina and her former brother-in-law?" Addy asked.

"There's one way to find out," Ginger said.

"We could all three go outside for a breath of fresh air," Janice said.

"No." Addy held up a restraining hand. "You two stay here and enjoy the party...and make sure Daddy doesn't come outside."

Nick Romero leaned his hip against the brick patio wall. Damn, his leg ached. He'd been standing too long. Ever since an Uzi had ripped his leg open nearly seven months ago, he'd had to learn to live with pain. Indeed, the pain had been his friend. As long as he could feel the pain, he was alive. While he'd passed in and out of consciousness, he'd kept reminding himself that as long as he could feel, he wasn't dead. And so he had embraced the agony, he'd clung to it. He'd been damned and determined that no maniac's sneak attack was going to kill him. After all, he'd lived through Vietnam, through almost ten years as a Navy SEAL and nearly a dozen years as one of the DEA's top agents. He hadn't overcome poverty and prejudice and the constant threat of death to let some psycho from his best friend's past destroy him. No, Nick Romero was made of stronger stuff.

He smelled her perfume before he saw her. Heavy, spicy, erotic. Even when Dina Lunden had been Dina Romero, his brother Miguel's wife, she'd bathed herself in cologne. Back then, it had been the cheap stuff, the kind you bought in dime stores for a dollar, the kind that Dina could afford on her waitress's salary and her husband's meager wages from farming. But once Miguel had gone to work in the oil fields, Dina started buying her perfume at the drugstore.

Funny, what a guy thought about when he smelled a woman's perfume. Of course, Dina wasn't just any woman. She was special. Despite the fact that what he'd once felt for her was long dead, she would always be special. A man never forgets his first love, especially if she was his brother's widow.

"Nicky." Her voice had that same soft, little-girl coo it had so many years ago. "I saw you come outside and thought now might be a good time for us to talk. Privately."

She was still a damned good-looking woman. Still sexy as hell. The one blonde he'd never been able to forget. "Talk away. I'm listening."

She moved forward, stopping hesitantly. She reached out, her long, slender fingers draping themselves around his forearm. "I've missed you, Nicky. It's been a long time."

"Not so long, Dina." She had such a hypnotic smile. A smile that promised so much and gave so little. Nick knew how deceptive everything about this woman could be. "I came to your last engagement party and your last wedding." He noticed that her smile scarcely altered, but the light in her eyes dimmed ever so slightly. "It couldn't have been more than three years ago."

"Almost five." She squeezed Nick's arm, her sculptured pink nails biting into the fabric of his tuxedo. "You haven't missed one of my weddings, have you, Nicky? Except..."

"Except the one that you didn't invite me to."

"I thought you'd forgiven me for marrying Briley Fuller so soon after Miguel died."

Nick tilted her chin with his index finger, looking directly into her big blue eyes. Like her lips, those eyes promised so much. False promises. "I've forgiven you for everything. It's myself that I've never been able to forgive."

"Silly boy, you didn't do anything wrong." She nudged her body closer, pressing her full breasts against his chest.

"I lusted after my brother's wife, and when he wasn't three months cold in the ground, I screwed her." Even, now, after all these years, he could still taste the bile as it rose to his throat, still hear the condemnation on his grandmother's tongue when she found Dina in Nick's bed. He'd thought he was in love. He'd been seventeen. And he'd been a fool.

"Miguel was dead. I was lonely." She ran the tips of her long nails across his jaw. "And we wanted each other."

Taking her by the shoulder, Nick pushed her away from him. "I was seventeen. I wanted a woman, and at that time you were my ideal. Blond, big-boobed and knowledgeable."

She laughed, the sound like a high-pitched bell. Clear and sharp and feminine. "I'm so glad we've stayed friends, despite the fact you wouldn't even speak to me after I married Briley. He was a mistake, but . . . he was so rich."

"You seem to like your men that way," Nick said, glancing over Dina's shoulder toward the French doors. They had just opened, and a tall, slender redhead was looking straight at him.

Nick's gut tightened. There was something familiar about the woman, her titian hair, her towering height, her strong features. She certainly wasn't classically beautiful, but she possessed an earthy appeal that not even her plain dress and subdued hairstyle disguised.

"You mean that I like rich men?" Dina asked.

"Yeah, rich mistakes. How many will this make? Five?"

The redhead walked out onto the patio, closing the doors behind her. She stood less than twenty feet away. And she was still staring at him. He felt an odd sensation in the pit of his stomach. Amazed at his reaction, Nick admitted to himself that the tall, skinny redhead turned him on. He couldn't remember the last time he'd been so fascinated by a woman.

He shook his head. *Damn, who would have believed it?* She certainly wasn't his type.

"Rusty will be my sixth husband. You never count Miguel."

"Do you know a tall, slim redheaded woman wearing a gray silk dress?" Nick asked.

"Why?" Dina's voice trembled slightly.

"She's standing just a few feet away watching us."

Dina swirled around, her most dazzling smile in place. "Addy, darling, do come over and meet my Nicky."

He surveyed *darling* Addy from the top of her curly red hair to the tips of her gray leather heels. Thick, unruly flame-red hair. Plain but expensive two-inch heels. A neat little gray silk dress covered her model-thin body. It didn't cling or drape; it simply covered. Despite the fact that this woman obviously didn't dress to attract men, Nick found her very attractive. Even though he truly liked women, all women, he usually preferred sexy blondes with round curves.

Darling Addy stared at him intently, as if she were trying to gauge the extent of his personal relationship with Dina. She seemed interested in him, but not enthralled the way so many women usually were. He didn't know exactly what it was about him that piqued female interest, but he wasn't about to deny himself the pleasures of being considered a Romeo.

"Oh, Nicky, do say hello to Addy McConnell, Rusty's daughter." Dina glanced nervously back and forth from Addy to Nick. "Addy, this is my brother-in-law, Nick Romero. He's flown in from Florida just for my engagement party."

Smiling, Nick held out his hand. "Ms. McConnell."

She stared at his hand for several minutes, then offered hers. "Mr. Romero."

When he didn't immediately release her hand, she tugged gently. He held fast, pulling her closer. When she was only inches away, he gazed into her eyes, almond-shaped green eyes—cat eyes—framed by thick reddish-brown lashes. "On closer inspection, I see a definite resemblance to your father. Same hair, without the gray. Same eyes, only brighter. And you're much prettier than Rusty. Your mother must have been quite a beautiful woman."

"She was, but I don't look anything like her. I'm pure McConnell. Through and through. Just ask Daddy." Addy jerked her hand out of Nick's. "We're pleased that you could fly in and share this special night with Dina. Will you be staying here at the house?"

"No," Dina said, her lips puckered in a seductive pout. "I told him there was more than enough room, but he booked into a hotel. Wasn't that naughty of him?"

"You should have stayed here." Addy nodded toward the house. "This place is almost as big as a hotel and there's no one living here right now except Daddy, Dina and Brett."

"Brett Windsor's living here?" Nick asked.

"Brett's considering some local investments. He'll be getting his own place soon." Dina patted Addy on the arm affectionately. "Brett thinks the world of Addy, but she won't give him the least little bit of encouragement."

"Is that right?" Nick tried to keep the sarcastic tone out of his voice. He'd just bet that Brett thought the world of Addy. He thought the world of Rusty McConnell's millions was more like it. Brett Windsor had inherited half of his father's estate and Dina had inherited the other half. That had been fourteen years and two husbands ago. Nick doubted if either one of them had a dime of Ashley Windsor's six-million-dollar legacy.

Dina glanced toward the French doors where the man in question stood. "There's Brett now. I should go and assure him that Nicky isn't a rival, shouldn't I, Addy?"

"By all means." Addy waved at Brett, who flashed her a brilliant smile and waved back at her. "I'll entertain Mr. Romero."

"What?" Dina laughed, fluttering her eyelashes. "Nicky, you behave yourself with Addy. After all, she's my Rusty's only child and he adores her."

"I promise to be on my best behavior." Nick glanced at Addy, wondering what she thought of her father's fiancée.

"I'll hold you to that." Giving Nick a flirtatious smile and Addy an affectionate pat on the arm, Dina sauntered toward her third husband's son.

"Your brother was one of Dina's husbands?" Addy asked.

"Her first husband." Nick realized that this woman didn't like Dina, and her curious green eyes said that she wasn't sure she liked him either.

"Then you've known her for a long time?"

"Since I was fifteen, and I'll be forty-four soon."

"She seems very fond of you."

"She is." Nick noticed the surprised expression on Addy's face. Had she been expecting a denial? "But then, Dina is very fond of a lot of men."

"And, if my father is any indication, a lot of men are fond of Dina."

Nick reached out and took Addy's hand, slipping her arm through his. She didn't resist. Grasping his cane in his other hand, he walked them toward the French doors. "Will Dina be your first stepmother?"

"If Daddy marries her, she will be."

"You don't like Dina?"

"Dina and I have an understanding," Addy said, hesitating before entering the house again. "We tolerate each other. In front of Daddy, we're always cordial."

"If it's any comfort to you, Ms. McConnell, Dina probably won't be a part of your life for more than a few years. As you already know, her track record in the marriage department isn't very good."

"Daddy's crazy in love with Dina, despite her—er—track record."

They stepped inside the house, into the throng of celebrants, into the midst of bright lights and loud music and the hum of hundreds of voices. People filled the downstairs of Rusty McConnell's three-story mansion.

When Addy took several steps away from him, Nick reached out, detaining her by grasping her slender wrist. "If I could dance, I'd ask you for the next one." He almost laughed when he saw the look of surprise on her face.

"Why would you do that?" she asked, a genuinely puzzled look in her eyes.

"Because I'd like to hold you in my arms." Nick knew what women liked to hear, and he'd always had a knack for saying the right thing, for pushing the right buttons. He was adept at using words to achieve his goal, and he usually meant most of what he said. He never blatantly lied to a woman or made promises he didn't keep.

"You're wasting your time flirting with me, Mr. Romero. I'm immune to charming men."

The moment she spoke, he realized that he had indeed meant what he'd said to her. He did want to hold her in his arms. For some odd reason he felt that Addy McConnell needed someone to hold her, to care about her, to protect her. Stupid notion. Why would the heir to a multi-million-dollar aerospace firm need a crippled ex-DEA agent to take care of her? "Some charming man broke your heart?"

"Some charming bastard married me for my daddy's money."

Her smile was as deadly cold as any Nick had ever seen. This woman truly was immune to charm. Did she hate men? he wondered. All men? Or just the charming ones?

"His loss, I'd say."

"Yes, it was," Addy agreed, then walked away from Nick.

He didn't follow, but he watched her. She was tall. At least five ten or eleven in her two-inch heels. Rusty Mc-Connell was Nick's height. Six three.

Addy was slender, but not too skinny. Her shoulders were broad, her waist tiny and her hips well-rounded. She paused by the side of a voluptuous creature in a red sequined dress, whose frosted blond head barely reached Addy's shoulder. Apparently the woman was a close friend. She and Addy were laughing.

Nick noticed how very different the two women were. The blonde was his type—bold and sexy and bosomy. So why did she pale beside Addy? Nick couldn't understand what it was about this redhead that made the blood run hot in his veins. The blood in her veins was probably mixed with ice water. And she didn't have any breasts, at least not enough to fill out the front of her plain little silk dress. She was small but no doubt firm. He guessed that her nipples were a pale coral to match the peachy tint of her creamy gold complexion. He wanted to see those small breasts, those tight little nipples.

Her hair intrigued him, that thick mass of fiery red curls. Nick felt certain that beneath the rather drab exterior a colorful woman existed. The very thought of discovering what treasures lay buried under that plain gray dress suddenly aroused him unbearably.

He noticed Addy turn abruptly toward the center of the room where Dina was tugging on the tail of Rusty Mc-Connell's tuxedo jacket. When Addy took a step away from her friend, Nick moved forward, following her. Suddenly she broke into a run. Nick couldn't keep up, his gait hampered by his limp. People moved back, making room for Addy's mad dash through the crowd.

"Get out of here, Carlton, or I'll throw you out myself!" Rusty bellowed, his deep voice loud over the band music that continued playing.

With Addy on one side and Dina on the other, the two women tried to hold Rusty away from a younger man who had stopped on the dance floor and still held his partner in his arms. The woman was quite young. No more than twenty-five. And very, very pregnant.

Nick moved closer, stepping up beside Brett Windsor who stood directly behind Addy. Windsor was a pretty boy. Tall, blond and muscular.

"Daddy, don't do this. Remember your blood pressure." Addy clung to her father's huge arm.

"Listen to her, Rusty darling." Dina clung just as tenaciously to his other arm.

"He wasn't invited," Rusty said. "How the hell did you get in here, Carlton?"

The other man, a good-looking guy in his mid-thirties smiled at Rusty. Nick thought the smile said a lot. It was actually a smirk.

"Lori and I received an invitation. I presented it at the door." The dark-haired young man gave his companion a gentle hug. "I thought perhaps you'd finally decided to let bygones be bygones."

"I didn't issue that invitation and neither did Addy. Do you honestly think that after what you put her through she'd want to see you and...and your pregnant wife?" Rusty yanked free of his women, came up to the other man, towering over him by a good four inches, and punched Mr. Carlton in the chest with the tip of his meaty index finger.

Addy stepped forward, slipping her arm through her father's. "Daddy, don't do this." She turned to the couple. "Gerald, you and Lori shouldn't have come here. You're not welcome, and whether or not you received an invitation, you weren't invited. Please go."

"I told you we shouldn't have come," Mrs. Carlton said, turning her brown, puppy-dog eyes to her husband beseechingly.

"I guess the McConnells hold a grudge for life," Gerald Carlton said, looking directly at Addy. "You certainly haven't changed, Adeline. Still as plain and understated as ever, and still letting Daddy fight all your battles. Too bad you didn't inherit his strength—and his sexual appetite."

Nick knew Rusty McConnell was going to deck the younger man. Hell, *he* wanted to hit the sonofabitch and he didn't even know him.

Addy gasped, then grabbed her father. "No, don't. It's what he wants."

Nick stepped forward. He slipped his cane between Gerald Carlton and Rusty McConnell. Both men stared down at the black cane, then up at the man who had dared to interfere.

"Rusty, despite the fact that you're Addy's father and would love to take care of this matter, don't you think it's my place?" Nick turned his cane, positioning the tip in the center of Gerald's chest.

Rusty glared at Nick, obviously dumbfounded by his action. "Why...what—?"

"What do you think you're doing?" Addy whispered, her voice a hiss.

"I'm doing what you've been trying to do," Nick said, low and soft, for her ears only. "I'm trying to stop your father from killing this man."

"Who are you?" Gerald Carlton asked.

"I'm the man who's asking you to step outside," Nick said.

Gerald Carlton studied Nick, taking in every aspect of his appearance. His gaze stopped on Nick's cane, the tip lying against his own chest. "You're not some sort of bodyguard for Rusty. He'd never hire a cripple to protect him, so just who are you?"

"Now see here, Romero—" Rusty said, his voice a snarling growl.

"You're right. I don't work for Rusty." Nick slipped his arm around Addy's waist, pulling her close to him. "This is personal."

Addy's mouth opened in a silent gasp, but Nick had to give her credit. She didn't say a word. She didn't panic. Instead, to his delight, she swayed slightly toward him, resting her body against his.

Gerald laughed, a rather boyish, unmanly laugh. "You can't mean to imply that you and Addy... that—"

"Let's just say that I'm a man who appreciates all the special qualities in Addy that you were apparently too blind to see, let alone appreciate." Nick removed his cane from Gerald's chest, then used it to indicate the foyer. "You have two choices. You and your wife can leave now, or... your wife can take you home after you and I have a little discussion outside."

Gerald laughed again, but the laughter did not reach his eyes. He glanced around the room. Except for the band playing on, the room was deadly quiet. People were gaping, mouths open, eyes wide, waiting. Gerald looked at Nick. Nick smiled. A part of him hoped this clean-cut, sissified Anglo would step outside with him. Nothing would please him more than to show Mr. Carlton that he was one cripple who could easily beat the hell out of him.

"Gerald, let's leave now," his wife pleaded.

"If you're really bedding her," Gerald said, a self-satisfied grin on his face, "then I hope Rusty is paying you enough to make it worth your while."

Rusty lunged for Gerald, but Nick stood firmly in the way. He loosened his hold on Addy, shoving her gently away. Only two people heard the deadly warning Nick uttered, the words vulgar and succinct. Rusty and Gerald stood dead still. Gerald's face turned ashen. He grabbed his wife by the arm and made a hasty exit. Stopping at the double doors leading into the foyer, he gave Nick a nasty look, fear and hatred in his hazel eyes.

Rusty McConnell, big and broad and in superb physical condition for a man well past his prime, slapped Nick on the back, then placed his arm around his shoulder. "Did you mean what you said to him? Would you do it?"

"In a hot minute," Nick said, then glanced over at Addy, who looked rather lost, her face pale, her eyes overly bright as if she might burst into tears at any moment. "I take it that

Gerald Carlton is the bastard who married you for your daddy's money?''

"How very astute of you, Mr. Romero." Addy stepped away from the woman in the red sequined dress who appeared to be trying to comfort her.

"Call me Nick." He smiled. She didn't. "After what just happened, everyone is going to assume that we're already on a first-name basis.''

"So you should be," Rusty said, giving Nick another strong pat on the back. "I could have handled that pipsqueak Carlton without any help, but I have to admit I like the way you stood up for Addy. You're the kind of man she needs.''

"Daddy!''

"Rusty, what a thing to say." Dina reached for Rusty's big hand, squeezing it tightly. "Nick and Addy just met, and I hardly think they're a suitable match.''

The crowd began moving about and talking again, several people taking advantage of the dance music, others seeking hors d'oeuvres and champagne. Brett Windsor stepped forward, placing a comforting arm around Addy's waist. Nick had the irrational urge to coldcock Mr. Ivy League. Windsor hadn't kept Addy's father from killing her ex-husband. Windsor hadn't defended Addy when Carlton bad-mouthed her in front of everyone. Windsor hadn't been willing to take the other man outside and teach him some manners.

If anyone should be taking Addy McConnell in his arms, it shouldn't be Brett Windsor. He, Nick Romero, should be the man. But before he could make his way to Addy, to claim her attention, she walked away with Windsor. Rusty still had his big arm draped around Nick's shoulder and Dina had slipped between the two of them, taking each by the arm.

Nick watched while Windsor led Addy out onto the dance floor, took her in his arms and waltzed away with her.

* * *

Addy accepted her wrap and purse from the maid, whom she didn't know. Someone new Dina had hired, no doubt. Since becoming engaged to Rusty, Dina had moved into the mansion and hired several new servants, claiming there wasn't enough staff to adequately care for such a large estate. Of course, Rusty was agreeing to anything Dina wanted these days. No fool like an old fool in love, Addy thought, hating herself for considering her father foolish. But he was. He didn't seem to care about Dina's past, about all her former wealthy husbands.

Stepping outside onto the large veranda, Addy decided the night was too warm to warrant her shawl. She looked around for Alton, her father's chauffeur. She didn't see anyone, not even one of the parking attendants. Maybe they were taking a break. After all, it was barely eleven and most people wouldn't even begin leaving until after midnight. But she'd had just about all of Rusty and Dina's engagement party she could take. The thought of celebrating her father's upcoming nuptials to a woman who'd been married five times and unashamedly used sex to get what she wanted from men didn't sit well with Addy.

What was it with men and sex? she wondered. No matter what their age, they all seemed to have their brains in their pants. Even her father. It really hadn't bothered her so much when she found out that he'd been having an affair with his secretary, Ginger, for nearly eight years or that there had obviously been numerous women during the years since her mother's death. Maybe even before... after Madeline Delacourt McConnell had shut herself in her room... after the delicately beautiful Mrs. McConnell had lost all sense of reality and retreated into a fantasy world of her own. A world that didn't include kidnappers who had murdered her nine-year-old son.

Shaking her head, Addy walked down the steps leading to the circular drive. She wished she had driven her own car here tonight, but her father had insisted on sending Alton.

Her father was overprotective where his only child was concerned. He had been ever since Donnie's kidnapping and death when she was six. He didn't like her driving from downtown Huntsville at night alone, even though the trip took less than twenty minutes.

Alton and the others were probably in the kitchen drinking coffee. Or they could be in the garage, where Alton would be showing them Rusty's antique car collection. She decided to wait a few minutes. After all, she wasn't in any hurry to go home, just in a rush to escape the party.

The party alone would have been bad enough, but three unexpected guests had turned the evening into a real nightmare. Addy suspected that Ginger had mailed Mr. and Mrs. Gerald Carlton an invitation to tonight's shindig. The woman would have done anything to ruin Dina's big night. Ginger probably hadn't even thought of how Gerald's presence would affect other people—namely Addy McConnell. And she hadn't cared how Addy would feel seeing Lori, carrying Gerald's third child. She had tried twice to give Gerald a child. She'd failed miserably both times.

Addy gazed up at the dark sky, at the softly glowing June moon and questioned the powers-that-be as she'd done so many times in the past. Perhaps she'd wanted too much, had dared to ask for more than was her due. After all, she'd been born with a silver spoon in her mouth. Her father was a multimillionaire by the time he was thirty-five. Her mother had been one of the loveliest and wealthiest young debutantes in the state of Alabama. Never once had she wanted for anything money could buy. But, oh, how she had longed for the things in life that were beyond price.

She had longed for a normal mother, one who wasn't under a nurse's care. She had longed to be just one of the kids, not "that rich girl," not Rusty McConnell's only child. She had longed for love and passion. She'd gotten an unfaithful husband who'd married her for her father's money. And she'd longed for a child. She'd lost two babies before her fifth month of pregnancy.

Engrossed in thought, Addy strolled farther and farther down the circular drive, past limo after limo, past several Mercedes, BMWs, Jaguars and Porsches.

Nick Romero had been the other unexpected guest, a man she couldn't even begin to understand. There was something about him that intrigued Addy, and something that frightened her. Suddenly she realized that the very thing that intrigued her was the same thing that frightened her: Nick's sensuality. When he looked at her, it was as if...as if he wanted her. She knew that couldn't be right. Tall, flat-chested, redheaded Addy McConnell wasn't the type of woman who evoked passion in men, and most certainly not a man like Nick Romero—big and dark and devastatingly attractive, a man who made women swoon.

Addy felt a steely arm slip around her waist, then saw the rag in the man's hand as it came toward her face. Dear God, someone had grabbed her from behind...someone was going to hurt her. When she opened her mouth to scream, the hand came down over her face, covering her mouth and nose with the rag, the smelly rag. Acting purely on instinct, Addy struggled, trying to free herself. She kicked backward with her heels, hoping to make contact with the man's legs. He held her tighter. She rammed her foot into his ankle and struck him in the stomach with her elbow. Groaning, he loosened his hold on her.

"Be still, bitch," he said, his voice sharp.

When he tried to cover her face with the rag again, she bit down on his hand. He snatched his hand away, cursing loudly. Addy took her chance, whirling around. For a split second, she saw his face in the moonlight. He was a stranger. He grabbed for her. She turned and ran. He ran after her.

He reached out, knocking her down on the pavement, then falling to his knees to straddle her hips. The force of his attack knocked the breath from her lungs. He jerked her up off the driveway.

"They wanted things done up all nice and neat. Said to use the chloroform. Said not to hurt you." He jammed a gun in her ribs. "But they didn't bother telling me that you were such a feisty bitch! So no more Mr. Nice Guy. Understand?"

Addy nodded. What was she going to do? She had to get away. This man could rape her, torture her, kill her. But who *was* he? Someone had sent this maniac after her. But who and why? Dear God, was this an attempted kidnapping? If Rusty McConnell lost his one remaining child to a kidnapper, he wouldn't be able to live through the tragedy a second time. All Addy could think about was her father.

Her high-pitched, ear-splitting scream shattered the nocturnal solitude.

Chapter 2

Nick didn't know why he'd followed Addy McConnell outside. He wanted to see her again? Yeah. He wanted to talk with her? Yeah. He wanted to get to know her better? Yeah. He wanted to drag her into the back seat of one of those big, shiny limos parked in the driveway and find out if she was as frigid as her ex-husband had implied? Damn, yes. Some gut-level instinct told him that Addy was as fiery as her hair, as hot and wild as the look he'd seen in her bright green eyes. But she would be that way only with him . . . only for him.

He heard the scream. A bloodcurdling scream of pure fear. And then he saw them. The tall redheaded woman and the muscular youth who held her. She wasn't struggling, she was just standing there in his arms, screaming. Nick moved forward cautiously, knowing he mustn't surprise Addy's attacker. He cursed his bad leg for slowing him down. Time was of the essence. He wouldn't have been the only one who'd heard her screams. Soon the lawn would be swarming with curious guests. No telling what the assailant would do if confronted by a mob of onlookers. He could panic and kill Addy.

Nick saw the gun held to Addy's ribs. The metal housing sparkled like shiny glass when the moonlight struck it from the right angle.

Nick eased off the veranda and out onto the drive, his steps faltering slightly as he leaned heavily on his cane. He could make out only the shadows of Addy and the man holding her captive. He crept along behind the parked cars, edging his way closer and closer to the woman he desperately wanted to save.

Nick saw several uniformed chauffeurs coming around the house, followed by five parking attendants in white coats. Damn! He hastened his lame gait, cursing the pain in his calf. He had to get to Addy.

The mansion's double front doors swung open. At least two dozen people ran outside, Rusty McConnell leading the pack. Double damn!

Nick crouched down behind the driver's side of a white Rolls, peering over the hood. If he reached out he could touch the hem of Addy's dress.

"Damn you, bitch," the man with the gun shouted. "See what you've done. See what you've done!"

He jerked Addy away from the passenger side of the Rolls, twisting her arm behind her back and pointing the revolver directly at her head. Addy had stopped screaming. Her face, only lightly covered with translucent makeup, was almost as gray as her dress. The fear reflected on her peachy flesh made the smattering of tiny freckles across her nose visible even in the moonlight.

Nick knew he had few options. Capturing the assailant wasn't his top priority. Saving Addy was. That meant disarming her attacker before he had the chance to use his gun.

"Good God, it's Addy!" Rusty McConnell bellowed like a wounded bull, his voice carrying loudly in the stillness.

Nick could hear the rumble of voices, the tantalizing moan of a saxophone from inside the house, the labored breathing of the sweating man who began walking backward, practically dragging Addy with him. Nick slipped around the side of the Rolls, keeping his head low, groaning silently as excruciating pain radiated from his calf up into his bent knee. Coordinating his movements perfectly to keep pace with Addy and her kidnapper, Nick reached the rear of the car the moment they did.

He had one chance and one chance only. If he failed . . . If the man panicked . . .

Nick made his move. The man, young and scared, his dark eyes riveted to Nick, swung Addy around hard, using her as a shield. His long, sandy ponytail flipped over his shoulder. He tightened his hold on Addy. For one split second, he raised the gun a fraction of an inch, the barrel shining brightly just above Addy's head, the man's white hand clearly visible against Addy's flame red hair.

Using his trained warrior instincts, Nick raised his black walking stick with split-second precision. The gold tip touched the assailant's hand. He reacted quickly, shoving the gun against Nick's cane. Nick pressed the concealed lever. A sharp stiletto sprang from the tip of the cane and pierced the attacker's hand, slicing through flesh and muscle. Blood gushed from the wound. The man yowled in pain, dropping the gun. The metal rattled as it hit the driveway. Using his good leg, Nick extended his foot and kicked the revolver under the Rolls. The young would-be kidnapper, having lost his gun and inadvertently released Addy, glared at Nick, who swiftly and adeptly pulled the knife out of the man's hand and, with a quick press of a lever, returned the knife to its secret bed within his black lacquer stick.

When the young man made a move toward Addy, Nick used the gold-tipped staff to ward him off. Twirling the cane around, Nick slapped him across the face, bloodying his nose.

Nick heard the sound of voices coming closer, the loud pounding of running feet. Panting, the assailant glared over

Nick's shoulder, then back at Nick. Easing away slowly, the man turned and broke into a full run. Nick made no attempt to follow. He leaned over to help a badly shaken Addy McConnell to her feet. Her tightly coiled topknot had come loose. Thick, heavy tendrils of bright red hair fell down her back, over her ears, and wispy curls framed her face. The sleeve of her unflattering gray dress was ripped, one of her two-inch heels was missing and there was a run in her panty hose that stretched from her ankle all the way up and beyond the hem of her dress. Her silver and black beaded purse rested at her feet where it had fallen from her shoulder.

The delicate fragrance of her expensive perfume mingled with the heady odor of her female perspiration. Nick could smell her heat . . . and he liked her uniquely sweet scent.

Leaning on his cane, Nick pulled Addy up against his body, hugging her close. Her breathing was labored, her eyes wild with fear, her full lips parted in the prelude to a sigh or a moan or a cry. Nick wasn't sure which. God, he wanted to kiss her. He wanted to hold her so close, so tight, that she would become a part of him. He wanted to run his hands all over her, from neck to knees, to make sure she was unharmed, to reassure her by his touch that she was alive.

The voices and running feet came closer. Within seconds a crowd would surround them. He looked at Addy. She looked at him.

"Oh, Nick..." Her voice was pleadingly soft, issuing both thanks and invitation in the way she uttered his name.

She leaned into him, resting against him. She put both of her arms around his waist, clinging to him. He'd never felt so much a man. Not in all his life. Was this what it felt like, he wondered, to protect your woman?

"You're all right, Addy." Nick lowered his head, his breath mingling with hers. "He didn't hurt you, did he?"

"No—not really—just...just scared me." She raised her lips to his.

Just as Nick's mouth covered hers, he felt the hardy slap of Rusty McConnell's big hand on his back. "What the hell was going on? Who was that man?"

Addy turned her face toward her father, but she remained in Nick's arms, her hands clutching at his back. "He...he was trying to rob me," she lied. "Nick showed up just in time. I...don't know what I would have done."

"The police have been called." Rusty stared at his daughter, doubt and fear raging in his dark green eyes. "Some of the men are trying to catch your attacker. I'd let the dogs loose if we didn't have guests wandering around out here."

Nick could feel the quick, hard beat of Addy's heart where her chest rested against his side. Her breasts were crushed into him. They weren't as small as he'd thought, but they were just as firm.

There was more to this attack than a man trying to steal a woman's purse. If that was all the man had been after, he'd have taken it and run. No, the man, whoever he was, had wanted Addy, had been trying to take her with him. That meant he was either a rapist or a kidnapper. If he'd been a murderer, he could have shot her before Nick saw them. Addy was lying to her father, and Nick didn't understand why. Who was she trying to protect? Surely not her attacker.

"Did you get a good look at his face?" Rusty asked. "Could you identify him?"

Addy nodded. Trembling, she clung to Nick.

"I'll get rid of everybody as quickly as I can," Rusty said. "You aren't going back to your house tonight. You can stay in your old room. I'll have Mrs. Hargett get it ready for you."

"The police will probably want to question everyone," Nick said. "Just in case anybody saw something. But I think Addy and I are the only ones who can identify her attacker. There's no need for them to grill her. I got as good a look at him as she did."

"I'll get Dina," Rusty suggested. "She can stay with you, Addy. A girl needs another woman at a time like this."

"No, Daddy. Really. I'll—I'll be all right." Addy twisted the back of Nick's tuxedo jacket in her hand, wadding it into a wrinkled knot. "If I can just go inside . . . get away from all these people staring at me. Something to drink. Brandy, maybe. Or a shot of whiskey. And—and—" she looked at Nick. "And Nick—Mr. Romero could go with me."

"Huh?" Rusty's gaze moved from his daughter's face to her arms that were clinging to Nick. "Take her inside, Romero. And stay with her. I'll take care of everything else. You take care of my daughter."

Nick heard both the entreaty and the warning in big Rusty McConnell's voice. The man knew he would protect Addy with his life. He also knew that Nick wanted her, and wanted her badly. A man could always tell when another man was proprietary about a woman. Nick had seen that look in many a man's eye. He'd never thought another man would ever see it in his. He hadn't felt possessive about a woman in twenty-five years. Not since he'd been seventeen and in love with his brother's wife.

"Well, they weren't a whole hell of a lot of help, were they?" Rusty McConnell stomped across the cream and gold Persian rug in his living room. Running a big hand through his thick, cinnamon-streaked white hair, he chomped down on his half-smoked Havana cigar.

"Now, darling." Dina draped her small, delicate arm around her fiancé's thick waist. "I think the officers did a thorough job. My goodness, they questioned every guest and gave all of us the third degree. It's two-thirty, and we're exhausted. Why don't we go to bed and—"

Unconsciously, Rusty jerked away from Dina's possessive hold, turning to Addy. "You're not going home. Do you understand? Mrs. Hargett's already got your room ready."

"I'll stay here tonight, Daddy, but in the morning, I'm going home." Addy refused to allow some maniac's attack to turn her father into the fanatically overprotective parent he'd been years ago. From the time she was six and her older brother had been killed by his kidnappers, Addy had lived in a gilded cage, a poor little rich girl unable to flee the golden chains that kept her *safe*. Not until her marriage to Gerald had ended had she found the strength and courage to escape Rusty's loving captivity.

Rusty's gaze swung around, focusing on his niece. "That boyfriend of yours is outside waiting. Why don't you go on home, Janice. And, if Addy isn't up to coming in to work Monday, you handle things."

"Now, Daddy, don't go making any decisions for me." Addy gave Janice a knowing nod and tried to smile. "Go on home with Ron. I'm fine."

"I'll see you Monday," Janice said, giving Addy a quick hug. Walking out, she paused. "Uncle Rusty, you know that M.A.C.'s day-care center can't function without Addy."

Rusty didn't acknowledge his niece's parting comment. Turning all his attention on Brett Windsor, he resisted Dina's attempts to put her arm around him. "What the hell are you still doing here? Go on up to your room, Windsor. I need to talk to Addy and Nick. Alone."

Addy bit her tongue to keep from chastising her father for his rudeness. A worldly wise man, a self-made millionaire, D.B. McConnell could be charming if the occasion called for it, but otherwise he didn't bother with the formalities of courtesy. Good manners were something that, even in her declining years of mental illness, Madeline Delacourt McConnell had instilled in her daughter, and Addy abhorred the lack of them in anyone, even in her own dearly loved father.

She reached out, placing her hand on Brett's arm. "I'll see you in the morning at breakfast."

His smile only enhanced his already handsome face. His dark blue eyes changed from brooding to pleasant. Addy returned his smile, thinking how attractive Brett Windsor was, with his sandy blond hair, his tall, muscular body, his quick wit and attentive manner. Too bad his interest in her was only monetary. As much as she liked Brett, there was no doubt in her mind that his sole interest in her was her daddy's money. Of course, he had no idea that she knew what was behind his phony smiles and attentive manner.

"Why don't you escort your stepmother upstairs?" Rusty said. "This hasn't been the best of nights for her."

"But, Rusty, darling, I should be here with you," Dina protested. "A wife should always be at her husband's side, sharing the good and the bad, giving him her support and love."

Addy wanted to say "poppycock." Dina protested being asked to leave because she didn't want Rusty making any decisions without her. After all, she wasn't his wife, yet, and she didn't want anything to postpone or prevent their upcoming nuptials. Without moving, Addy saw Nick in her peripheral vision. He was staring at Dina, a quirky little smile on his face. He knows her, Addy thought, and can see straight through her the way I can.

"You're exhausted," Rusty said. "There's nothing you can do for Addy or for me, tonight. I'm sorry our engagement party ended on such a sour note." He pulled Dina into his arms, her small body lost in his enormous bear hug. "I just want to go over things again with Addy and Nick."

"All right, Rusty, whatever you want." Reluctantly, Dina accepted Brett's arm and the two left the room.

The moment the door closed, Rusty turned to his daughter. "Now, little girl, I want you to tell me what you didn't tell the police."

"I don't know what you're talking about. I told the police everything." Addy crossed her arms over her chest and plopped down into the cream brocade Queen Anne chair by the fireplace.

"Don't play the innocent with me. I know damn well what happened tonight! Somebody tried to kidnap you."

Rusty hovered over Addy, glowering at her, daring her to deny the truth.

She'd been afraid this would happen. Her father was too smart, but it had been worth a try, to protect him from worry and to protect herself from his reaction. "The man was trying to rob me, Daddy."

With an exasperated grunt, Rusty turned to Nick. "Do you think he was trying to rob her?"

"No, sir." Nick glanced at Addy, who glared up at him, a slight tremor moving her head, as if she wanted to give him a negative warning but realized her father was watching her. "The man was either a rapist or a kidnapper. My guess is that your daughter can tell us which."

How was she going to fight both of these men? Addy wondered. Obviously, Nick was on her father's side. She glanced back and forth from the big dark Hispanic to the big fair Scot, both men of equal height and similar physiques, although Rusty's body had broadened and softened slightly with age. *Birds of a feather.* Two strong, overbearing, macho men.

She realized Nick and Rusty were staring at her. "All right. He was trying to kidnap me, but he didn't. I'm fine. Nick foiled his rather clumsy attempt."

"Why the hell didn't you tell the police?" Rusty bent over, placing his meaty hands on the armrests of Addy's chair. Lowering his head, he narrowed his green eyes and frowned. "You didn't want me to know. Is that it, little girl?"

Shoving on her father's burly chest, she pushed him away, then stood up. "Daddy..."

Rusty turned from her, walking across the room to the long windows that faced the veranda of his white-columned mansion. "I'll call the police in the morning and tell them. We'll have to take the proper precautions."

"Daddy...don't." No, she couldn't bear it. Never again. She was free and she intended to stay free. "If you want to hire someone to follow me around, keep watch on my house, that's fine. Even put on some extra guards at work, that's okay, too. But—I will not move back here and I will not be kept under lock and key.''

''We'll discuss this in the morning after we've all had some rest.'' Rusty nodded toward Nick. ''Alton's brought Nick's things over from his hotel and Mrs. Hargett has put him in the room beside you.''

''What?'' Addy exclaimed, her gaze riveted to Nick's smiling face. Just what was going on here? She felt as if these two had telepathically decided what was best for her.

''I'd prefer him in the room with you, but I didn't think you'd ever agree to that.'' Rusty's grin was pure masculine superiority.

''Why on earth would you put Nick—Mr. Romero next to me? I'm sure you've already called in an army of guards to surround this place.''

''We'll have more than enough security by tomorrow,'' Rusty said. ''But regardless of that, Nick's the kind of man I want close to you if there's any trouble.''

''How do you know what kind of man Mr. Romero is?'' Addy asked.

''Are you forgetting he saved you from a kidnapper tonight, little girl?''

''For heaven's sake, stop calling me that! I'm thirty-five years old.''

Completely ignoring Addy's demand, Rusty surveyed Nick from head to toe. ''I ran a check on Nick. Just a preliminary check, when Dina said she'd invited her brother-in-law to come for the party and to stay a few days. Did the same thing with Brett Windsor. No big deal.''

''But why, Daddy? That's an invasion of privacy.''

''Brett Windsor has shown an interest in you. I wanted to see just how much money he did or didn't have. I wouldn't want you to have to go through the same kind of mess you did with Gerald.''

"Give me some credit, Daddy. You didn't have to run a check on Brett. I've known all along that it's your money he wants and not me."

"So we're both smarter than we used to be, but it's better to be safe than sorry."

"Some of us are smarter," Addy mumbled under her breath.

"Insulting Dina in front of her brother-in-law?" Rusty laughed.

"I'm going to bed," Addy said, heading for the door. "And in the morning, I'm going home."

"Nick, you go on with her, see her tucked in all safe and sound." Rusty commanded, but a trace of chuckling humor softened his words.

Addy stopped dead in her tracks. Without turning to face either man, she said, "What did you find out about Mr. Romero that makes you think he's so trustworthy?"

"He fought in Nam. Spent ten years in the SEALS. Went in when he was eighteen. He was a DEA agent for nearly a dozen years." Rusty paused, as if waiting for his daughter to comment. When she didn't, he continued. "He came from nothing and made something of himself, just like I did. I think Nick and I are a lot alike. Besides, he's one of Sam Dundee's best friends, and Dundee said that, despite Nick's bad leg, he's one of the toughest, meanest sonofabitches he's ever known. The kind of man you'd want on your side in a fight."

Addy knew she'd made a mistake in asking. Obviously, Nick Romero possessed all the requirements her father considered important in a man. Close friendship with Sam Dundee, whose private security agency her father had used on more than one occasion, was a definite plus in his favor. What more could Rusty McConnell ask for? "With such glowing credentials, I think you should just adopt him— then Dina would have someone around to amuse her when you're too busy."

Rusty's big body shook with laughter. "Dina has Brett for that. Besides, I was thinking I wouldn't mind having a man like Nick for a son-in-law."

Nick's gut twisted. His heartbeat accelerated. What the hell kind of game was McConnell playing? When he saw the stricken look on Addy's face, he wondered if she hated the idea of marriage or just the idea of being married to him. "Don't worry, Addy, I'm not the marrying kind." He gave Rusty a hard stare. "Maybe you'd better just adopt me."

"You take care of our Addy." Rusty walked over and draped one arm around Addy's shoulder, then reached out and placed his other arm around Nick. "If you hear the least little peep out of her during the night, you rush right on in. You—" he turned to Addy "—behave yourself and cooperate."

Rusty walked them to the double doors leading out into the foyer. Stepping away from them, he laid Addy's hand on Nick's arm.

"Why don't you just play along with your father?" Nick whispered. "It'll make it easier for both of us."

"It's obvious that you don't know Rusty McConnell, Mr. Romero. He doesn't respect easy compliance, especially not in his daughter. He expects me to fight back."

"Have you always?"

"No, I haven't." Addy allowed Nick to lead her up the winding staircase. "Daddy has always loved me. Adored me, really. But when I divorced Gerald and moved out of this house, Daddy learned to respect me and accept what I wanted."

"And you're afraid this kidnap scare will somehow turn back the clock to the way things used to be?"

"I won't let that happen."

Nick didn't doubt her. There was more to Addy Mc-Connell than met the eye. Was that why he felt so attracted to her? He couldn't figure it out. She was far from his type. Hell, she wasn't much to look at. Too flat-chested, too plain, too tall and too hostile toward men. He liked women who liked men. Soft, fluttery females. Sultry, sexy ladies who enjoyed flirtation and seduction. Experienced women who knew the rules and played the game to perfection.

Addy McConnell didn't fit the description. But there was something about her, something lonely and vulnerable, and something filled with raging hunger. She hid it well, but Addy was a woman in need. And Nick wanted to be the man to fill that need.

Addy opened her eyes. Dawn light filtered through the sheer panels that covered her bedroom windows. She'd forgotten to draw the yellow drapes last night. An early morning hush enveloped the room. Stillness. Quiet. Then she heard the woman's voice coming from the room next to hers, the room her father had assigned to Nick Romero.

Addy scooted to the edge of the bed, slipping into her blue house slippers. Feeling around at the foot of her rumpled bed, she found the blue robe that matched the lace-trimmed cotton gown she wore. When she'd moved out of her father's mansion nearly seven years ago, she'd left everything behind. She wanted nothing that reminded her of the three years she'd spent with Gerald or the two heartbreaking miscarriages she'd suffered. But her father had kept not only her room unchanged, he'd kept every one of her possessions, including her clothes.

Walking softly, Addy made her way to the door, cracking it slightly open. When she heard Nick's door opening, she closed her own, leaving just enough space so she could peep into the hallway. Dina slipped out of Nick's room. He stopped in the open doorway. She stood close, her body grazing his. Dina wore a sheer black silk negligee. Addy gasped at the sight of Dina's near nakedness. My God, had the woman no shame?

Dina ran her long nails down Nick's cheek, then across his lips. Addy sucked in her breath.

"We're in agreement, then," Dina said, breathlessly. "You won't say a word to Rusty about—about what happened, will you? He might not understand."

"It's none of my business." Nick looked down at the small blond woman who had once tempted him beyond reason. Strange how age and experience change a man. "But Rusty McConnell is nobody's fool. My guess is that he already knows exactly what you're all about and he wants you anyway. Why not be totally honest with him and see what happens?"

"Silly boy. You know better than that. You men are all such fools when it comes to women. You get so possessive and can't bear to think that we might be as experienced as you are. We're supposed to be thankful to all the women who taught you how to be studs in bed, but you're jealous of the men who taught us how to be pleasing."

"Hell, Dina. Rusty knows you've been married five times, doesn't he?"

"Yes, but—"

"Go back to bed before Rusty wakes up and finds you gone. It would be easier to explain everything about your past to him than it would be to explain what you've been doing in my bedroom at five-thirty in the morning."

She ran her fingers down his throat, across his bare chest to the undone snap of his tuxedo trousers. "All we've done is talk."

Nick grabbed her hand, shoving it away. "And that's all we're going to do, now or ever. I'm not a sex-hungry seventeen-year-old."

Addy didn't want to listen. She wanted to close the door and forget what she'd seen and heard. But she couldn't. She owed it to her father to find out what was going on between Dina and Nick, didn't she? Of course she did. *Liar,* her conscience screamed at her. *You're jealous.* How could this have happened? she wondered. How could she have allowed herself to become interested in a man like Nick Romero?

It was because he'd rescued her that she'd started thinking of him as a knight in shining armor. During the few hours of restless sleep she'd had, she'd dreamed of Nick. Black eyes. Bronze skin. Big and broad and strong. She didn't want to think of him as her champion, as her own personal paladin, but she did. He had defended her from her ex-husband's insults and then saved her from an attacker. Nick Romero, no matter what else he was, was quite a man.

Dina reached out, allowing her hand to hover over Nick's bare chest. "If you're entertaining any fanciful notions about Addy, I'd advise you to forget them. Rusty keeps a close watch on his little girl's love life and he wouldn't approve of you."

"Now that's where you're wrong," Nick said. "Rusty McConnell wholeheartedly approves of me. Just earlier this morning, after you and Brett went upstairs, he told Addy that he wouldn't mind having me for a son-in-law."

"What?" Dina's voice screeched loudly.

"Quieten down before you wake Addy." Nick glanced at Addy's partially open door and smiled.

"You're leaving in a few days. Going—going to El Paso to visit your grandmother."

"I might stay around a while longer."

"Are you doing this to make me jealous?" Dina asked.

"Go back to Rusty's bed, Dina, and leave me alone."

"You can't ever forgive me, can you?"

"Leave, Dina. Now."

Swirling the floor-length robe as she turned, Dina marched down the hall, her chin tilted high. Addy watched until her father's fiancée turned the corner leading to the west wing of the house. She started to close the door. Nick Romero stuck his foot inside the narrow crack. Addy tried to shove the door closed. Ramming his shoulder into the door, he pushed it open.

"Up awfully early aren't you, Addy?"

"Something woke me."

"Something or someone?"

She glared at him, the corners of his mouth curving upward in a self-satisfied smile. He knew she'd seen Dina leaving his room in her see-through nightie and he didn't know whether or not she'd tell her father.

"I think we should have a little talk," Nick said, his body pressing against hers. "In private."

He was warm, his thickly muscled bronze chest like a hot pad where it touched her. Even through her gown she could feel his heat. The tremors began in her stomach, radiating upward and outward until every nerve in her body tingled. The reaction was totally unexpected. Being near a man had never shaken her so badly.

When he grasped her elbow, maneuvering her backward into her room, she made no protest. But when he shut the door, she stepped away from him, wary of his intentions. She didn't know this man, this brother-in-law of Dina's, this former DEA agent. How did she know he was trustworthy, despite her father's approval? Rusty had liked Gerald in the beginning, had been impressed with his knowledge of aeronautics and the day-to-day running of a company like M.A.C.

"Stop looking at me as if you're afraid." Nick took a tentative step toward her, then stopped suddenly when he realized she was genuinely scared. "I don't ravish unwilling women if that's what's worrying you."

"I want you to leave."

"Not until I explain what Dina was doing in my bedroom."

"I don't care what she was doing, or what you were doing or if the two of you were doing something together."

"Adamant about it, aren't you?" Nick grinned at her, taking in the way Addy McConnell looked first thing in the morning. With her long red hair hanging freely halfway down her back and her tall, slender body encased in a cute little blue cotton nightgown and matching robe, she looked about twelve years old. Her face, scrubbed clean of the light makeup she'd worn earlier, radiated with a healthy glow.

Her skin was golden tinted, with only a smattering of freckles here and there. A few on her nose. A few more on her throat and arms. He wondered how many there were on the rest of her body.

"Daddy knows that Dina isn't as pure as the driven snow..."

"But my guess is that Rusty wouldn't be pleased to find out that his fiancée, the woman he's bedding, was in my room trying to seduce me." Nick watched Addy closely.

"Was that what she was doing, seducing you?" Addy maintained a calm control over her voice, praying that the quivering she felt inside wouldn't manifest itself in her words.

"It's an old game between Dina and me. Has been for years. She *tries* to seduce me. I reject her. She likes to think she's tormenting me, that I have to call forth all my strength in order to resist her." Not since that once, twenty-five years ago, when he'd succumbed to his brother's widow, had Nick ever given in to that specific temptation again. After he'd gone against his better judgment and made love to Dina, she'd told him she was going to marry another man. An older man. A more powerful man. A richer man. And he'd spent the rest of his life feeling guilty for bedding Miguel's widow, feeling as if he'd betrayed his brother. Oh, he'd been hot for her then, so hot he'd thought he'd die. But that fire had burned itself out a long time ago and he and Dina had somehow come through it as friends. Friends of a sort, that is.

"My father is very possessive. He wouldn't want to share her."

"He doesn't have anything to worry about where I'm concerned, but he might want to do a nightly bed check in Windsor's room." Nick didn't know it for a fact, but he was reasonably sure that Dina and her stepson had been lovers for years, between her marriages and perhaps even during them. He'd bet his last dime that Rusty McConnell wasn't aware of that little fact.

"What a hateful thing to imply!" Addy said. "You're probably trying to place blame on Brett to save your own hide. After all, I didn't see Dina coming out of Brett's room, did I?"

"Jealous?" Nick moved toward her, slowly, deliberately, like an animal stalking his prey.

"Of you and Dina?" Addy laughed, the sound blatantly phony. "Don't be ridiculous."

Nick reached out, slipping his hand beneath her hair, circling her neck. She gulped in huge swallows of air. Her eyes widened in a mixture of shock and excitement. He pulled her closer. In her bare feet, she stood five inches shorter than he did. The perfect height for him.

"You don't like me very much, do you, Addy?" He touched the tip of his nose to hers, and smiled when he heard her indrawn breath.

"I...I don't know you." Decently clothed in her gown and robe, Addy felt naked, bare to his gaze and touch. Vulnerable. Nick Romero made her feel vulnerable.

"I remind you of your daddy, don't I?" His breath mingled with hers as he lowered his head just a fraction. "All the qualities you dislike in Rusty, you see in me."

"He was right, wasn't he? The two of you are a lot alike."

"Probably." Nick watched her intently, amazed by his own desire for this tall, flat-chested redhead. "It's obvious that you love your father, why is it that you don't like him?"

"I—I do like him. It's just that—that he's so damned macho and controlling. So overprotective because he loves me. He thinks because I'm his daughter, he should be able to protect me from everything and everyone. He—he smothers me, sometimes."

"A man tends to be that way with the people he loves. His woman, his children, his family." Nick tightened his hold on Addy's neck, forcing her head upward toward his until only inches separated them. He touched her bottom lip with the tip of his finger.

She knew he was going to kiss her. What she didn't know was whether or not she wanted him to. "Why—why are you doing this?"

"Damned if I know," he said, then took her mouth.

His kiss was gentle and seductive, a practiced perfection. Addy trembled, her own lips responding, surrendering to a power she'd never known, an enticement she was unable to resist. She sighed, longing for more. Placing his hand on her hip, he stroked her through her cotton gown as he deepened the kiss.

Addy eased her hands upward, twining them around his neck. The minute his tongue entered her mouth, he felt himself spiraling out of control. It had been a long time since he'd gotten aroused so quickly, so thoroughly. If he didn't stop things immediately, he'd be flinging her down on her bed and ripping off that little-girl gown she wore. He'd be finding out how many freckles she had on her body and exactly where they were located.

He broke away from her, releasing her, gently pulling her arms from around his neck. "You're wearing a disguise, Addy McConnell. You wrap yourself up in your Plain-Jane clothes and pretend you're an iceberg, that you dislike sex."

"It—it isn't a disguise." Her words came out choppy, on quick, heated little breaths. Nick had kissed her more thoroughly than she'd ever been kissed in her life, and she was still reeling from the aftereffects. "I am a Plain Jane who dislikes chest-beating Neanderthal men. And I am an iceberg. Just ask my ex-husband."

Nick walked away from her, then turned when he reached the door. "Why should I ask that bastard anything, when I got all the proof I needed, first hand, that you're hot as a firecracker?"

"I am not!"

Nick grinned. "That was a compliment, Red. I like my women hot."

"I am not one of your women."

Nick opened the door, paused briefly, then looked back at Addy. "But you will be." Before she could reply, he walked out and closed the door behind him.

She stood, speechless, her mouth agape, her gaze focused on the door. A riot of emotions exploded inside her. Desire. Anger. Passion. Outrage. She wanted to hit something, preferably Nick Romero. "Of all the overconfident, strutting peacocks! He's insufferable! If he thinks for one minute that—that..." Addy couldn't finish her sentence. Visions of Nick Romero's big body filled her mind. Nick, pressing down onto her, into her, his dark eyes devouring her as he took her. Addy shook her head, trying to erase her erotic thoughts.

In a few hours, after she'd pacified her father by having breakfast with him, she would go home. She had no intention of being around Nick Romero one minute longer than she had to. After today, she'd never have to see him again.

Chapter 3

Addy had delayed going downstairs for breakfast as long as she possibly could. Her father had already sent Mrs. Hargett upstairs twice, the last time relaying a command that she join the others at once.

Glancing out the windows onto the front lawn of her father's estate, located about ten miles outside of Huntsville, Addy thought again how much the rich green lawns and towering old trees reminded her of her mother's ancestral estate where they'd lived until Madeline's death. Wanting to escape all the agonizing memories of his son's kidnapping and subsequent murder and his wife's suicide four years later, Rusty McConnell had taken Addy away, moved her into a sparkling new mansion, pure and untainted by any reminders of a past too painful to remember. She had missed Elm Hill, the vast acres of rolling pastures and thickly wooded forests. Even now, she dreamed of someday returning and living out the rest of her life in the house where five generations of Delacourts had been born and raised. Someday...when she had laid all her fears to rest.

Her mother and Janice's mother had been the last of the line, both women now dead, leaving only the two cousins as heirs to family pride and genteel breeding. And Elm Hill had stood vacant for twenty-five years, Janice having neither the desire nor the money to renovate the old place and Addy, with more than enough money, but not enough courage to fight the demons from her childhood.

Instead, she'd bought a house in Huntsville's historic district, Twickenham.

A sharp, loud knock at her bedroom door snapped Addy out of her rambling thoughts. "Yes?"

The door opened. Mrs. Hargett stood outside in the hall-way. "I'm terribly sorry to keep bothering you like this, but—"

"Is he threatening to come and drag me downstairs kick-ing and screaming?" Addy laughed, remembering how many times during her difficult adolescent years her father had issued similar warnings. Having a daughter with her mother's old-fashioned breeding but none of her delicate blond beauty had often confused Rusty McConnell. But not nearly as much as the mixture of personality traits she had inherited from Madeline and himself. Cool, calm and ever the lady. Rusty liked that. What he didn't like was her stub-bornness, which was one of his own most prominent qual-ities.

"Yes, ma'am. That's what he said." Mrs. Hargett, small and skinny, with round black eyes that were the only bright spot in her pale colorless face, smiled, crinkling the feath-ery wrinkles that lined her eyes and mouth. "He ordered me to give you that message, but then he told me to wait. He looked over at that Mr. Romero, you know, Mrs. Lunden's brother-in-law."

Agitating circles formed in the pit of Addy's stomach. "You don't have to tell me. He said to let me know that if I didn't come down, posthaste, he'd send Ni—Mr. Romero up to fetch me.''

''Mr. McConnell can be outrageous sometimes, can't he?'' Mrs. Hargett shook her head, not disturbing one curl of her neatly permed short gray hair that was coated with a hair spray with the sealing powers of a good lacquer.

''There'll be no need for a return message.'' Addy picked up her purse from the nightstand. ''I might as well get this over with.''

Together, she and Mrs. Hargett descended the staircase, but once in the foyer the housekeeper turned toward the kitchen while Addy squared her broad shoulders and marched into the dining room.

Rusty McConnell disliked antique furniture. Elm Hill had been filled with five generations of acquisition. Every stick of furniture in this mansion was expensive and new. Rusty sat at the head of the dark oak dining table, a traditional-style buffet at his back, an enormous matching china cabinet at the opposite end of the room, directly behind Dina, who turned and glared at Addy, a look of resentment in her cool blue eyes. Addy wondered what had prompted that look. Something was going on. More than she'd bargained for, she feared.

''About time you got down here.'' Rusty flicked the ashes from the tip of his cigar into a small brass tray. ''We've all finished with breakfast.''

''I'm not hungry.'' Addy, her steps quick and unfaltering, sailed past Dina, not even acknowledging her presence. She stopped briefly to touch Brett on the back. He turned his bright smile on her. ''Good morning.''

''Why the hell did you put on that dirty, ripped dress you were wearing last night?'' Rusty asked, scooting his chair backward, preparing to stand. ''You've got a closet full of clothes in your room.''

Standing by her father's chair, Addy placed a restraining hand on his shoulder. ''Don't get up, Daddy.'' She bent down, kissing him on the cheek. ''You really should have given those clothes to Goodwill or the Salvation Army years ago.''

Rusty grunted, then gave his daughter a quick kiss on her forehead. "Sit down. We've got a lot to discuss."

"Make it quick." Addy didn't sit down. Picking up a cup filled with hot, black coffee, she brought it to her lips. "I'm going home, so don't try to stop me."

"I knew you wouldn't want to stay here," Rusty said. "So I've made arrangements to keep you safe in your own home."

Addy sipped the strong, eye-opening coffee. Suspiciously glaring at her father, she tried to figure out why he was being so agreeable. She'd been sure she'd have a battle royal on her hands this morning, certain he'd insist she move back into the mansion and be kept under lock and key twenty-four hours a day. "What's the catch?"

"I've hired protection for you." Rusty ran the tip of his big, meaty finger around his empty cup. Smiling, he glanced up at Addy, a mischievous twinkle in his green eyes.

"What did you do, call Sam Dundee this morning and have him fly in some of his men?" Addy hated the thought of someone following her every move, but it was an acceptable alternative to moving back to her father's house.

"I talked to Sam. He's arranging some extra security, but he suggested a private bodyguard for you, someone he thinks is the best my money could buy." Sticking his cigar back in his mouth, Rusty inhaled deeply, then released a cloud of smoke.

Addy felt the tension in the room, an underlying tremor of emotions coming from the others sitting around the table. She glanced over at Brett, handsome, syrupy sweet Brett, who simply smiled at her. But there was something in his eyes, an odd look that Addy didn't understand. Turning her attention to Dina, she again noted the resentment the other woman couldn't disguise.

Taking a deep breath, she finally looked at Nick Romero, whose tight jeans and cotton knit shirt took nothing away from his aura of sophistication. The tiny diamond stud glistened against his bronze earlobe. Addy tried not to remember the way he'd kissed her, the way he'd made her feel. She didn't want to have any more romantic fantasies about him being her personal champion, her paladin. But the minute she looked at him, her control slipped. A tingling warmth spread through her. She fought it, annoyed. Nick stared at her, his face blank.

"What do you mean, a private bodyguard?" She didn't like the sound of it.

"Sit down, little girl." Rusty reached into his pants pocket and pulled out a rumpled sheet of paper. "Take a look at this."

Addy picked up the paper, scanning the typewritten words. *Addy McConnell will not be harmed if you follow our instructions. We will contact you soon with our demands. Do not involve the authorities. Your daughter's life depends on your cooperation.*

Pulling out a chair, Addy sat down beside Brett Windsor. He casually laid his arm across the back of her chair. "It came in the morning mail," he said. "Rusty's been horribly upset since he read it."

"These kidnappers were so sure of themselves that they mailed this yesterday." Rusty grabbed the letter out of Addy's trembling fingers. "Nick has already talked to the police and the FBI as well as Sam Dundee."

Jerking around, Addy glared at Nick, whose face was still as unreadable to her as hieroglyphics. "You've put Nick in charge?"

"Considering his background and connections, he volunteered." Rusty cleared his throat, and Addy knew he was trying not to reveal how overwrought he was, how deeply disturbed he was by the memories of that long-ago kidnapping that had ended so tragically. Addy would give anything to prevent the pain she knew he was feeling. Rusty McConnell was a good man. He didn't deserve such torment.

"The letter and envelope it came in will be thoroughly tested, but my guess is that it will be clean, the stationery the kind you can buy anywhere." Nick tapped the edge of the table with his index finger. "The type is computer printer. Most likely from a computer available to a vast number of people."

Addy watched Nick's finger as he continued tapping lightly on the table. She hated herself for remembering the way that finger had caressed her lips. "I suppose I should thank you, once again, for all your help, Mr. Romero. Too bad you're leaving in a couple of days. Going to El Paso to visit your grandmother, aren't you?"

Addy glanced at Dina, whose perfectly made-up face paled slightly, the lush pink blusher on her cheeks seeming overly bright. Her father's fiancée now knew that she'd overheard part of her early morning conversation with Nick.

"Maria is going to be so upset by your change in plans," Dina said, clasping her hands in front of her, cushioning them against her breasts. She looked pleadingly at Rusty. "She's eighty-five, you know, and hasn't seen Nick in over a year."

"Why have you changed your plans?" Addy's heart sank. She didn't want this man here, disrupting her life, especially not now when she was going to have to fight her father to maintain her hard-won independence. She wasn't sure she had the strength to fight two domineering men.

"Your father has asked me to stay on, to help out." Nick leaned back in his chair, glancing first at Addy while he talked, then turning to Rusty. "You might as well go ahead and tell her. She's not going to like it."

"Addy—"

"Tell me what? About the extra security Sam Dundee has arranged, and about these private bodyguards?" Addy hated the way her father hesitated, realizing that he dreaded what he had to say. "More security here at the house? At the company?"

"Some, yes, but mostly for you," Rusty said.

"At the M.A.C. day-care center, right? And bodyguards to watch my house and follow me wherever I go?" She did hate the thought of losing her privacy and a good deal of her freedom, but she wasn't stupid. She knew when her father did something out of overprotectiveness and when it really was for her own good. "I don't like it, but I realize that it's necessary until the authorities discover whoever's behind this kidnap scheme."

"You're being very sensible about this," Dina said. "Rusty was so sure you'd rebel."

Addy thought that her future stepmother sounded disappointed that she wasn't fighting her father. "As long as Daddy understands that I'm not going to leave my home or give up my job, then he can hire a dozen bodyguards for all I care."

"He hasn't hired a dozen bodyguards for you," Brett said, his dazzling smile still in place. "Just one."

"I don't understand." Addy turned to her father. "One man can't stay awake twenty-four hours a day."

"He won't need to if he's sleeping at the foot of your bed." Brett glanced across the table, giving Nick a hard look.

"What?" Shoving her chair backward, Addy jumped to her feet.

Rusty slammed his big fist down on the table, the jar bouncing the china, crystal and silverware, creating sharp tinkling sounds. Creamed coffee sloshed out of Brett's cup. The centerpiece vase of roses teetered, but didn't topple over.

"Sam Dundee is sending some men for around-the-clock surveillance, at your house and at work, but I want someone right by your side, twenty-four hours a day, keeping you safe. Somebody with experience as a fighter, a warrior. A man who can kill to protect you if it comes to that."

"You've asked Sam Dundee to send a man to stay with me twenty-four hours a day?" Hot, spitting indignation filled her. She could not accept this decree. "No, absolutely not! I'm willing to agree to almost anything else, but not a live-in caretaker.''

"I'm sorry, Addy, but I can't give you a choice in the matter.'' Rusty stood up and reached out for his daughter, then dropped his arms when she moved away from him.

"What if...if I agree to move back here?'' Did her father have any idea what that offer had cost her? She was willing to take a step back into her sheltered past, if only he'd be reasonable.

"Wherever you stay and whatever you do, Nick is going to be with you. Do you understand that from now until the kidnapper is caught, Nick Romero is going to be your shadow?'' Rusty tried again to touch his daughter. Again she retreated.

"Nick Romero?'' Addy exclaimed.

"Sam Dundee agreed that he was the best man for the job,'' Rusty said. "I thought so myself, but had a few doubts because of Nick's....er...well, his bum leg. But Sam assured me that he doesn't have a man as capable as Nick. Sam said Nick Romero was the best.''

"I tried to convince your father that Nick wasn't fully recovered, that his being crippled would prevent him from being able to do the best job of protecting you.'' Dina clutched the white linen napkin in her small hands, twisting it around and around, her sharp pink nails biting into the material.

"His being crippled certainly didn't prevent him from rescuing me last night,'' Addy said, then realized, too late, that she'd just defended the last man on earth she wanted protecting her.

"Romero always has been the physical type,'' Brett said, surveying Nick's big body with a touch of superiority and a great deal of disdain. "Brawn over brains, so to speak.''

"A Navy SEAL and a top DEA agent has to have plenty of smarts,'' Rusty said, eyeing Brett with contempt. "And he's the only man I know, besides myself, that I'd trust to take care of my little girl.''

Addy didn't like the look her father gave Nick. It said they shared some special secret. Why did her father trust Nick so completely, especially with her life?

Dina voiced Addy's thoughts. "You certainly took an instant liking to Nick, didn't you?"

"Sure did," Rusty said.

"Of course, I've known Nick almost all my life and I trust him, but—well…Addy's life will be quite safe with him, but I'm not sure about her virtue." Dina's smile radiated a frosty warning.

Addy glared at the older woman. Brett appeared shocked. Nick smiled. Rusty bellowed with laughter.

"Addy can protect her own virtue if she wants to," Rusty said, still chuckling. "I'm well aware of your brother-in-law's reputation with the ladies. I've got one myself. Nothing wrong with a man liking women!"

"Are you saying that you don't mind if Addy has to fight Nick off every night?" Dina ran her gaze over Addy's slender body encased in the simple gray dress, spotted with dirt and ripped on one sleeve. "Even though Addy's hardly his type, sooner or later, she's bound to appeal to him if the two of them are together constantly."

"Addy's not his type, huh?" Rusty reached out, pulling his daughter close to his side. She didn't resist. "Likes 'em shorter and fuller and sexier, huh?"

"I think Addy is lovely," Brett said. "She has a real cameo beauty, and such elegance."

"Thank you, Brett." Addy jabbed her father in the ribs with her elbow.

"If the time comes when Addy starts looking good to Nick, then I think she'll know how to handle him," Rusty said. "Addy not only looks like me, she's smart like me. She'll know exactly what to do with a man like Nick."

There was a conspiracy afoot. Addy was certain. Her father and Nick Romero knew something that no one else in this room knew. Something about her and Nick.

"I'm totally opposed to Nick getting involved in all this." Dina dropped her twisted napkin on the table. "He isn't physically sound. His last operation was only six weeks ago."

"I know how fond you are of Nick," Rusty said. "But he's quite fit. Sam Dundee told me himself that he'd offered Nick a job with him as soon as he'd finished his visit to El Paso."

"Well, Addy, what are we going to do with these men?" Dina asked, but she didn't look at the younger woman.

"You can do whatever you want," Addy said. "I'm going home."

"Not without Nick," Rusty said, giving her a tight hug.

Addy pulled out of her father's embrace, turned to Nick and smiled. "We can go in your car. Mine's at home since Daddy sent the limo for me last night."

Nick stood, retrieving his cane from its resting place against the side of the table. Walking toward Addy, he offered her his arm. She glanced from his smiling face to his big arm, then looked over at Dina, who was watching them intently, a frown marring her perfect features. Addy slipped her arm through Nick's. "I wouldn't dream of making you sleep at the foot of my bed," Addy said, loud enough for everyone in the room to hear.

"I could take that as an invitation to share your bed."

"It is an invitation—for you to sleep in my guest bedroom."

"That won't do," Nick said. "I'll be too far away."

"It's the room next to mine."

"I should be in the room with you."

Addy realized that three pairs of eyes watched them and three sets of ears listened to every word they said. When they reached the door leading into the foyer, she paused, glancing around the room. Her father seemed a little too pleased with himself. Brett was still smiling, but that odd look hadn't left his eyes. Dina was positively seething with jealousy. Addy wondered if her father was too blind to see it.

"We'll work something out," Addy said, then lowered her voice to a whisper as she and Nick stepped out into the foyer. "You are not staying in my room. I—I'm not going to fight Daddy about this. He's scared. Anything could happen with his high blood pressure and bad heart. I may have to endure your presence twenty-four hours a day, but I will not have you invading my bedroom."

"I never enter a lady's bedroom uninvited."

"Good. That settles it, then."

"Does it?" Nick asked, his smile widening at the look of surprise on Addy's face.

Huntsville traffic, especially on a Saturday morning, was maddening, but no better or worse than in any bustling city its size. Nick maneuvered his '68 silver Jag out of slow moving lanes and into more rapid ones, deftly avoiding the areas under construction as much as possible. The drive from the McConnell estate to the Twickenham district took almost twenty minutes. During the entire drive, Addy had been subdued. He'd wondered if she was pouting, but decided she wasn't the type. She was too direct. More likely, she was thinking about what had happened last night, how close she'd come to being a victim, and how drastically her life would change during the following days, maybe even weeks or months. There was no way to tell how quickly the authorities would nab the would-be kidnapper, or even if they would ever discover his or her identity. Money, if that were the true motive for the kidnapping, was a powerful inducement. There was the constant danger that he or she would try again.

"Turn here," Addy said pointing. "It's the second house. White with black shutters."

He parked the car in the small narrow driveway, killed the motor and glanced at Addy's home. Where her father's house was a replica of antebellum splendor, sporting huge white columns and a wraparound veranda, this house was authentic. Nick didn't know much about styles, but he could tell the house was old. Built long before the turn of the century would be his guess. Glistening snowy white in the noonday summertime sunshine, the house boasted a fresh coat of paint as did the glossy black shutters. Someone had spent a fortune restoring this place. That someone was probably Addy McConnell.

Opening the car door, Addy stepped out onto the sidewalk, stretching her long, slender frame that had been cramped in the confines of the small sports car. Nick watched the way she moved, all fluid and graceful. Her arms arched above her head, hiking up her skirt. He got a good view of her legs—small ankles, well-shaped calves, and long, trim thighs. Nick felt a tightening in his gut, and cursed himself for being a fool. Kidding Addy about seducing her was one thing, but actually doing it would be quite another matter. Kidding her was fun; the thought of making love to her actually scared him.

"Are you getting out or are you going to sit there staring at me all day?" she asked.

"I'll get my bag." He grabbed the battered brown leather suitcase he'd used for countless years and followed her up the steps leading to the small front portico supported by double columns on each side. "How long have you lived here?"

"For five years." She unlocked the front door. "Before that I shared an apartment with Janice. Before Ron came along."

"Ron's the boyfriend, right? The sulky-looking guy who picked her up last night?" Nick stepped over the threshold and felt as if he'd been transported back in time. The pale yellow walls added warmth to the wide foyer. A dramatic staircase, built against the left wall, curved upward.

"I didn't know you'd met Ron." Addy soaked in the beauty of her home, glancing around, proud of each familiar piece of furniture, each picture on the wall, every detail over which she'd fretted. "He's all right, I guess. Janice loves him and says they're getting married eventually. He's got a big chip on his shoulder when it comes to people with money. I think he's the type that would like to be rich, but doesn't want to work for it."

"Is Janice rich?" Nick ran the toe of his shoe over the blue and cream wool rug that covered the wide plank floor.

"It's a nineteenth-century Chinese rug." Addy pointed to Nick's feet. "And, no, Janice isn't rich. Her father squandered most of her mother's inheritance. All she has left is half interest in our grandparents' home, Elm Hill."

"Is everything in this room old?" Nick asked.

"Almost every item is antique," Addy said. "From the Federal period piano built around 1815," she pointed to the small musical instrument placed directly beneath the staircase, "to the Chippendale cherry side chairs, to that original Jan Weenix still life on the wall."

"Mmm . . . Is Elm Hill worth anything?"

"Yes, Elm Hill is definitely worth something. Why do you ask?"

"If Janice isn't rich, why doesn't she sell her half of the estate?"

"Our grandparents' will prohibits Janice from selling her half to anyone but me."

"Has Janice asked you to buy it?" Nick wondered about Janice's boyfriend. Rusty had told him that Ron Glover was a low-life creep who'd spent most of his teen years in and out of juvenile court. He'd been arrested numerous times as an adult, but had never been convicted.

"No. Why?"

"Just curious."

"Curious about Ron Glover, wondering if he's money-hungry enough to plot my kidnapping?" Addy placed her foot on the bottom step of the staircase.

Gripping his walking stick with one hand, Nick tightened his hold on his suitcase with the other. "Is he?"

Addy continued up the stairs, Nick following. "I don't know about Ron. It's possible. He's not a very nice man, but then neither is my ex-husband."

"Gerald Carlton? You think he might be behind the kidnap plot? Why? Rusty said his second wife's father is quite wealthy, that he made Gerald a vice-president in his company."

Addy opened the door to the first bedroom. "Gerald's *wife* is wealthy, not Gerald. Believe me, he's far more money-hungry than Ron Glover and far smarter."

Nick walked into the guest bedroom, a medium-sized square room. The upper walls were pale cream, the bottom wainscoted surface had been painted a light olive green. The bed, with tall, thin posters, stood in the middle of the room, an embroidered chenille spread covering it. To the left of the bed a wooden cupboard filled with knickknacks fitted neatly into the corner and a huge bedside table rested on a large area rug to the right. A stack of books lay atop the old chest nestled at the foot of the bed.

"Reminds me of a bed and breakfast I stayed in once a few years back." He set down his leather suitcase. "You really hate your ex-husband, don't you?"

"I did hate him for a long, long time. Now—now, I'm not sure. I don't wish him dead, but—but I hate seeing him so happy with his wealthy wife and fat, healthy babies."

"So we have two suspects," Nick said, sitting down on the bed, testing it by bouncing lightly up and down. "New mattress?"

"What do you mean we have two suspects?"

"Well, not counting the fact that the kidnapper may be some stranger, some unknown criminal out to get rich quick, we have an ex-husband who obviously hates you and your father as much as you hate him . . . and we have your cousin's boyfriend, who'd like to get rich without earning his money the old-fashioned way."

"I see." Addy's face paled. "My room is right next door. I'm going to take a bath and change clothes. Why don't you look around and check the place out for yourself?"

"What sort of locks do you have on the doors? Dead bolt? And what about the windows? Is there a security system?"

"I don't know about the doors and windows, but, yes, there is a security system. It isn't on right now. I often forget to turn it on. I forgot last night. Daddy's always fussing at me."

"What about some lunch?" Nick suggested.

"Are you cooking?" she asked, then walked outside into the hallway.

"How about if we order pizza?"

"No anchovies," Addy said, "and lots and lots of black olives."

Nick inspected the room, wondering if the entire house looked like this. Picking up his suitcase, he lifted it onto the bed, then looked around for a closet. There wasn't one. Instead he found a large, mahogany armoire, empty except for several ladies' straw hats lying across the single top shelf.

Within a few minutes, he heard water running. Addy was taking a bath. His mind quickly spanned the short distance between Addy's bath and her naked body. He wished he wasn't so damned curious about what she looked like without her clothes. Probably skinny, he thought, then remembered the glimpse of her shapely thigh. Hell, he'd been a fool to agree to Rusty's request. He had no business playing bodyguard to Dina's future stepdaughter. He should have insisted Sam Dundee send in one of his best men from Atlanta.

Nick hated admitting that he didn't want another man guarding Addy McConnell night and day for God knew how long. She was a needy woman, ripe for the picking and he couldn't bear to think of her giving herself to some other guy, some guy who would break her heart. He, on the other hand, had the willpower to stay with her and protect her without seducing her, despite what he'd led her to believe.

And...he didn't trust anyone else to keep her safe. That was the bottom line. Addy was in danger, and there was something about her that brought out all the possessive, protective instincts deep inside him. The only way anyone was going to hurt Addy was over his dead body.

Addy and Nick sat in shield-back chairs with cane bottoms. The crusty remains of a large sausage pizza, with extra black olives, covered the grease-stained box lying in the middle of an oak trestle table. Nick took a deep swallow from his beer, sprawling his long legs outward, resting his heels against a braided throw rug.

"You know, Addy, you're taking this awfully well. A lot better than I expected. You've been playing the part of the perfect hostess ever since we got here."

"I don't want you in my house." She picked up a canned cola. "I don't want anyone acting as my live-in bodyguard. But my seventy-year-old father has high blood pressure, a bad heart, and he refuses to stop smoking those awful cigars. Things are going to be difficult enough without my acting childish. I plan to cooperate with you as much as I can."

"You're being too nice to me." Nick glanced around the huge, oak-paneled kitchen. The floors boasted their original wide planks, and a chest-high brick fireplace covered a third of one wall. "Are we playing some sort of game?"

"You're the one who seems to enjoy playing games." Addy sipped her cola, then frowned at him. "My father wants you here. So be it. Despite the fact that I will not allow anyone, not even Daddy, to keep me locked up for my own safety, I know I'm in danger and I want protection, for my sake and for Daddy's. If anything happened to me—"

"Rusty told me about your brother."

"They—they shot him in the head. Daddy gave them a million dollars, and they killed Donnie anyway. He was only nine. I was six."

"And after that, Rusty kept you in a gilded cage?"

She nodded. He noticed the shimmering moisture glazing her eyes. She looked down at her lap, avoiding his scrutiny.

"You're right," Nick said, staring directly at her. "I do like to play games, especially with women. And I can't promise that I won't play games with you, from time to time. You jump to the bait so quickly. I can get you riled up in no time and I admit I enjoy kidding you."

"You annoy me by making sexual suggestions." Addy jumped up, pouring what was left of her cola down the sink drain. "If you keep doing that, we're going to be fighting all the time. Is that what you want?"

"A little harmless flirtation is good for you, didn't you know that?" Nick picked up the pizza carton. Looking around for a garbage can, he saw none. "Where's the trash?"

"In the pantry." She pointed him in the right direction. "Save your flirtation for Dina and other women who enjoy it."

"You might enjoy it, if you'd give me half a chance. Most women think I'm irresistible." Nick tried not to laugh when he saw the anger in her eyes. Somewhere along the way, Addy McConnell had forgotten how to have a good time, how to joke and laugh and be carefree. Maybe, during their stay together, he could teach her a thing or two about enjoying life. When the image of her lying upstairs in his bed, her curly red hair spread out and covering her naked breasts, flashed through Nick's mind, he groaned.

"I'm not into one-night stands or brief, meaningless affairs." Addy clutched the edge of the sink.

"I said I liked flirting with women. I didn't say I bedded every woman I found attractive." In recent years, Nick's tastes had become very discriminating and he'd sought more than sex from his relationships. Maybe he was getting old, but the idea of finding *the right woman* appealed to him more and more. Of course, she'd be curvaceous and blond. She'd have a sense of humor, enough to laugh at his jokes, anyway. Naturally, she'd be dynamite in bed and no more interested in marriage than he was.

"Since Dina pointed out that I'm not your type, why waste your time with me? Is it that important for all women to fall swooning at your feet?"

Nick laughed, picturing Addy swooning at his feet. He liked the idea, and wondered if there was any possibility that she—

The insistent ring of the telephone interrupted Nick midthought. Addy reached for the wall phone.

"Hello? Yes, he's here." She handed the red telephone to Nick.

"Nick Romero. When? . . . Where? . . . Yes, the wound would be in his right hand. A stiletto blade . . . Powerfully built. Young, maybe early twenties. Long brown hair . . . Okay. We'll be there shortly."

Addy gazed at Nick, wide-eyed. "What was that all about?"

"The police think they've found your would-be kidnapper."

"What? Has he told them who hired him?" On trembly legs, Addy walked over to Nick, grabbing him by the arm.

"He couldn't tell them anything. He's dead. Been dead since early this morning." Nick put his arm around Addy to steady her. She swayed into him slightly, then righted herself immediately, pulling out of his comforting embrace.

"What do they want us to do?" she asked. "Identify him?"

"Yes." He hated seeing that pale, haunted look on her face. "I can't leave you alone here, so I'll have to take you with me. But I can identify the body. There's no need for you to see him."

"Whoever hired him, killed him."

"It looks that way."

"He—or she—will try again."

"Probably." Nick wanted to pull her back in his arms and comfort her. He wanted to promise her that he'd take care of her, not let anyone hurt her. But Addy was afraid of him, scared of him as a man. And as much as he hated to admit it, maybe she had a right to be. He couldn't ever remember feeling so possessive and protective. Hell, maybe his taste in women was changing. Could it be that after all these years of chasing some bosomy blond dream, the woman destined to change his life was a skinny redhead?

Chapter 4

The room was cool. Nick was hot. He'd sprawled his big body out on the soft cream sheet, kicking the covers to the foot of the bed. Normally he slept in the raw, but considering the possibility that he might have to rush to Addy McConnell's defense at a moment's notice he'd left on his briefs.

He wasn't sure of the time, but figured it was close to midnight. After a quick supper of cold ham sandwiches and potato salad, he and Addy had sat in her small den adjacent to the kitchen and listened to one of her favorite tapes, the musical score from *Phantom of the Opera*. Having been raised in Texas, Nick preferred the elemental sounds of country, but over the years he'd learned to appreciate various types of music. He found that Addy's tastes were more select. She preferred classical and semi-classical above all else. She was a patron of the arts, having season tickets to the symphony.

More than one luscious blonde from Nick's past had exposed him to the social world of the ultrarich. He fit in just as well with multimillionaires as he had with his Navy SEAL comrades and his fellow DEA agents. If Nick Romero was anything, he was adaptable. He had discovered early in life that the people who succeeded were those who found a way to use the system to their advantage. Even a half-breed Mexican kid with an illiterate dirt farmer for a father and a whore for a mother could rise above his humble beginnings if he had the guts and determination to change, to learn and grow, to assimilate every new experience. In other words, to adapt.

Listening to Addy move around in her room, Nick figured she was as restless as he, and was probably having a difficult time getting to sleep. Going to the police station had been far more upsetting for Addy than she'd been willing to admit. Nick was accustomed to crime, was used to being exposed to the seamier side of life where murder was a common occurrence. But Addy was not. When he'd tried to discuss the attempted kidnapping with her, she'd shied away from the subject and had downright refused to talk about the untimely death of her assailant, who had died from a fall off a steep embankment on Monsano Mountain.

Addy was scared, but was trying hard not to show it. Nick wanted to assure her that it was all right to be afraid, that it was not only normal but smart. Bravery and fear were constant companions, as inseparable as life and death. Fear could save your life, whereas fearlessness often proved fatal.

He heard the door to Addy's bedroom open, then the click-click tapping of her shoes. Suddenly, all sound ceased. He sat up in his bed, listening. The stairs creaked. Someone was walking up or down.

Easing open his own bedroom door, Nick surveyed the darkened hallway. Moonlight spread out over the wooden floor like creamy yellow-white butter across dark toast. Still hearing the sporadic creaking, Nick eased carefully down the hall until he reached the landing. Addy, her satin high-heel slippers dangling from her fingers, tiptoed down the stairs. Nick sucked in his breath at the sight of her retreating back. Her tall slender body, visible in the soft moonlight, was draped in a pale lavender confection of gossamer silk and lace.

What the hell was she doing? She looked like a woman running away, trying to escape from someone or something. He'd like to go back to bed, go to sleep and forget that Addy, upset, uncertain and scared, was wandering around downstairs. But he couldn't. She was his responsibility.

He returned to his room, slipped into a pair of jeans and made his way quietly down the stairs, the faint tapping of his cane echoing in the stillness. From the foyer, he could see light under the kitchen door. He hated to intrude on her, to interrupt her privacy, but dammit, he wouldn't be doing his job if he didn't check on her.

Easing open the door, he stopped dead still when he saw her standing in profile, slowly pouring herself a glass of chilled white wine. Her red hair, deep and rich and gloriously bright like the rusty, red clay earth of Alabama, hung in curly disarray down her back and across her shoulders. The silky peignoir set she wore swept the floor. The robe, a sheer concoction edged with heavy lace at the hem and across the bottom of each long sleeve, had fallen open to reveal an empire style gown of the same diaphanous lavender material. The bodice, cut low and revealing the slight swell of Addy's breasts, was covered with matching lace.

Dear God, had he ever actually thought this woman, this smoldering female temptation, was plain? If Addy McConnell chose to dress circumspectly in public, she revealed her true sensuous self in her sleepwear. Nick's whole body tightened with anticipation. He didn't think he'd ever seen anything as desirable as the vision before him, one he found difficult to believe was real.

"Addy?" Even to his own ears his voice sounded rough and hard.

She jumped, startled by his invasion. With her green eyes glaring and her pink mouth opening to a perfect oval, she stared at him. He noticed that her hand, holding the wineglass, trembled ever so slightly.

"Sorry if I frightened you." He walked through the doorway and into the kitchen. "I heard you come downstairs and wanted to make sure you were all right."

"I'm fine." She set the glass on the counter. "I'm sorry if I disturbed your sleep."

"I wasn't asleep." He eyed the wine bottle. "I'm your bodyguard, remember? I don't sleep unless you do." He nodded toward the sauvignon blanc. "Pour me a glass, too, if you think it'll help us both get a good night's rest."

She looked at him with pleading eyes. "Couldn't you leave me alone? I'm not used to having someone else around, watching me, monitoring my every move."

"It can't be helped, so we'd both better try to make the best of it." Moving slowly, Nick stopped just short of touching her. His gaze traveled over her, from fiery hair to bare feet. "What did you do with your shoes?"

"I tossed them in the chair." She nodded toward her slippers. "There." Addy wished he would stop looking at her. He made her nervous staring at her as if he could see straight through her gown. But then, maybe he could. She wasn't accustomed to men seeing her in her underwear or her sleepwear, so she indulged herself in her passion for sexy, frilly and very feminine attire that she alone would see. But Nick could see her. All of her, here in the kitchen light.

She could feel a delicious warmth spreading through her, casting a delicate pink hue to her naturally golden complexion. This man had a strange effect on her, creating a desire in her to experiment with the danger she knew he offered. Nick Romero would be an exciting, demanding lover. Something she'd never known. But she was a failure at intimacy, unable to respond properly, incapable of achieving fulfillment. She didn't dare risk the utter humiliation she'd feel if she disappointed Nick. She'd been devastated by

Gerald's frustration over her inadequacies, and Gerald was certainly no match for a man like Nick, a man whose every look, word and move reeked of sensuality.

Nick caressed the neck of the wine bottle absentmindedly, wishing it was Addy's soft throat. Retrieving a glass from the row of crystal goblets inside the open cupboard, he poured the clear golden liquid.

Addy watched the way his big hand moved over the wine bottle and the crystal glass. She could almost feel his touch on her. Instantly her nipples hardened.

Taking a sip of the chilled dry wine, Nick looked up at Addy, his dark eyes conveying a message of desire. She tried to look away from him, but his gaze held her spellbound. When he glanced down at her breasts, she sucked in a deep breath, willing herself not to sway toward him.

"Why don't we take our wine into the den," he said. "We'll be more comfortable in there, and we can talk."

For a split second she thought he was going to touch her. She was half afraid he would and half afraid he wouldn't. "I . . . I don't want to talk. I just want to be left alone."

"But I can't leave you alone. You know that. It's my job to guard you against danger twenty-four hours a day." He could see that she was on the verge of angry tears. He suspected that she was as upset over her reaction to him as she was over the turmoil in her life. She was a woman who seemed to pride herself on her independence and self-control, and here he was undermining both. As long as the threat of a kidnapping hung over her head, Addy would require his presence as a bodyguard. And, as long as the two of them were together, sparks were going to fly and both of them were at the mercy of their own baser instincts. He didn't doubt for a minute that Addy wanted him as much as he wanted her. He could see it in her eyes, feel it in her body's response to him.

"Nick, please . . . don't—"

"Don't what, Red? I haven't done anything."

Did he honestly think he had done nothing? Addy wondered. Surely a man as experienced as Nick Romero knew only too well what effect he was having on her. Circumstances might have forced her to accept his presence in her home. Her life could be in danger, and she knew her father's health and peace of mind were at risk. If only the man her father had chosen as her bodyguard was anyone else on earth beside this devastatingly handsome man with the power to awaken her long dormant sexual longings.

"Come on, Red, let's have a midnight powwow. We'll swap old war stories." He placed his hand on the small of her back, opening his palm to cover a wide expanse of her silk-clad body. She tensed immediately. "Relax." He gave her a slight nudge. "This has been a hell of a day for you. You don't really want to be alone. You want to talk and yell and scream and maybe even cry."

"You think you're so damned smart, don't you?" Addy walked away from him, removing herself from his warm, caressing hand. "For your information, Mr. Romero, I seldom cry. I used up a lifetime supply of tears years ago."

He followed her into the den, not replying to her comment. Somewhere behind the security wall she'd built around herself, Addy's deepest emotions still existed, waiting to be released. Nick wanted to be the man to penetrate that wall, to tear it down—brick by brick if necessary. He wanted to be the man to bring those buried feelings back to life.

Entering the dark den, Addy turned on a small brass table lamp decorated with china roses and covered with a parchment shade. A warm, mellow glow filled the room, revealing pale eggshell walls and an orderly clutter of antiques, from a painted Pennsylvania German chest to a Queen Anne curly maple chair.

Addy sat down on the old sofa which was covered with a paisley throw and held a variety of crewel, cross-stitch and needlepoint pillows. She clutched the crystal goblet in her unsteady hand, her eyes focusing on the liquid shifting back

and forth. Bringing the glass to her lips, she sipped the wine
slowly, trying to ignore Nick Romero when he entered her
cosy, private hideaway. She'd been forced to share several
hours with him before bedtime, all the while wishing she
were alone. She'd been able to handle both Nick and her
own emotions earlier, but now she felt vulnerable, less able
to protect herself.

Nick walked across the wooden floor, barely noticing the
throw rugs he stepped on as he made his way toward Addy.
She sat on the small sofa. There was room for him, but he
could tell by her stiffly arched back, her tilted chin and her
cool manner that she would prefer he didn't join her. He sat
down in a sturdy flowered wingback chair to the left of the
sofa, a large round end table separating them.

He watched her. He'd seen people who tried to keep everything bottled up inside. Sooner or later they exploded like
a time bomb. Addy needed to release some of her pent-up
emotions.

"Do you think Gerald Carlton could be behind the kidnapping attempt?" Nick asked, pleased when Addy glared
at him with fiery green eyes. "Is he capable of murder?"

Taking another sip of her wine, Addy closed her eyes,
knowing that images of her life with her former husband
would flash through her mind. How many times, she wondered, had Gerald made her feel worthless as a woman?
How many nights had she waited for him to come home
from some other woman's bed? How many times had he
accused her of being unattractive and frigid? But was he
capable of murder?

"Gerald is capable of almost anything if there's enough
money in it for him." She set her wineglass down on the end
table and turned to Nick. "Could he kill for money? I don't
know. Possibly. Probably."

"He really did a number on you, didn't he, Red?"

"I would prefer not to talk about my marriage."

"You prefer letting all that pain fester inside you like an
infected wound? That's a mistake."

"What would you have me do? Pour out my heart and soul to you so that you can comfort me? Is your male ego so enormous that you think you have to prove to me how wrong my ex-husband was about me? Is that what this is all about? You want to prove that you're man enough to make the ugly, frigid, little rich girl enjoy sex for the first time in her life?"

Nick hadn't expected such a vehement reaction. Obviously, he'd struck a nerve, a sexual nerve. He took a generous sip from his own wineglass, then set it beside Addy's on the table. "Did you love Carlton when you married him?" Nick wasn't sure why he wanted her answer to be negative. What difference did it make if Addy had loved her ex-husband? It was apparent she despised the man now.

"What?" Dammit! How could she have allowed herself to lose control the way she had? She hadn't meant to blurt out such personal information, but Nick had angered her. Somehow this man she'd known for a little over twenty-four hours had a way of provoking her strongest emotions. Her first impression of him had been right. He was a dangerous man.

"Did you love Carlton?"

"I think so. It was no grand passion or anything like that. I was twenty-five and I'd lived a fairly sheltered life. Men weren't exactly beating a path to my door. Gerald was charming and attentive and—and Daddy liked him."

"But you weren't in love with him?"

"I have no idea what being in love means." Addy jumped up, her hands knotted into fists as they rested against her hips. "I don't want to talk to you about Gerald or about love or sex. Daddy's paying you to be my bodyguard, not my psychiatrist, so just leave me alone."

Nick stood up, reached down, picked up her wineglass and handed it to her. "I'd say you've been left alone for too long."

Hesitating briefly, she took the glass, making sure their hands didn't touch. "I like being alone. It's preferable to spending time with insufferably macho men who think a Plain Jane like me should be grateful they've shown an interest.''

Nick laughed aloud at her words. Plain Jane indeed. Was it possible, really possible, that Addy had no idea how incredibly lovely she looked right this minute? Had her ex-husband totally destroyed her confidence in her sexual attractiveness? Damn, what Nick would give for five minutes alone with Gerald Carlton!

Stepping away from Nick, Addy downed the remainder of her wine, then set the glass on a nearby chest. Nick set his glass beside hers, then with a swift move that alarmed Addy, he stepped behind her, grasping one shoulder.

"What are you doing?" Her voice was breathless. His big hand clutched her silk-covered shoulder as he gave her a gentle nudge forward. "Nick, stop it!"

"I want to show you something," he said, giving her another shove. "Move, woman."

She balked, refusing to budge another inch. "Stop shoving me around and stop giving me orders. What's gotten into you?"

"I want you to walk out into the foyer."

"Why?"

"I told you. I want to show you something."

"This is my house. What could you possibly show me that I haven't seen a hundred times?" she asked, trying to pull away from him. He held her shoulder firmly.

"You have two choices," Nick said. "Either you march your little fanny out into the foyer or I'll carry you."

"You wouldn't dare." She eyed his cane.

"Try me."

She didn't bother to turn around and face Nick. She didn't have to see the look on his face to know he was serious. She could hear the determination in his voice. She knew that if he had to carry her, he would, even if walking unaided by his cane might be painful for him.

"Oh, all right." The day had been almost more than she could bear. Accepting Nick as a live-in bodyguard despite her desire to remain free. Finding out that the man who'd attempted to kidnap her last night had met a deadly fate at the hands of some unknown person or persons still intent on harming her. Realizing that, for the first time in her life, she was sexually attracted to a man. Strongly, irrationally attracted to a man she had begun to think of as her personal champion.

She simply wasn't up to any more emotional upheaval. She didn't have the strength to fight Nick. Not right now.

With his hand firmly planted on her shoulder, Nick guided her out into the foyer. Momentarily releasing her, he flipped the switch that turned on the chandelier. Light, glittering off the cut crystal, flooded the entrance hall.

Nick led her to the enormous gilt-framed mirror that hung on a side wall. He set his cane aside. Confusion filled Addy's mind and heart when Nick, standing behind her, his big, dark hands draping her shoulders like bronze claws, positioned her directly in front of the rectangular looking glass.

She tried to avert her eyes, as if afraid of what her reflection would reveal. When she gazed down at her feet, Nick released one shoulder, taking her chin in his hand and tilting her face upward. She closed her eyes. Whatever he was trying to do, she wanted no part of it. She wasn't going to let him make her see something she didn't want to see.

With his lips close to her ear, he whispered, "Open your eyes, Addy, and tell me what you see."

He ran his hand down her neck, caressing her throat. Then he reached out and encircled her waist with his arm, pulling her back against him. She felt his hard arousal against her buttocks. Inadvertently she cried out.

"Open your eyes."

"No." The word escaped from her throat on a tormented breath.

"If you're afraid to take a good look at yourself and tell me what you see, then just listen and I'll tell you what I see."

"Please, Nick—don't."

He splayed his hand across her stomach. She jerked, an instinctive reaction that could have been fear or passion. Nick knew enough about women to understand that Addy was afraid. More of herself than of him.

"I see a woman, Addy. A woman. Not a girl and not even a lady, though I know that you are a lady in every sense of the word."

She squirmed against him, trying to pull away, wishing she could escape before he said any more. "I hate you."

"No, you don't." His voice was deep and dark and incredibly sensuous. "You hate yourself, don't you, Addy? I'm making you feel like a woman and that frightens you."

"Why are you doing this to me?" She struggled against him. He held her tightly.

"God, Red, stop that! You've already got me so hot I'm about to lose it."

She stopped moving and stood perfectly still. His words seeped into her consciousness. Her body stiffened with denial, not wanting to admit that she was every bit as aroused as he was.

He ran his fingers through her hair, lifting it and watching the titian strands fall back to her shoulders as he released them. "You have beautiful hair. It's like fiery silk. Thick, wavy flames."

When he pulled her closer and closer against him, she didn't resist. He was weaving a spell with his words, words that she warned herself didn't mean a thing. Nick was a practiced lover, a Latin Romeo with the ability to charm any woman. She couldn't let him charm her. She didn't dare.

"Your skin," he said, caressing her neck, pushing aside her silk robe to fondle her shoulder. "Your skin is soft and smooth. All of your little freckles intrigue me. I'd like to kiss every one of them, and someday—someday soon—I will."

Addy drew in deep breaths trying to calm her raging senses. *Don't listen to him,* she told herself. *He doesn't mean what he's saying.*

He moved his hand downward, over her breasts, barely grazing her tight nipples. She closed her mouth, biting off a cry of excitement. Both of his hands spanned her waist. "Your body is sleek and slender and infinitely fascinating. When I first saw you, I thought you were flat-chested. I was wrong." He covered her small breasts with his hands, lifting their delicate weight, brushing her nipples with his thumbs. "They're high and firm and fill my hands. And I love the way your nipples hardened at my touch. You're a very responsive woman, Addy. Did you know that?"

She was beyond speaking, so she nodded. He buried his face against her neck, his mouth opening, his tongue lavishing seductive moisture on her heated flesh.

She leaned backward against him, unable to stop herself from succumbing to the enchantment of his words and the lure of his big hard body. Releasing her breasts, he slid his hands farther down her slender frame, stopping to grasp her hips, then gently kneading her buttocks. "Full and firm and tight." His hands skimmed the sides of her thighs. "Legs like a thoroughbred. Long and trim. Do you have any idea how much I want those long legs of yours wrapped around me?"

She groaned when he eased both hands across the front of her legs, delving between them, easing the silky fabric of her gown up against the hot moistness she could not hide.

"Open your eyes, Addy, and take a look at a beautiful, sensuous woman... a woman I want desperately."

She opened her eyes, took one look at herself in the mirror and squeezed her eyes shut. "No, no... no."

"You dress yourself in plain, unattractive clothes trying to disguise the beautiful woman you are, but you sleep in frothy negligees. I'll bet all your lingerie is utterly sexy and feminine, isn't it?"

She didn't respond. His hands still rested between her thighs. He lifted up, pressing his fingers against her. Thrashing her head from side to side, she moaned.

"I want to make love to you. To you, Addy. I don't give a damn about Rusty's millions and I don't care what your ex-husband says. With me...with us...sex would be different. Open your eyes, Red. Take a look at us and tell me that you know what I'm saying is true."

Addy opened her eyes slowly, forcing herself to look in the mirror. God, was that her? The woman she saw staring back at her *was* beautiful. She was filled with a beauty born of passion, her face flushed with desire, her body taut with longing. And Nick stood behind her, his big body hard against her, his maleness pounding demandingly. He moved his hands over her as she watched.

"What do you see, Addy? Tell me."

"It's not me," she said, her voice hoarse with mounting desire. "You've turned me into someone I don't know."

"It is you, Addy. The real you. The real woman who wants and needs. You're on fire. You're on fire for me."

"Nick?"

He turned her around, taking her in his arms. The image of the wanton woman in the mirror burned brightly in Addy's mind. Nick Romero was a sorcerer, a wizard, a magician. He possessed the power to drive her wild with desire, to make her look and act like a beautiful, desirable woman.

He was her defender...her champion...her paladin. And she longed to be his woman.

He nibbled at her lips, teasing them apart. She sighed, opening for his possession. He took her with a force that shook them both. He deepened the kiss. She clung to him, running her hands over his bare shoulders and back, pressing herself against him, hot and ready and desperate.

It was the most difficult thing he'd ever done, and he knew he would probably hate himself in the morning. But he couldn't take advantage of Addy. He realized that all he had to do was lead her to the nearest bed, and she'd let him make love to her all night. But tomorrow, she'd hate him and hate herself. He didn't want Addy McConnell's hate.

Releasing her mouth, he ran his hands up and down her arms. "We've got to stop, Red, or we won't be able to."

"Nick, I . . . please—"

He caressed her cheek with the tip of his finger. "I wanted you to see what a beautiful woman you are. Don't ever doubt that you're desirable. I want you, but I can't take you now when you're so vulnerable." The sad, puzzled look in her eyes told him that she was hurting, and it was his fault. Dammit all, the last thing on earth he wanted to do was cause this woman any more pain than she'd already suffered. "Do you understand what I'm saying and why?"

She stepped away from him, deliberately avoiding any eye contact with the mirror. "You're good, Nick Romero, damned good. A Latin lover and a Southern gentleman all rolled into one. A deadly combination. No wonder women can't resist you."

"Addy—"

She held up a hand to warn him off, then backed away slowly. "From now on, don't try to teach me anything else about myself, okay? Just do your job as my bodyguard and keep me safe. I—I'm not ready for a man as lethal as you . . . and I'm not sure I ever will be."

He watched her walk up the stairs. Her shoulders were erect, her head held high. He had no idea what was going on inside her, but he knew one thing for sure. Addy McConnell would never forget how beautiful and desirable she'd looked tonight. Unfortunately, neither would he.

Chapter 5

Nick wondered if Addy felt as if she were inside an armed camp. M.A.C. already had its own security force, but Rusty McConnell had ordered some highly trained professionals from Sam Dundee. The four men and two women who'd flown in from Atlanta the day before were on the job that morning when Nick and Addy arrived at the M.A.C. day-care center. Giving credit to Sam Dundee's superb training, Nick admitted that the six extra workers were as unobtrusive as possible, seeming to fit in as if they were long-time employees. But Addy McConnell could do little more than breathe without constant surveillance. Nick felt a little redundant and had told Rusty so when the two had shared an eight o'clock cup of coffee in the executives' office building. Rusty's long-time secretary Ginger Kimbrew had served them. The luscious brunette hadn't tried to hide her interest in Nick, and any other time he might have accepted her unspoken invitation, but, right now, the only woman who interested Nick was in an adjacent building trying her best to avoid any direct contact with him. Besides, Nick figured that Rusty and Ginger shared more than a business relationship, one that she wasn't quite ready to dissolve despite Rusty's engagement.

After fending off Ginger's blatant advances, Nick convinced Rusty that the hours Addy spent at M.A.C. would be the best time for him to play detective, using D.B. McConnell's money and power and his own government contacts.

Nick had decided that he'd make spot-checks on Addy during the day. His brain told him that it was part of his job. His male libido told him that he wanted to be near the desirable woman he'd held in his arms Saturday night. His heart refused to take part in the discussion.

A florist delivery boy accidentally bumped into Nick when they both reached out at the same time to open the door leading to the M.A.C. day-care center.

"Sorry, sir," the youth said.

Nick held the door open for him. "No problem. Go ahead. It looks like you've got your hands full." The overpowering sweet aroma of roses filled Nick's nostrils as he gazed down at the huge floral arrangement the boy held.

"Yeah, some guy must have it bad, huh? Two dozen red roses on a Monday morning."

The room they entered was a beehive of activity. Children of various ages, sizes, sexes and races were engaged in supervised play and work, while one select group of what Nick judged to be three-year-olds were lining up for mid-morning break. Janice Dixon handed out individual apple juice cartons while her helper gave each child a napkin and straw.

Nick saw Addy. Even though she only vaguely resembled the sexy woman from Saturday night, his body recognized the sensual beauty that lay behind the mask of baggy navy cotton slacks and oversized green T-shirt. He'd bet his silver Jag that underneath those nondescript casual clothes, Addy wore some skimpy pieces of lace and silk. Nick imagined her wearing emerald green bikini panties and match-ing bra, both the color of her incredible eyes.

Suddenly Nick noticed that Addy was deep in conversa-tion with a slender dark-haired man in a three-piece busi-ness suit. Nick didn't like the way the man looked at Addy, as if he had some type of claim on her. And he hated the way Addy smiled and then laughed at something the guy said. She'd never smiled at him that way, and he realized that he wanted to hear her laugh—with him, and not another man.

While Nick stood back watching and brooding, the de-livery boy approached Addy. "I'm looking for Addy McConnell."

"I'm Addy McConnell."

The boy handed Addy the huge green vase of red roses. "These are for you, ma'am."

Addy accepted the floral gift. Nick noted the surprised look on her face. Obviously it wasn't her birthday or any other special occasion. She turned toward her office, mo-tioning for her companion to follow. Nick took several ten-tative steps forward, stopping just outside her open office door.

She set the flowers on her desk, then removed the at-tached card. Her smile widened. Her green eyes bright-ened. Nick wanted to know who'd sent the flowers that gave Addy such pleasure.

He marched into her office. "Morning." He looked di-rectly at Addy, then shifted his gaze first to the flowers and then to the man standing beside her. "Just checking in. If you have a few minutes, we need to talk."

"All right. Come on in, Nick, and have a seat." Addy sensed Nick's displeasure, but couldn't quite figure out what was bothering him. Did he feel as awkward about Saturday night as she did? Neither of them had spoken about the in-cident in front of the mirror. All day yesterday they had walked on eggshells around each other. "I'd like you to meet Jim Hester, a friend of mine who just happens to be one of

M.A.C.'s top engineers. Jim, this is Nick Romero, the man Daddy's hired as my personal bodyguard.''

What was it with her? Nick wondered. Did she have a thing for engineers, or just engineers who worked for her father? And who was this guy, really, in whom Addy had confided about the attempted kidnapping? "Hester." Nodding to the other man, Nick held out his hand.

Jim Hester shook hands with a firm, forceful grip that surprised Nick. The guy looked like a typical desk jockey with his pale complexion, thinning brown hair and slender build. "I'm certainly glad to know that Addy's in such good hands, Mr. Romero. She's a special lady and we wouldn't want anything to happen to her. Tiffany and I are both very fond of her.''

"Tiffany?" Nick asked

"My daughter. She's one of the three-year-olds taking a juice break right now. So, if you two will excuse me, I'll go join her while y'all talk business." Jim headed for the door, then stopped and turned around. "You never did say who sent the roses.''

Nick didn't realize that he was holding his breath until Addy read the name on the card. "Brett Windsor."

"What the hell is Windsor doing sending you flowers?" Nick's outburst seemed to have startled Jim and angered Addy, both of them turning to stare at him.

"Brett Windsor? I thought you'd convinced him months ago that you weren't interested," Jim said, smiling.

"I did, but Brett occasionally still sends me flowers." Addy glared at Nick. "Gentlemen do that sort of thing, you know. They treat you with respect and consideration. Things that Latin lovers obviously bypass on their way to seducing women into their beds.''

Jim Hester cleared his throat. Addy's face flushed. Nick badly wanted to hit something.

"I'll stop back in and say goodbye before I return to work. If you two will excuse me, I'll see if Janice has an extra apple juice." Jim made his way out the door as quickly as possible.

Nick slammed closed the door to Addy's office. "So little Plain-Jane McConnell has two men in her life, huh?"

"It's not what you think." She didn't know why she was trying to explain to Nick about her relationships with Jim and Brett. Neither man loved her or desired her physically. One was only a friend and the other—

"Brett Windsor is good-looking and charming." Nick flung his arm out in a gesture of disgust as he pointed toward the roses. "He knows all the right things to say and do to impress a lady, but you know as well as I do that he's far more interested in Rusty's millions than he is in you."

"You don't think that I'm attractive enough to interest a man like Brett?" She threw out the challenge, daring Nick to reply. Smiling she leaned over and smelled the roses.

"Whether or not Windsor finds you attractive has nothing to do with this. The man is a user. He's been living off Dina for years." Propping his cane against the desk, Nick reached out, grabbing Addy by the shoulders. "Don't you realize that Brett Windsor is just as capable of a kidnapping scheme as your ex-husband? Encouraging him, for whatever reason, is a mistake."

"I have done nothing but discourage Brett. I'm not a total fool. Besides, I think you're overreacting because you're jealous of Brett's relationship with Dina."

"Dammit, Red, you say such stupid things! Dina is nothing more to me than a friend. I found out at an early age that she's poison to any man who cares about her." Nick pulled Addy close, so close that her breasts crushed into his chest. "Windsor is on my list of suspects. Stay away from him."

Addy twisted and turned in Nick's arm, trying to free herself. She hated the way he made her feel—all hot and damp and eager. "You're only my bodyguard. That doesn't give you the right to interfere in my personal life. The next thing I know you'll be telling me that Jim is on your list of suspects so I shouldn't see him anymore."

"Jim Hester isn't a suspect. Not yet." Nick lowered his head until his eyes met Addy's and his lips hovered over hers. "What's this Jim got that interests you so? He looks like a pretty ordinary guy. Is he divorced or widowed?"

Addy swallowed. She was hot. Nick was too close. She couldn't think. "Widowed. Why?"

"I just wondered…because of his daughter. She doesn't have a mother, then, does she?"

"No." Addy slipped her hands between her body and Nick's, giving him a shove. He held fast.

"I take it that you're very fond of Tiffany Hester."

"Stop questioning me like this. I don't like it." She struggled against him. "And I don't like your manhandling me whenever the notion strikes you. I may be your responsibility, but I'm not your personal property."

"That's a matter of opinion." Nick had never felt so possessive, so proprietary about a woman. He hated the thought that Addy might actually be interested in Brett Windsor or Jim Hester. Neither man was right for her. If either of them had been able to stir Addy's passions, she wouldn't turn into a smoldering flame every time he touched her. He, Nick Romero, was the right man to teach Addy what a sensuous woman she really was. No other man could do it. No other man would be allowed to even try. Hell, he was the only man who was ever going to touch her.

"When you interrupted Jim and me you said that you needed to talk to me, so say whatever you came here to say and leave. This place is crawling with security. I don't need you here and I certainly don't want you."

Nick glared at her, his black eyes boring into her. "How upset is Ginger Kimbrew that Rusty is marrying Dina?" Releasing Addy, Nick picked up his cane and stepped away, turning his back toward the wide expanse of windows that covered the back wall of Addy's femininely decorated office.

Addy sat down behind her white desk. "Ginger was Daddy's mistress for a number of years. She probably had high hopes of becoming the second Mrs. D.B. McConnell."

"How do the two of you get along?" Nick glanced around the room, taking note, for the first time, of the dainty lavender-flowered wallpaper, the matching gingham checked curtains at the windows and cushions on all the chairs. Ferns and green plants in various sizes filled every available space where sunlight could touch them.

"Ginger and I have never been close, but we've always been friendly. Why do you ask?"

Nick saw the realization dawn in Addy's eyes. "A woman scorned is capable of almost anything, right? What I'm wondering is if Ginger wants revenge against Rusty enough to plot the kidnapping of his only child."

"Oh, Lord, I'd never considered Ginger."

"Consider her. It won't pay to overlook any possible suspect and every conceivable motive."

"You don't think the motive is money?"

"I don't know. Hate and revenge are often as powerful as greed." Nick turned to her, wishing that he could give her the answers to all the questions he saw in her eyes. "Just don't trust anyone. Except your father and me."

"I hate living like this. I despise having to suddenly distrust people I know and like. But most of all I hate having you in charge of my life." Swinging around in her swivel rocker, Addy stared up at Nick. "Get out of here and leave me alone. Okay?"

He hated the pleading sound in her voice, knowing how difficult it had been for her to gain her independence and what a struggle it was for her to keep Rusty from controlling her life. "I'll check back in around lunchtime. Maybe we could go out for a bite."

"I'm sorry, but I'm having lunch with the children today."

"Then I'll join you and the romper room crowd. It's been years since I've eaten peanut butter and jelly sandwiches."

Addy's eyes widened. She hadn't expected him to invite himself to join her. "Fine. Be here at noon."

"You've got a date." Nick smiled all the way out of the office, not once turning around to see the expression on Addy's face.

Damned obstinate man. Overbearing. Bossy. Of all the men in the world, why was Nick Romero the one who'd come to her defense and rescued her from a kidnapping attempt? And why did her father like and trust him so much that he'd handed her over into Nick's safekeeping? And why, dear Lord, was he the first man since her divorce who made her think about risking her pride, her heart and her body?

Five minutes later, Addy looked up from her desk to find Jim Hester standing in the open doorway. She'd been so lost in her thoughts that she didn't know how long he'd been watching her.

"Come on in, Jim."

Closing the door behind him, Jim took a seat across from her desk. "Mr. Romero is a very interesting man."

"I imagine most people find him interesting." Addy wasn't quite sure where this conversation was going.

"Women in particular, I guess," Jim said.

"I understand he has a reputation. Why are you so interested in Nick?"

"Because you're so interested."

"I am not...I—Is it that obvious?" Addy couldn't deny her feelings, not to Jim. He was too good a friend, too dear and kind a man.

"I had hoped that someday you and I—Well, Tiffany and I are both terribly fond of you and—"

"There's nothing going on between Nick and me. Daddy's hired him as my bodyguard until this kidnapping threat is over. I'm not Nick's type. He isn't interested in a permanent relationship and I can't handle a temporary affair.''

"Then you'd better watch out, Addy. That man wants you. And I'd say he's used to getting what he wants. I'd hate to see you get hurt.'' Jim stood, then walked over to Addy's side, placing his arm around her shoulders. "I admit that I'd rather not be on the receiving end of Nick Romero's wrath, but if you want to try to use me as a buffer, I'll take my chances.''

Addy laughed, thankful that Jim understood her so well. If only she'd fallen in love with him instead of the idea of being a mother to his child. "Thanks. I—I don't think you'll be in any danger. I doubt if Nick would actually fight over me.'' Then she remembered Friday night when he'd come to her defense against Gerald at her father's engagement party.

"Don't sell yourself short, Addy. The way that man was acting today, I'd say he'd do more than fight for you. I think he'd kill for you.''

"That's what Daddy's hired him to do, if it's necessary. But that's his job. It isn't personal.''

"Don't kid yourself. It's definitely personal with Mr. Romero.''

Janice Dixon rushed into Addy's office. "Sorry to interrupt, but Brittany McKinney has thrown up all over the bathroom and won't let anyone touch her. She's crying for her mother.''

"Go take care of Brittany,'' Jim said. "I'll see you tomorrow when I stop by for juice with Tiffany.''

"Call Brittany's mother,'' Addy said. "She works in the secretarial pool. I'll walk Jim out and go see if I can calm Brittany down until her mother gets here.''

"Looks a bit out of place, doesn't he?'' Janice whispered to Addy while the two women watched Nick Romero, who was sitting between a couple of three-year-old girls.

Addy's gaze moved over the big man whose very size dwarfed the small stool on which he sat. He had removed his jacket before sitting down to share vegetable soup and grilled cheese sandwiches with the children.

"He doesn't seem too uncomfortable, but then he has the awed attention of two females." Addy laughed, amazed that Nick could charm even preschoolers. His easy camaraderie with the children had surprised her, considering his background. She couldn't help but wonder if he'd ever thought of becoming a father. For one unguarded moment the thought of giving Nick a little girl of his own flashed through Addy's mind.

"He's looking this way," Janice said. "What's going on between you two?"

Addy fixed her gaze on Nick, then smiled and waved at him from her position at the table opposite his. "He's teaching me how to play games."

"What?" Janice choked on her iced tea.

Raising her voice, Addy called out, "Are you enjoying your lunch, Mr. Romero?"

"The food's not bad," he said. "And the company is— entertaining." He looked around the table where children of various sizes and sexes were munching on their sandwiches, slurping their soup and loudly sipping their milk.

"If you'd care to stay for nap time, I'll let you read them a story." Addy couldn't help noticing how totally at ease Nick seemed, crouched there in the middle of so many toddlers. Many men, especially hard-edged military types, would have been nervous, even wary, around small children.

A little brown-eyed girl sitting beside Nick looked at him and smiled. When he smiled back, she held up her unopened milk carton.

"I can't get it open," she said, handing the milk to Nick.

He took the carton, pulled apart the spout and returned the open container. "Here you go."

Just as the little girl's fingers tightened around the carton, the boy sitting next to her lost his balance on his stool and fell over on her. The milk sloshed out of the open container and splattered across Nick Romero's pale blue shirt.

Stunned, Addy watched the milk soak into Nick's clothing. She jumped up, rushing over to where the little girl sat crying.

"It's all right," Nick tried to assure the child. "It's just milk. It'll wash out."

"I didn't mean to do it," the child wailed when Addy crouched down beside her. "It was Barry's fault!"

"Stop crying, honey. Mr. Romero isn't angry." Addy motioned for one of her assistants, a heavyset, matronly lady, to take charge of the children at the table.

As soon as the assistant had lined up the three-year-olds and ushered them into another room for nap time, Addy turned to Nick. "You'd better come into my office and get out of that wet shirt. Lucky for you we have a washer and dryer, so we can clean you up in a few minutes."

"I take it by your calm manner that accidents like this are a daily occurrence." Nick grinned when she gave him a you've-got-to-be-kidding look.

"Accidents like this are an hourly occurrence, sometimes more often than that. We're dealing with preschoolers here."

Nick followed Addy into her small, cheerful office. She closed the door and turned to him. "Take off your shirt." She held out her hand.

He looked at her outstretched hand, then up into her sparkling green eyes. "Just what I like, a forceful woman."

Letting her hand drop to her side, Addy willed herself not to blush. "Nick . . ."

He began unbuttoning his shirt, very slowly. Addy steeled herself against her body's reaction. She refused to look away shyly. Nick would know for sure that the sight of his naked chest excited her.

"I'm afraid I don't have anything large enough for you to put on while we're washing and drying your shirt. I could send someone over to Daddy's office for one of his shirts." Addy tried to concentrate on Nick's face, focusing her attention on the glittering diamond stud in his ear. But when he pushed his shirt apart and tugged it out from beneath his belted slacks, her gaze traveled downward to the wide expanse of darkly tanned, thickly muscled chest.

"I'll be fine. It's warm in here." Removing his shirt, he handed it to her.

She grabbed the shirt quickly, but couldn't keep herself from staring at his chest. He was magnificent. Big. Manly. A thick matting of black hair covered his chest from nipple to nipple, a thin dark line trailing down to his navel and beyond. Addy didn't think she'd ever seen anything quite so sexy.

"Sit down. I'll put this in to wash and be right back." She opened the door, grateful for the excuse to escape.

"Addy?"

She stopped, but didn't turn around. "Yes?"

"I don't suppose you've got a cup of coffee in this place, do you?" He sat down on the lavender gingham cushion padding her chair.

"I—I'll bring you some."

"Thanks."

Leaning back in the wooden swivel desk chair, Nick slipped his hands into his pants pockets. He hadn't been blind to Addy's reaction when he'd removed his shirt. He liked the idea that just looking at him had turned her on. Sex was always better when both parties were equally aroused, and despite what Addy thought of herself Nick had no doubts that she would be one of the hottest women he'd ever bedded.

"What do you mean you don't have it?" a loud masculine voice demanded.

Nick sat up straight, listening. He glanced at the slightly ajar door that led to the small hallway separating Addy's office from the main playroom. He eased himself out of the chair. Leaving his cane against the wall, Nick clung to the side of the desk as he made his way closer to the door.

"I mean I don't have it!" Janice Dixon hissed. "How could I ask Addy for another loan right now when she and Uncle Rusty are half out of their minds worrying about the kidnapping? It would look rather strange, don't you think?"

"Maybe you're right, but we've got to figure out something. I've got to have that two thousand soon or I could wind up as dead as Addy's kidnapper."

"Ron, I'm scared. What if the police question you, and they just might, considering your background?"

Nick hobbled away from the desk, grabbing a chair near the door to steady himself. Peeking through the narrow opening, he saw the back of Janice Dixon's ripe little body. Ron Glover, tall and dark, faced her.

"They've got nothing on me, sugar. I was nowhere near Addy McConnell Friday night until long after the kidnapping, and nobody can trace me to the guy who fell off Monsano Mountain." Ron reached out, circling Janice's neck with his hand, pulling her closer. "See what you can do about getting me the money."

"Shhh! Don't talk so loud. Nick Romero is in Addy's office." Placing her fingertips over Ron's mouth, Janice nodded.

"What? Why the hell didn't you tell me?" Ron's voice lowered to a whisper. "That guy's bad news, Jannie!"

"He can't hurt you, Ron."

"That's right, sugar. No two-bit, crippled, ex-DEA agent is a match for me." He lowered his head, taking Janice's eager mouth.

Just as Ron kissed Janice, Addy rounded the corner, a mug of steaming black coffee in her hand. The minute Nick saw her, he hobbled back across her office and sat down behind her desk.

"Hello, Addy," Ron said. "Hope you don't mind me stopping by to see my girl."

"Janice's personal life is her own business," Addy said, then walked past the couple, pushed open the door and went into her office.

Addy set the coffee mug down on her desk in front of Nick. "There's sweetener and creamer inside the top drawer on the left."

"I take it black, remember?"

"I didn't remember. Why should I?"

"No reason." He smiled. "Thanks anyway."

Sitting down in the maple Boston rocker a few feet from her desk, near the corner by the windows, Addy began rocking back and forth. "As soon as your shirt is ready, you can leave and get back to *playing detective*."

"I've been *playing detective* right here in your office."

"Oh? How's that?"

"By eavesdropping." He picked up the mug she'd set before him.

"On Ron and Janice, no doubt."

"They were having a very interesting conversation about money." Nick put the mug to his lips, sipping the dark rich coffee.

"It's no secret that Janice supports Ron, and I know that several loans I've given her have been for him." Addy stopped rocking. "I've tried to make her see what a sleaze-ball he is, but she refuses to listen to reason. She's crazy about him."

"Yeah, well, *love* can make people do strange things."

"Are you an expert on love?"

"Hardly, but I've been around enough to know that people who think they're in love can do some pretty stupid things. Take your cousin Janice. If she's that hung up on Glover, she might be persuaded to do anything he asks of her."

"Like helping him plot my kidnapping. Is that what you're saying?"

"Like I told you earlier today, Red, don't trust anyone except your father and me." Nick hated throwing suspicion on Addy's cousin. It was obvious the two women were genuinely found of each other. But if Ron Glover did have Janice completely under his control, she could be dangerous to Addy.

"I can't believe—" The jarring ring of the telephone cut off the rest of Addy's comment.

Nick glanced at the white phone sitting atop the desk. "Want me to answer it?"

Addy jumped up, quickly making her way to the phone. "Hello, M.A.C. Day Care. Addy McConnell speaking. May I help you?"

A muffled masculine voice said, "If you know what's good for you, you'll tell your daddy to follow my instructions."

The color drained from Addy's cheeks and her eyes widened. "What did you say? Who is this?"

"What's wrong?" Nick asked.

"Unless I get what I want, accidents could start happening," the voice said.

"Accidents? What sort of accidents?" Addy's fingers tightened around the receiver.

Standing, Nick retrieved his cane and walked around the desk to stand beside Addy. "Give me the phone."

"It would be terrible if something happened to you. You can't be protected from everything. What if a bomb were planted at the day care? Not only would you get blown into a zillion pieces, but so would all those little kiddies. Tell your daddy that I'll be in touch soon." The sinister voice on the phone snickered several times before hanging up.

Addy trembled, her heartbeat accelerating. When she tried to replace the receiver, her hand shook so badly she almost dropped the telephone. Nick grabbed her by the shoulder, turning her to face him. He could tell by the glazed look in her eyes and the deadly pallor of her normally golden complexion that the caller's message had frightened her badly.

"Come on, Red, tell me what that was all about."

She stared at him, and for one split second she wanted to scream. "It—it was a man." Addy looked into Nick's black eyes, eyes filled with genuine concern. "His voice was muffled . . . like he was talking through cloth or something."

Nick tightened his hold on her shoulder. "What did he say?"

"He warned me that, if Daddy doesn't follow his instructions, he'll get to me somehow, even if— Oh, Nick, he said that something could happen here at the day-care center . . . that a bomb could explode, that—" Addy choked back tears and blinked several times in an effort not to cry, but the thought of anything happening to her precious children played havoc with her emotions.

"My God!" Nick pulled her into his arms, stroking her back with one hand. Resting his cane against the desk, he cradled her head with the palm of his other hand. "If this was no idle threat, then we're dealing with a madman."

Addy snuggled against Nick, knowing she was safe. The warm masculinity of his hairy chest sent a current of desire spiraling through her. She laid her head on his naked shoulder. She couldn't explain her reaction to this man. He was practically a stranger, a man who made no secret of the fact that he was a ladies' man, and yet she trusted him. Held within the comforting security of his strong arms, she realized that Nick Romero would indeed protect her at all costs.

He *was* her paladin.

"Oh, Nick." She swallowed the tears, refusing to give in to the overwhelming urge to cry. "The voice said that he'd be in touch with Daddy and give him his instructions!"

"Whatever's going on here is more complicated than any of us thought." He grabbed Addy's chin in one big hand and tilted it upward, forcing her to face him directly. "I swear that we'll catch this man, whoever he is."

Tears caught in her throat making it impossible for her to reply immediately. She simply stared at Nick, trying to convey what she felt in the expression on her face. Her eyes, moist with unshed tears, softened with tenderness, and she forced a weak smile.

"Trust me to take care of you, Red." Nothing had ever been so important to him. He wanted her trust. He wanted to make her feel safe and protected.

"I trust you, Nick. With my life if not with my heart." She reached up, placing her hand on his cheek.

He covered her hand with his own, brought it to his lips and kissed her palm. "I don't want to break your heart, Addy, but I'm beginning to think that you just might break mine."

She clung to him unashamedly, absorbing his strength, his raw masculine power. "Oh, Nick, what are we going to do?"

It hurt him deeply to see her like this, so vulnerable and unsure. With a possessiveness he knew only with this woman, he lowered his lips to hers. "I won't let anyone hurt you. No matter what I have to do, I'll protect you." He covered her mouth with his, sealing his promise with a kiss that claimed ownership.

Chapter 6

Addy slipped the navy blue dress over her head. Zipping it quickly, she turned to face her image in the cheval mirror. She looked...presentable. Not strikingly beautiful, not sexy and desirable, but neat and well-groomed. So what difference does it make? she asked herself. Over the past seven years since her divorce, she'd learned to appreciate her ordinary appearance—her plain face and thin body. But in the five days since she'd known Nick Romero, he had undermined her contentment, making her long for the kind of beauty men appreciated.

Sitting down on the edge of her pencil-post bed, Addy picked up her sedate navy pumps off the Oriental carpet and slid her feet into them. She stretched one of her long legs out in front of her, scrutinizing the shape and length. Her legs weren't bad; they just might be her best feature. *Dammit! Stop doing this to yourself.* She hadn't felt so insecure about her looks since she'd been married to Gerald, who'd taken every available opportunity to remind her of how inadequate she was. But Nick had never once implied that he found her less than attractive. Indeed, his every word, his every action, had suggested the opposite.

Last Saturday night, when they'd known each other for only twenty-four hours, Nick had held her in front of the foyer mirror and practically made love to her, forcing her to face herself, to see herself as an aroused and sensuous woman. She had tried all week to erase that memory from her mind, but she couldn't forget how she'd felt or the way she'd looked. She had been beautiful in those moments of passion. Nick's praise and adoration had made her beautiful.

But Nick Romero was a temporary fixture in her life, a man who, once the kidnapping threat ended, would leave her life as quickly as he had entered it. No matter how he made her feel, she couldn't risk letting him break her heart. He'd made it perfectly clear that he wasn't averse to having an affair with her, and she'd made it equally clear that she wasn't interested. She could handle friendships with men; however, a sexual relationship was taboo unless the man in question could prove his love for her. Only a man who loved her would be patient and understanding, helping her overcome her deficiencies as a woman. Only a man who truly loved her wouldn't give a damn about her daddy's millions.

Addy glanced at the colorful flowered scarf lying on her dressing table. She'd bought the scarf in a moment of weakness, thinking it would brighten up some of her drab outfits. But she'd never worn it. It was too flashy.

Picking up her delicate gold watch out of her small jewelry case, Addy focused on the row of violets sitting atop the pine chest of drawers. She smiled, remembering how for the past three days the florist delivery boy had brought her a large container of violets, each with a small lavender and white ribbon. No card had been included, but she knew who'd sent them. Each day she'd brought the violets home with her, and Nick hadn't said a word. But she knew they were from him. Laughing, Addy fingered the velvety softness of one tiny leaf. No wonder Nick was so popular with the ladies. He was a romantic. Most men sent red roses. Roses were pretty standard, but only a man who really understood women would take the time to choose a flower that matched a woman's personality. She supposed Nick saw her as a shrinking violet. Or was there another meaning behind the flower he'd chosen for her?

She heard the rap of Nick's cane as he walked down the hallway from his bedroom to hers. Without giving any more thought to the matter, Addy grabbed the large, colorful scarf and draped it across her right shoulder.

Nick stopped in the open doorway, surveying Addy from head to toe. Damn, he wished her outer garments were half as sexy as her lingerie. At least the scarf added a touch of color to the plain navy dress. He wondered what had prompted her to act so impulsively. In the five days he'd known her, not once had Addy worn anything stylish, colorful or alluring—except her lingerie. He hadn't seen her sleeping attire every night, but on the nights that he had, she'd worn frothy concoctions that took his breath away.

"It's almost seven-thirty." He stepped just inside her open doorway. "Time to leave."

Smiling, Addy turned to face Nick. "Try to be cordial to Jim if you see him today, and at least be civil to Ron when he picks up Janice."

"I'm having a more complete check done on Glover. From what my contacts have already found out, he's more than capable of plotting your kidnapping, and he's just the type to use threats."

"Do you think he's capable of murder? After all, the person behind my kidnapping has already killed once." Addy walked over to Nick and the two stepped outside into the hallway. "If I thought Janice was in danger—I mean, if Ron is really—"

Nick put his arm around Addy's waist, giving her a reassuring hug. He couldn't tell her that there was a possibility that Janice, so enamored of a hood like Glover, was actually his accomplice. Of course, both Ron and Janice could also be completely innocent. "I don't think Janice is in any danger, whether or not Glover is the kidnapper. He'd have no reason to harm her."

Together they descended the stairs, Addy slowing her stride to accommodate Nick's limp. His big hand stayed on her waist, warm and reassuring. She liked it when Nick touched her, even casually, and he'd touched her often in the last few days, despite her coolness toward him. There had been no more kisses, and Addy knew she should be grateful. Nick's kisses were lethal.

He escorted her outside to his Jag, opening the door and helping her into the seat. Before starting the car, he turned to her. "You look lovely."

Swallowing hard, Addy stared directly at Nick, wishing her heart would stop beating so rapidly. "It's the shawl. It adds color to—"

"It's not the damned shawl." Nick revved the motor, his big hands clutching the steering wheel. "It's you, Addy. You're lovely."

"Tha—thank you." Nick wasn't the first man who'd given her compliments, and, unfortunately, he wasn't the first one she'd believed. Did she dare trust Nick Romero? Did she dare listen to her heart?

"You've got three men chasing you." Nick backed the silver sports car out of the driveway. "How the hell can you consider yourself unattractive and undesirable?"

Addy sat up straight, looking away from Nick's lean, hard face. Glancing out the window at the stately old homes and towering green trees as they drove past Jefferson Street, she remained silent, unsure how to answer Nick's question.

Nick chose the route leading through downtown. He didn't like Addy's silence any more than he liked the way she'd turned all moody and distant the last few days. He'd done everything he could to reassure her, but the waiting—the endless waiting—for word from the threatening phone caller had played havoc with her nerves. It hadn't helped any that Rusty McConnell had been growling like a papa lion, frightened for the safety of his only cub. Nick knew that Addy worried more about her father than she did about herself.

But Nick worried about Addy. In less than a week's time, she had become important to him. Far too important.

Within ten minutes they turned into Research Park. Grassy green fields and majestic, tall trees lined the streets of the park, each street named after a space shuttle—Columbia, Discovery, Endeavor. Nick pulled the Jag into Addy's private space in the M.A.C. day-care center parking lot.

When she clasped the door handle, Nick reached across the console, taking her hand. "He's bound to contact Rusty soon. Then we'll know what we're dealing with and how to handle the situation."

Looking down at Nick's big hand grasping hers, she sighed. "I hope you're right. I don't know how much longer Daddy's going to be able to endure the waiting."

Nick squeezed her hand. "Your father's tough, Red. He can stand a lot more than you think he can."

"It's not fair for him to have to go through this again—living in fear of losing a child to a kidnapper."

"That's not going to happen. I won't let it."

Turning her head slightly, Addy glanced at Nick. A shiver of something akin to excitement raced through her. How had she allowed herself to become so dependent on this man? And why did his protectiveness make her feel safe and yet vulnerable all at the same time?

Nick met Addy in the hallway leading to her father's office. Rusty had summoned them both on an *urgent matter*. Addy's face was flushed, her eyes overly bright. Nick could see the way her hands nervously clutched her leather purse. Only someone who knew her well, someone who'd spent endless hours with her, could tell that Addy was upset. Although their acquaintance was less than a week old, Nick had come to know Addy in a way he'd never known another woman. Except Dina. The truth of the matter was that he'd never spent as much time with another woman. Day and night. Sharing meals with her, sleeping in the room next to hers, listening to her talk and laugh and argue, and catching glimpses of her elegantly slender body covered by nothing more than her sexy lingerie.

Addy McConnell, taken in small doses, could be dismissed as nothing more than a skinny redhead. Nick understood why so many men had overlooked the real value that lay hidden behind her Plain-Jane facade, and had taken an interest in Addy solely because of Rusty's money. But Nick had learned, to his own detriment, that Addy McConnell, taken in large doses, could prove fatal to a confirmed bachelor who'd always prided himself on being a love 'em and leave 'em ladies' man.

He couldn't remember ever wanting a woman so badly— not even when he'd been seventeen and thought he'd die from wanting his brother's wife. At forty-three, he'd known his share of women, and could easily have his pick of dozens of beauties. So, why didn't the idea of bedding some bosomy blonde appeal to him?

"Ginger wouldn't tell me anything," Addy said, her long legs slowing their pace to keep step with Nick's slower, halting gait. "Did she tell you why Daddy wanted to see us?"

"No. She just said to get to Rusty's office pronto, that it was urgent." Reaching out, Nick pulled one of Addy's trembling hands away from the purse she clutched at her waist. "Whatever it is, we'll take care of it. Rusty, you and me. The three of us together."

Addy halted her steps, stopping to stare at Nick. "You mean that, don't you? You actually think I'm capable of being part of the solution."

Nick paused, then squeezed her hand. "You're a smart lady, and from what I've seen, you're pretty tough. You're the one whose life is in danger, so it stands to reason that you'll want to cooperate with the two men who'd die trying to protect you."

"Nick...I—" She'd never known a man like Nick Romero. He overwhelmed her by almost everything he said and did. And he constantly surprised her. Did he, she wondered, realize how possessive he sounded, how much like a man in love? Dear Lord, she couldn't allow herself to indulge in that particular fantasy.

"Come on, Addy, your father's waiting." He tugged on her hand. She gave him a half-hearted smile and started walking again.

The receptionist stood up when they walked past, watching them enter Ginger's office. She wasn't at her desk, but stood in the open doorway to Rusty's office.

"He's on the phone with the police." Ushering them inside, Ginger closed the door. "Can I get either of you something to drink?"

"No, thanks," Nick said.

Addy simply nodded.

Rusty slammed down the telephone, the crashing sound reverberating around the room. He turned his dark green gaze on Nick. "From now on, I want you so close to her that she can't breathe without you hearing her." He glared at Addy. "And if it takes handcuffing you to him, then I'll see to it. Understand me, little girl?"

Addy rushed to her father, putting her arms around him. He crushed her in his arms, almost pressing the breath out of her. She knew that something terrible had happened. Rusty's ruddy face was flushed crimson, his thick lips drawn in a fine line of pain, and his big, meaty hands shook with the force of his rage.

"What is it, Daddy? What's happened? Has *he* called?"

With one big arm still draped around Addy, Rusty leaned down, picked up a sheet of paper off his desk and handed it to Nick. Nick took the paper, reading it silently, then looked at Rusty holding his only child protectively in his arms. Dammit, he wouldn't want to be in Rusty's shoes.

But, in a way, he was. Addy wasn't his beloved child, but she was going to be his woman and her safety was as important to him as it was to her father.

"What's this?" Addy asked, reaching out for the paper Nick held in his hand.

Nick released the paper, allowing her to take it. Rusty kept his supportive arm around her. She scanned the letter, similar to the one her father had received almost a week ago, the morning after the failed kidnapping attempt.

"Oh my God!" The letter fell from Addy's fingers and floated to the carpeted floor. "Now we know what the kidnapper wants."

"If M.A.C. doesn't withdraw its bids on the NASP contract, then Addy's life is in danger," Rusty said. "That contract is worth millions. Hundreds of jobs that are threatened because of the economy can be saved."

"The kidnapper isn't some madman who wants a ransom, is he?" Addy's mind rioted with a dozen different thoughts, finally calming to focus on one possibility. "Gerald! It's Gerald, isn't it? If M.A.C. doesn't bid on the NASP contract, then New Age Aerospace has a good chance of becoming a NASP contractor, and not only would that add greatly to Gerald's standing with his father-in-law, but it would be the perfect revenge on us, wouldn't it?" Looking up at her father, she knew that he'd come to the same conclusion.

"New Age Aerospace isn't our only competitor," Rusty said. "We can't rule out someone at one of the other companies."

"Rusty's right," Nick said. "Just because Gerald Carlton has a personal reason to want to see M.A.C. lose the contract doesn't mean he's the only suspect."

"You can't agree to this." Addy pulled away from her father. "We have to make a bid on the NASP contract. There's too much money and too many jobs at stake to buckle under to this threat."

"Baby girl, we're talking about your life." Tears clouded Rusty's vision as he took his daughter's slender hands into his enormous grasp. "Nothing is more important to me than you."

"Oh, Daddy, I know that." Addy wanted to comfort her father, but she was incapable of easing his fears. "There's no way anyone can get to me with all the protection I have." She focused her attention on the big, dark man whose very presence in the room made her feel safe. "My God, how do you think anyone could get through Nick?"

"We have to consider all our options," Nick said, his heart thumping at a deafening roar. Addy trusted him! Really trusted him. "First, tell me about this NASP contract."

"NASP is the National Aero-Space Plane, the X-30. It's one of the boldest concepts that the Air Force and NASA have ever conceived," Ginger Kimbrew said, making her presence known for the first time since Addy and Nick had entered Rusty's office.

Nick turned to Ginger, understanding how intricately involved she was in every aspect of the McConnell Aerospace Company. "I'll contact Sam and have him check out all the competition, all the possible contractors who'll be bidding."

"The five prime contractors that comprise the NASP National Program Office are based near Air Force Plant No. 42 in Palmdale, California." Rusty helped Addy into his huge leather chair, then sat on the edge of his desk. "There's no need to run a check on those guys. Their part in NASP is a done deal. But the big boys are ready to let Huntsville in on the deal, and M.A.C. wants to be part of the team."

"This is a visionary aircraft," Ginger explained. "It would enable the U.S. to have routine access to space from a runway. Access embodied in the X-30."

"Propulsion is NASP's biggest worry. That's where M.A.C. comes in. Our engineers are primed and ready for this project." Rusty's excitement danced in his eyes, vibrated in his deep, strong voice.

"You understand why Daddy can't give in to this threat, don't you?" Addy asked Nick.

"There's one possibility that we're all overlooking," Nick bent over and picked up the threatening letter, then laid it on Rusty's desk. "What if the NASP contract isn't the real motive? What if someone is using it as a red herring?"

"What are you saying?" Addy scooted to the edge of her father's chair.

"It never pays to jump to conclusions." Tapping his finger on the letter, Nick glanced from Addy to Rusty. "This letter would have us believe that the person behind Addy's kidnap attempt doesn't want several million in ransom money, but does want Rusty to lose millions on an important government contract. Reputable competitors don't deal this way. They have families of their own."

"Carlton is too hot-headed and bent on revenge to consider anything but getting what he wants." Rusty struck his desk with his closed fist. "So help me, if he's behind this, I'll—"

"Rusty, calm down." Ginger rushed forward, reaching out pleadingly. "This isn't doing your blood pressure or heart any good."

"She's right, Daddy. If Gerald is behind this, he'd like nothing better than to see you drop dead from a heart attack."

The outer office door swung open. Dina Lunden and Brett Windsor swept into Rusty's private domain, the haggard receptionist following them, screeching that they couldn't interrupt Mr. McConnell, who'd given strict instructions not to be disturbed.

"What's this about you dropping dead from a heart attack?" Dina asked, making her way directly to Rusty. Dina eyed Ginger, who had her hand on her boss's arm. Releasing Rusty, Ginger stepped aside.

"Nothing for you to worry about, honey." Rusty jerked Dina up against him. She buried her face in his chest.

"But I do worry about you, darling. Especially now that Addy's in such danger." Purring like a kitten, Dina rubbed her head against Rusty as she slipped her arm around his waist. "Has something else happened?"

"Is there some reason you and Windsor came by today?" Nick asked, barely giving Dina a glance as he concentrated all his attention on Brett Windsor.

"I'm meeting Rusty for lunch. It's almost noon." Dina took a quick look at her diamond-studded wristwatch. She ran her hand up Rusty's chest, caressing him. "What's wrong, darling? Tell me."

"We received another threatening letter," Rusty said.

Nick groaned. Why couldn't Rusty keep his mouth shut? He was a smart man, but damned stupid when it came to Dina. He shouldn't trust her so completely, and he sure as hell shouldn't trust Windsor. "The police have already been informed, and we're calling in the FBI."

"The FBI?" Dina's big blue eyes darted a startled expression from Rusty to Nick.

"I'll fill you in on all the details at lunch," Rusty said, stroking Dina's back. "Ginger, you take Dina and Brett here on into your office and get them some coffee or tea or something until Nick and I finish making a few phone calls."

"Oh, Rusty," Dina whined.

"Now, now, honey, go on."

"Are we going to be awfully late for lunch? Our reservations are for twelve-thirty." Dina pulled away from Rusty, a pouty look on her beautiful face.

"Ginger, call and have our reservations changed to one o'clock." Rusty glanced over at Brett. "Entertain your stepmother until I'm free."

"Of course." Brett came forward, taking Dina's arm and leading her toward the door.

Addy watched the way Nick stared at Dina, as if he found her disgustingly fascinating. A hot surge of jealousy ripped through Addy. Dina looked so feminine in her chic little summer suit. The beige silk draped and caressed her body as if it loved to be next to such voluptuousness. Suddenly, Addy felt like a frump in her navy dress, despite the colorful scarf draped across her shoulder.

Watching Dina and Brett make their exit, Nick thought what a perfect pair they made. Except for the twelve-year difference in their ages, they suited each other to a tee. Both were blond and beautiful, flawless in appearance but sickeningly self-centered and selfish. It was a pity they'd gone through old man Windsor's fortune so quickly. The only thing lacking in their relationship was money, which both of them seemed to value above anything else.

Brett halted just as he ushered Dina into Ginger's office. He turned, flashing his brilliant, toothy smile at Addy. "Why don't we join Dina and Rusty for lunch? Ginger could make the reservations for four."

"I...I don't know." Addy didn't want to go to lunch with her father and Dina. She wanted to go back to the day-care center and share a meal with Nick, who always showed up just in time for lunch each day. She glanced at Nick, wishing he would say something that could prevent their having to join the others.

Nick didn't say or do anything. He didn't even look at her.

"She'll go. It'll be good for her to get out." Rusty glanced at Nick. "Make the reservations for five, and have a couple of Dundee's boys tag along behind us."

"I need to take care of some things at the center before we go to lunch," Addy said. "Give me a buzz when y'all are ready to go."

Addy walked through Ginger's office. Her father's secretary was on the phone changing Rusty's lunch reservations, and Brett was pouring himself a cup of coffee from the machine on a nearby table. Dina reached out, grasping Addy by the wrist as she passed her.

"We need to talk."

"About what?" Addy asked, glancing down at Dina's long, sharp nails. She jerked her wrist free.

Dina looked over at Ginger, then at Brett. "Why don't we go on into the receptionist's office? I'll send her on an errand and we can have a little privacy."

Addy didn't want to talk to Dina about anything, and she certainly had no desire to be alone with her. She didn't like Dina. And she didn't trust her.

"I'm in a hurry, Dina. If Nick and I are going out to lunch with you and Brett and Daddy, I have to get back to the center and handle some problems there."

When Addy walked away, out into the reception area, Dina followed. "I need to talk to you about Nick."

Addy slowed but didn't stop. Dina Lunden was the last person on earth with whom she wanted to discuss Nick. "I don't have time."

"Ms. Harkin, go find me some aspirin. I feel a terrible headache coming on," Dina told the receptionist.

"I have some aspirin in my desk." Ms. Harkin opened the center desk drawer and reached inside.

"Don't be obtuse, Ms. Harkin. Find somewhere to go for a few minutes and leave Ms. McConnell and me alone."

"I—I don't know if I should, Mrs. Lunden. I mean..." The young woman floundered in an attempted explanation.

"It's all right, Joyce," Addy said. "Go ahead and take an early lunch."

The moment Joyce Harkin left, Dina turned to Addy. "I want you to ask Rusty to replace Nick with another bodyguard."

"What?"

"You may feel extremely flattered by Nick's attentions, but I can assure you that, in the long run, he'll only wind up hurting you." Dina's cool gaze traveled over Addy's slender body with the scrutiny of a trained spy seeking to discover any hidden detail. "You can't possibly believe that *you* could capture and hold a man like Nick Romero."

Addy felt the sting of Dina's words as if they'd been a physical slap. She didn't need the other woman to remind her of how totally inadequate she was. "My relationship with Nick is none of your business."

"But of course it is. After all, I'm practically your stepmother." Dina moved to Addy's side, a false show of concern on her face. "I love you because you're Rusty's child, and I like you, too. You're such a nice person, Addy. Really too nice for a bad boy like Nick."

"If you're so concerned about Nick acting as my bodyguard, why haven't you said something to Daddy yourself?"

"I have, but he simply won't listen to me." Dina sighed dramatically. "Men are such stubborn creatures, aren't they? Your father has this mistaken notion that Nick would make the perfect husband for you."

Addy couldn't stop the bubble of laughter in her throat from erupting. "I can't picture Nick as anyone's husband."

"Certainly not. Nick's too much of a free spirit." Dina seemed to relax, placing her hand on Addy's arm. "I should have known you would be sensible about this. After all, you're too smart to allow yourself to be used again."

"Yes, I am," Addy agreed. "But Nick isn't the sort of man who'd use me. I've learned that much about him. He's nothing like Gerald, and I honestly believe money doesn't mean anything to him."

"Nick isn't interested in Rusty's money the way your former husband was, that's true enough." Dina tugged on Addy's arm. "Why don't we sit down and I'll tell you some things you need to know about Nick so you'll understand my concern."

Addy stared at Dina, trying to figure out what the woman's real motive was. Could she actually be concerned, or was she jealous? "I don't need to sit down. Just tell me what you think I need to know."

"Very well." Dina's words escaped in an aggravated huff. "Nick sees you as a challenge, I'm quite certain of that. Women usually succumb to his good looks and charm quite readily, but since you haven't, he'll use whatever means necessary to seduce you. His rather substantial male ego is involved. Women don't say no to Nick."

"What makes you think he hasn't already seduced me?" Addy didn't like the smug look on Dina's face.

"He hasn't. I'd know if you and Nick were lovers. I've known Nick since he was fifteen. The two of us have no secrets."

Pulling away from Dina, Addy said, "Nick told me that you and he play a game where you try to seduce him and he resists." Addy watched for any change of expression on Dina's face or in her eyes. She saw only the slight flickering of Dina's long, dark eyelashes. "Are you sure the real reason you want Nick replaced as my bodyguard is because you're worried about me?"

"What other reason could there be?"

"Perhaps you're afraid that I might mean more to Nick than a conquest, that his feelings run deep enough to consider making a commitment to me."

The reaction Addy had been waiting for appeared on Dina's face. Her rosy cheeks flushed brightly and her blue eyes burned with indigo fire. She tightened her hold on Addy's arm, her nails biting into soft flesh. "Don't be an idiot. You aren't Nick's type. I'm Nick's type. Ever since we became lovers when he was seventeen, he's looked for me in every woman he meets. I have no doubt that when he's making love to those other blondes, he pretends he's making love to me."

Salty, burning bile rose in Addy's throat. She had suspected that Nick and Dina had once been lovers, but hearing the woman admit it was almost more than Addy could bear. She tried to keep her reaction from showing, from being so blatantly obvious. Nothing would appease Dina's spiteful jealousy more than seeing Addy upset by her scandalous admission that Nick had bedded his brother's wife. Addy had never dreamed Nick would have betrayed his own brother. Maybe she didn't know him as well as she thought she did.

"I couldn't care less about you and Nick," Addy lied. "But I think Daddy might care." Addy was pleased to note Dina's shocked expression.

Dina's face paled noticeably. "I'd rather Rusty didn't know, but if telling him is the only way to get Nick out of your life and end Rusty's obsession with the idea of marrying you off to Nick, then perhaps you should tell him."

Brett Windsor opened the door connecting the reception area to Ginger Kimbrew's office. "Addy, I'm glad you're still here." Brett glanced from Addy to Dina, then back to Addy. "Is there something wrong?"

"No," both women replied simultaneously.

"Well, Ginger has changed the reservations. All she had to do was mention Rusty McConnell's name. Amazing what wealth and power can do, isn't it?" Brett stepped between the two women, giving Dina a questioning glare before turning to Addy. "Has Dina said something to upset you?"

"I'm afraid Addy wasn't prepared to hear the truth about Nick. It seems she's quite smitten with him. Such a shame to see a dear, sweet girl like Addy making a fool of herself over a man—"

"I think you've said enough, Dina." Brett put his arm around Addy's quivering shoulders. "Addy has better sense than to fall for Nick Romero's rather obvious charms. Despite his smooth exterior, your brother-in-law is still as rough and uncivilized as he was when he was in the SEALS."

"I'd rather not discuss Nick with either of you." Addy started to pull away from Brett, but hesitated when she saw Nick standing in the open doorway, his dark eyes glowering at her. She leaned into Brett's embrace, slipping her arm around his waist. "Why—why don't you come over for dinner some night soon?'' The minute the words escaped her mouth, Addy regretted them. How could she act so childishly, trying to use Brett to make Nick jealous?

Brett's smile dazzled Addy with its perfection. "I suppose Nick will have to be there, won't he?''

"You've got that right, Windsor, but you and Addy can just pretend I'm not there.'' Nick glanced back into Ginger's office where her shapely behind was bent over her desk. "I could ask Ginger if she'd like to make it a foursome.''

"Good idea.'' Brett leaned down, planting a sweetly romantic kiss on Addy's lips.

Shocked, Addy had no intention of responding until she heard Nick's feral growl from across the room. In her peripheral vision, she saw Nick take a tentative step in her direction. Without thinking of the consequences, she responded to Brett's kiss with a passion born of her own anger and jealousy. Damn Nick for making her care about him when he was probably still in love with Dina.

Nick stopped dead still, then walking as fast as he could hampered by his bad leg, he fled past Addy and Brett and a cattily smiling Dina as if the hounds of hell were on his heels.

Addy pulled away from Brett, staring at Nick's wide back as he exited the reception area. She swallowed hard, wondering why she suddenly felt afraid of the man in whom her father had entrusted her life.

Despite the cool flow of air from the overhead fan, Nick's body glistened with sweat. He'd been punishing himself with a series of sit-ups he had hoped would exhaust him enough to sleep. He'd been seething with anger all day, ever since he'd walked in on the sickeningly sweet sight of Addy returning Brett Windsor's caress.

Clutching his fists at his sides, Nick beat the mattress, wishing it was Windsor's pretty-boy face. What the hell did Addy mean responding to Windsor with such passion? She didn't love the guy, and by her own admission, she didn't trust him. Just what had been going on?

He suspected that Dina had something to do with it. That mocking smile on her face had given her away. He knew Dina and all her little tricks. She had done or said something to Addy that made her angry with him, had made her want to get back at him. And by God, she had, in the worst possible way. He hated these feelings of jealousy. The last time he'd been jealous, he'd thought he was in love with Miguel's wife. He'd been a fool! Damned if he would ever let another woman make a fool of him.

The last thing he should be worrying about right now were his possessive feelings for Addy. Not when she was in real danger, when her very life could be at risk. He should be concentrating on keeping Addy safe, not succumbing to the powers of the green-eyed monster. Somewhere out there was a man or a woman primed and ready to kidnap Addy if Rusty McConnell allowed M.A.C.'s bid on the NASP project to stand. Nick knew that all his energy should be focused on making sure that didn't happen, regardless of what decision Rusty made about the contract bid.

He and Rusty had discussed the situation with Ned Johnson, the FBI agent assigned to the case. The federal government didn't like any type of threats being made that involved one of their pet projects—and the NASP project was a number one priority for both NASA and the Air Force.

Sam Dundee had assured Nick that he would run a check on all of M.A.C.'s competitors and have a complete report faxed to him by Monday morning at the latest. Nick knew he could count on Sam. They didn't make men any smarter, tougher or more trustworthy. Sam was one of the best friends Nick had ever had. They'd shared more than danger during their days with the DEA. They'd shared their pasts, their problems and occasionally their women.

Somewhere in the back of Nick's mind a damned pesty little suspicion wouldn't go away. What if the NASP bid had nothing to do with the kidnap attempt? What if there actually was another motive? Did he dare risk Addy's life by not paying attention to his gut instincts? Often, in the SEALS and as a DEA agent, the only thing that had saved him was his instincts.

He had pretty well ruled out Ginger Kimbrew as a suspect. The woman was too much in love with Rusty McConnell to be a threat. If the NASP bid turned out to be the real motive, Gerald Carlton headed the list, but if there was another motive—money, for instance—then Ron Glover jumped to the number one spot, followed closely by Brett Windsor. And there was always the off chance that Janice Dixon could be helping her boyfriend or... Nick hated himself for suspecting Dina. She was spoiled, self-centered and money-hungry, but he honestly didn't think she was capable of kidnapping or murder.

A loud tapping on his bedroom door drew Nick from his thoughts. Rising up on his elbows, he stared at the closed door. He made no response. The tapping began again, then he heard Addy's whispered voice.

"Nick? Nick, may I come in?"

He flipped the switch on the bedside lamp, positioned himself against the headboard and wiped the sweat off his face with the palm of his hand. "Yeah, come on in."

The door opened slowly, Addy peering in before she stepped inside and took several steps toward Nick. Seeing him lying in bed, wearing nothing but a pair of nylon shorts, she halted, staring at him with questioning eyes. "I—I want to know what's wrong."

"Why do you think something's wrong?" Damn, did she have any idea how she looked, standing there in the dim light, her titian hair tumbling down her back and onto her shoulders? She was wearing gold satin pajamas that hung loosely on her slender frame, but they didn't disguise the elegant line of her body or the pouting tips of her nipples. Just the sight of her aroused him.

"You haven't spoken two words to me since before lunch today." With slow, deliberate steps she made her way to the side of the bed.

Nick didn't move a muscle. At least not intentionally. One part of his body had a mind of its own. "I thought it best if I kept my mouth shut. Once something is said, you can't take it back."

"You're angry with me, aren't you?" She held her hands, twined together, in front of her. She didn't look directly at Nick, but down at the chenille spread folded back at the foot of the bed.

"You're too smart to try to use Windsor to make me jealous, so why did you?" He reached out, grabbing her wrist, tugging her down onto the bed beside him.

She gasped, but didn't struggle. "What makes you think that's what I was doing?"

He released her, then waited to see if she'd get up. She didn't. She sat, ramrod straight on the edge of the bed, close to but not touching him. "You don't care anything about Windsor, and you know he's only interested in Rusty's money, so what other reason could there be?"

"I am not going to become just one more of your women." Her voice trembled with emotion.

Nick ran his hand up her back, savoring the feel of her rich satin pajama top beneath his fingertips. He knew Addy's flesh would be twice as soft and smooth. She jerked, but didn't pull away. "What did Dina say to you?"

"What makes you think Dina—"

Wrapping his arm around her waist, he jerked her up the bed and to his side. She faced him then, glaring at him with both expectation and challenge in her glittering green eyes. "Let's stop playing twenty questions, Red. What did Dina say that made you so upset with me that you used Brett Windsor to hurt me?"

"My kissing Brett hurt you?" There was genuine awe in her voice, as if she were dumbfounded that she held that much power over Nick's feelings.

He grabbed her chin in his big hand, squeezing tightly but not painfully. "You know damned well that it ate me alive seeing you kiss him that way."

"Dina told me that—that you and she had been lovers."

Nick didn't respond. His hand on Addy's back stilled. He took a deep breath. "Yeah. A long time ago, when I was just a green kid whose raging hormones ruled his body." He felt her quiver.

"You—you slept with your brother's wife?"

"I slept with my brother's widow. Once."

Addy released the breath she'd been holding, then reached out to cover Nick's hand that held her chin so firmly. "Did you love her?"

"Look, Addy, what happened between Dina and me was so long ago that it has no bearing on the here and now. On the two of us." He didn't think Addy would understand if he admitted the truth. How could he explain to her that there was more than one kind of love, and that what he'd felt for Dina had been the absolutely worst kind—the most destructive kind?

"She thinks you compare every woman to her, that she's still the woman you want."

Nick flung off Addy's hand and released her chin. He jumped up off the bed, knocking Addy over in the process. She gazed up at him. "If I wanted Dina, I could have had her a thousand times over." The truth of his words rang in his ears like a dozen clanking bells. There hadn't been a time in the past twenty-odd years that he couldn't have bedded Dina. Between husbands or even during her marriages. She had no conception of the word "fidelity," and in other women, it didn't matter. But in the woman he loved, it was of paramount importance. He'd spent his entire life seeking a replacement for Dina, when in his heart he'd known she was his for the taking. He didn't want her. And he sure as hell didn't love her.

Pushing herself up with her elbows, Addy sat in the middle of Nick's bed. "I want to trust you completely...in every way, but—but I'm not prepared to take that kind of risk unless I can be sure of you."

"Sure of me how?" He glared at her, his big bronze body towering over her.

Addy had never wanted to touch a man the way she wanted to touch Nick. He was so utterly masculine that the very sight of him took her breath away. "If you want me, you're going to have to earn the right to make love to me."

"I'm going to what?"

"I want to be sure that I'm important to you, that you really care about me, that your desire for me is real."

Nick grabbed her hand, shoved it against his arousal and held it there. "That's real, Addy, as real as it gets."

She felt the throbbing evidence of his desire, and the shocking realization that she had evoked such a strong response in him tempted her almost beyond reason. Almost, but not quite. "Gerald could get hard, and he could ram himself into me, but he didn't care anything about me. I didn't mean anything to him but a way to get Daddy's money. When I give myself to a man again I don't want to have any doubts that I'm all he wants, all he cares about, above and beyond anyone or anything else."

Nick dropped his hand. Addy's hand slid down the front of Nick's shorts, her fingers caressing him. He groaned. "How the hell do I prove something like that to you?"

Addy walked toward the open door. "I don't know, but I'm sure you'll find a way."

With that said, she left. Nick stood, watching her as she disappeared into the hallway. Damned stubborn woman. She was asking too much of him. There was no way he could prove himself to her, was there? She was asking for the kind of love that didn't exist—not in his world.

Hell, he'd never had to prove himself to a woman. If she thought that he'd ever come to her begging, then she'd better think again.

Nick fell into the bed, his hot, aroused body pulsating painfully with a need that he knew only one woman on earth could appease. And that woman had just told him that if he ever wanted to find release between her long silky legs, he'd have to earn the right to make love to her.

Chapter 7

Hot June sunshine played hide-and-seek with gray, mid-morning rain clouds, creating a hazy, overcast daylight. Standing at her kitchen window, Addy watched the warm breeze floating through the trees and shrubs in her backyard, swaying the tops of the red azaleas and teasing the clematis vine clinging to the wooden fence. Everything looked the same as it had for the past few years since she'd purchased the house in Twickenham, since she had begun a new life, totally on her own. She had grown to love the sameness, the routine pattern of peacefulness, and, above all else, she had learned to appreciate her independence.

But things were not the same. An unknown person's threats had changed her life, throwing her cherished order into chaos, reverting her father back into the overprotective parent he'd once been, and utterly destroying her hard-won privacy and independence.

Addy placed the last lunch plate into the dishwasher, then wiped her hands and laid the towel on the counter. Glancing out onto the rock patio behind her house, Addy saw

Nick Romero, his broad back facing her, as he sat drinking a tall glass of iced tea. As much as the menacing kidnapper, Nick had altered the course of Addy's life, his very presence a disturbing force she found difficult to handle.

More than anything she wanted to believe that his interest in her was genuine, that he truly desired her as a woman and not as the heir to a fortune. If she allowed her romantic nature to override her common sense, she would give herself to Nick, heart and soul. Already, she fantasized about him, seeing him as her knight in shining armor, the man who would cherish her and protect her... forever. But Addy had learned to control the romantic girl within, giving her realistic self the upper hand. Trusting her life to Nick was easier than trusting her own heart.

The portable phone sitting outside on the patio table rang, jarring Addy out of her thoughts. Opening the door, she stepped outside just as Nick answered.

"Hold a minute, I'll get her," he said, then shoved the chair back and stood.

Before he could turn around, Addy walked over to him. "Is that for me?"

Nick gave her a long, hard look, then handed her the telephone. "It's Jim Hester."

Addy returned Nick's scrutiny as she accepted the phone. "Hello, Jim." Addy walked around the patio, savoring the feel of the warm sun and the pleasant breeze.

"I just wanted to check on you before I leave for Washington," Jim said. "I need to know that you're all right."

"I'm fine. Honestly."

"Addy?"

She could tell by the unusual edge to his voice that something was bothering him. "What is it, Jim? What's wrong?"

"Well, I—I thought you should hear it from me."

"What?" She had never known Jim Hester to be so mysterious.

"I'm taking Tiffany with me on this trip, and... I'm taking Carol Stilwell with me."

Addy could hear Jim's deep breathing, could feel the utter stillness. "You're taking your sister-in-law?"

"Yes, well—"

"It's all right, Jim." Addy walked farther away from Nick, knowing he was listening to her every word. "If you're trying to tell me that you and Carol are—are involved, I understand."

"I just didn't want you to think that I'd been leading you on and fooling around with Carol at the same time." Jim's voice sounded strained, pleading. "I guess I've always known that nothing would ever come of our friendship. And since Romero showed up... Well—I need someone, Addy, and so does Tiffany."

"Of course you do, and believe me, I understand. Good luck, Jim. I—I hope everything works out for you and Carol."

They said their goodbyes. Addy punched the off button. Nick came up behind her, leaning over to take the phone out of her hand.

"You didn't want Jim Hester, despite the fact that he's a nice guy. You wanted to be a mother to his daughter."

She would have preferred not to discuss that situation with Nick, even though it was obvious that he'd overheard every word of her conversation and had jumped to the correct conclusion. As foolish as the notion seemed, Addy couldn't help feeling like she'd been dumped. "I thought you didn't like Jim."

"I changed my mind about Hester. I wanted to dislike him, but I couldn't. He's all right, Addy, but he's not the man for you." Nick tossed the phone into a cushioned lounge chair.

Addy fiddled with the drawstring on her yellow walking shorts. "Let me get this straight. You've warned me off Brett Windsor because he's only interested in my money and you think Jim was the wrong man for me because all I wanted from that relationship was to be a mother to Tiffany."

"That about sums it up."

"I'm surprised you aren't telling me that you're the right man for me. Now would be the perfect time, wouldn't it?" Addy couldn't bring herself to face Nick. Somehow she knew he was smiling, that self-assured, macho smile.

"I am the right man for you, and we both know it."

"You're wrong, all wrong." She turned, forcing herself to look at him, determined to remain in control. "What you want is another conquest. You want—"

"I want you." Nick focused all his attention on Addy, his dark eyes reaching out, pulling her to him, mesmerizing her by their look of heated desire. "I don't want another woman, and I couldn't care less about Rusty's millions. All I want is you. Your body, your mind, your heart. Everything that makes you Addy."

When Nick reached out and took her hand, she jerked away from his touch as if he'd hurt her. "Don't do this to me. I can't handle it."

She ran from him, her bare feet racing over the warm flagstones. Nick didn't follow her immediately. Running his fingers through his thick black hair, he cursed himself for a fool. He couldn't seem to get it right with Addy. With other women he'd always been the smooth Romeo, who knew exactly what to say and do. With Addy it was different. She was different. The woman was driving him crazy. She wanted him to prove himself to her, and he had no earthly idea how to go about doing it.

He gave her five minutes alone—four minutes more than he wanted to give her. He found her in the den, staring out the window. She'd wrapped her arms around herself. Her shoulders drooped in defeat.

"Addy?"

Her body stiffened, but she didn't turn around or reply. He walked over to her. More than anything he wanted to pull her into his arms. He didn't dare. At this precise moment she'd fight him like a wildcat. Addy was a woman who needed persuasion, and he was damned and determined that he was going to be the man to persuade her.

"Come on and sit down," Nick said, his big hand hovering over her shoulder. It was all he could do to keep from touching her. "Why don't we just sit and talk for a while?"

"I don't want to talk to you." Addy kept her back to him. "I want you to leave me alone."

"Were you this stubborn as a little girl? If you were, Rusty must have had his hands full raising you."

Some of the tension drained from her body. It wasn't a visible thing, yet Nick sensed it. He lowered his right hand to her shoulder, making sure his touch was light and non-threatening.

Addy felt the warmth of his touch through her blouse. His hand was big and hard and strong, yet his grip on her shoulder was unbearably tender. Hating herself for enjoying the feel of his hand on her body, she refused to look at him. She didn't trust herself to remain in control if his eyes were still filled with desire.

"I'll never lie to you." Nick balanced his cane against the wall, then placed his left hand on her other shoulder, turning her around toward him. "I'm not looking for love and marriage and I'm not making you any forever-after promises."

Addy glanced down at the Sarouk rug beneath her bare feet. Her vision focused on the intricate gold, rust and blue pattern. "What—what can you give me, Nick, in return for my blind faith in you?"

He reached out, slipping his fist beneath Addy's chin. "I can give you passion and fulfillment. I can make you glad that you're a woman."

She was tempted, so very tempted. But men said whatever they thought necessary to get what they wanted. They sought out your weaknesses and used them against you. Men did that sort of thing. Gerald had.

He tilted her chin upward, forcing her to face him. Her eyes widened with a mixture of anger and embarrassment.

Every word he said was true, but how could he make her believe him? "Addy?"

"I'm not going to sleep with you, so you might as well give up on me. I—I don't like sex, and I refuse to become one more in a long line of women who've shared your bed."

Releasing her chin, Nick stepped away from her, but didn't break eye contact. "You didn't like sex with Gerald. That doesn't mean you won't like sex with me."

"You are, without a doubt, the most egotistical man I've ever known. I'm no good at sex, and not even a Latin stud like you can change what's lacking in me. I'd disappoint you, Nick, so why don't you stop pursuing me and put us both out of our misery?"

"The only thing that's going to put us out of our misery is making love. I've just got to figure out a way to prove myself to you." Walking over to the stereo unit hidden inside the huge oak cupboard, Nick checked through Addy's tape and disk collection. "Don't you have anything except classical and semi-classical stuff?" He held up a tape. "Well, what have we here? It's not exactly Ricky Van Shelton, but it's not Beethoven either."

Addy couldn't stop looking at him, puzzled by the sudden change in his conversation from something extremely personal to something totally insignificant. What was he trying to do, throw her off guard?

Nick inserted the tape in the player, then leaning heavily on his cane, walked over and sat down on the sofa, tossing several pillows onto a nearby round table. Suddenly the sound of soft, romantic music permeated the room. The mixed voices of men and women sang "Close to You." Nick patted the sofa. "Come sit down and we'll talk."

Addy gave him a wary stare. "I don't trust you."

"Yes, you do. It's yourself you don't trust."

Addy moved toward Nick, slowly, cautiously, intent on proving him wrong. A show of bravado was called for here. She wasn't a silly young woman eager to believe a man's sweet lies. She was a woman who'd gone through her trial

NO RISK, NO OBLIGATION TO BUY ... NOW OR EVER!

CASINO JUBILEE
"Scratch'n Match" Game

Here's how to play:

1. Peel off label from front cover. Place it in space provided at right. With a coin, carefully scratch off the silver box. This makes you eligible to receive two or more free books, and possibly another gift, depending upon what is revealed beneath the scratch-off area.

2. Send back this card and you'll receive brand-new Silhouette Intimate Moments® novels. These books have a cover price of $3.50 each, but they are yours to keep absolutely free.

3. There's no catch. You're under no obligation to buy anything. We charge nothing – ZERO – for your first shipment. And you don't have to make any minimum number of purchases – not even one!

4. The fact is thousands of readers enjoy receiving books by mail from the Silhouette Reader Service™ months before they're available in stores. They like the convenience of home delivery and they love our discount prices!

5. We hope that after receiving your free books you'll want to remain a subscriber. But the choice is yours – to continue or cancel, anytime at all! So why not take us up on our invitation, with no risk of any kind. You'll be glad you did!

YOURS FREE!

This lovely Victorian pewter-finish miniature is perfect for displaying a treasured photograph – and it's yours absolutely free – when you accept our no-risk offer.

of fire, and she could handle anything, including the likes of Nick Romero.

Addy sat down, making sure she was as far from Nick as she could possibly get while sharing the same small sofa with him. "I don't want to talk about sex."

"Fine. Let's talk about Addy McConnell when she was a little girl." Nick scooted several inches toward her, then propped his big feet on a tiny needlepoint footstool. "What did you do for fun?"

"I—I took riding lessons, swimming lessons, tennis lessons, piano lessons—"

"Whoa, Red! I asked what you did for fun. Lessons aren't fun."

"I enjoyed my lessons, even if there were never any other children around...only my bodyguards." Addy shifted nervously when Nick draped his arm across the back of the sofa.

An entirely instrumental rendition of the "Gone with the Wind" theme filled the room. Addy sighed. Nick smiled.

"You really were a poor little rich girl, weren't you? An overprotected, pampered Southern belle in a golden cage. Didn't you ever spend any time with other kids?"

"No. Only when Janice was allowed to visit and when Daddy gave me my yearly birthday party." Addy remembered those precious visits with Janice, who had become her dearest friend—her only friend. And the parties had been like dreams fulfilled when the children of M.A.C. employees were brought out to the mansion to celebrate her birthday.

"What about school?" Nick inched closer to Addy. She didn't seem to notice.

"I had private tutors. Public school was never considered, and Daddy thought private schools weren't safe."

"Are you saying that you never did anything just for fun? Spontaneous things? Crazy things?"

"Everything I did had to be supervised, otherwise it was unsafe. I—I did have privacy in my room. I learned to escape into books. They became my friends.'' It had been in those books that she had become a part of the fantasies, the romantic legends, the tales of knights and their ladies. As a child she had first read of Charlemagne and his twelve paladins—the *douze pairs* who were his bodyguards and companions.

When Nick eased his arm around her shoulders, she started to pull away, but realized that she didn't want to leave the warm comfort of his embrace.

''There was a world of difference in our childhoods. Nobody ever watched over me. The only person who even cared where I was or what I was doing was my grandmother. My father was a field hand who was either working or boozing it up. He finally drank himself to death.'' Nick tightened his hold on Addy when she snuggled against him, bending her knees as she lifted her feet onto the sofa.

''What about your mother?'' Addy asked.

''My mother.'' Nick grunted. How could he possibly explain a woman like Kitty Romero to Addy? ''My mother liked men. All men. While my father drank, she whored around. She left us, my brother Miguel and me, when I was ten.''

''Oh, Nick, I know how difficult it is to lose a mother.''

''Red, losing my mother was a godsend. She was nothing but white trash. My grandmother was the only mother we ever really knew. Kitty did us a big favor by leaving.''

Addy could hear the pain in Nick's voice, the anger he tried so hard to deny. When she laid her head on his shoulder, she felt him stiffen and then relax. ''My mother committed suicide when I was ten. She—she had a nervous breakdown after Donnie... when Donnie was murdered.''

''I didn't intend for us to talk about gloomy subjects.'' He loved the feel of her so close to him, her head resting against him, her whole body snuggling to him with such trust.

''Then maybe we shouldn't talk about our childhoods.''

''Mine wasn't all bad,'' he said, reaching down to take her hand in his, holding it palm up. ''Miguel and I were close, and we had a lot of fun together. He was five years older, but he never tied to brush me off so he could run with the older guys. He took me everywhere with him." Suddenly, Nick's whole body tightened, his face rigid. "Damn!"

"What's wrong?" She gazed up into his face and almost cried at the sorrow she saw in his dark eyes.

"I can't seem to steer clear of gloom and doom." When she stared at him questioningly, he said, "Miguel was killed in an oil rig accident when I was seventeen. God, I thought I'd die when we lost him!"

"He—Miguel was married to Dina."

"Yeah." Nick squeezed her hand, then released it and withdrew his arm from around her shoulders. He looked at her, sensing the waves of sympathy flowing from her, washing over him. He grabbed her face in his big hands, cradling her gently. "Tell me about your birthday parties, Red. I never had a birthday party in my whole life."

Instantly Addy realized that he didn't want to talk about Miguel and Dina and his relationship with them. Addy smiled at Nick. "Oh, my birthday parties were grand affairs. We had them at Elm Hill before Mama died, and then at Daddy's new house afterward. All of M.A.C.'s employees' children came. It was always a catered affair with a huge cake, ice sculptures that held the ice cream and thousands of helium balloons released into the air. And entertainment. A pony ride, a clown, and a band when I got older." Tears gathered in her eyes. She willed them away. She didn't cry. Not ever. Not anymore. "I always loved my birthdays. It was the only time I never felt—confined."

"I got invited to a birthday party once. One of the kids at school. I don't think I ever envied another kid so much in all my life." Nick ran his hands down Addy's neck, across her shoulders, and down her arms. He stopped at her waist. "It was no big production like your parties. Just cake and ice cream. A few drooping balloons. But what I remember were the presents. All that bright wrapping paper and ribbons and all those gifts." He pulled Addy toward him. She went willingly. "I was lucky if I got one present at Christmas, and never on my birthday. Grandma would always remember. When I was little she'd give me a dime to go to the store for ice cream. We were so damned poor."

"My father grew up poor, too." Addy could not resist the hunger in Nick's eyes. "You and Daddy really do have a great deal in common, don't you?"

"Yeah, in more ways than you'd ever imagine." Nick lowered his head, his lips brushing hers. "We both care a hell of a lot about you."

Being kissed by Nick Romero was very much like being burned by a painless fire, a fire that consumed and left you hot but unharmed. His lips were warm and damp and demanding. He nibbled, he teased, then parried before thrusting. She groaned into his open mouth, accepting the invasion of his tongue, feeling herself slowly but surely unraveling from within. Spiraling tension built low in her stomach, the pressure mounting as it invaded the very core of her. Her nipples tightened. Her small breasts suddenly felt very heavy.

She clung to him, not wanting these strange but wonderful new feelings to end. Nick wasn't just her bodyguard. He wasn't just some Latin lover out to score. He was a man who'd known his share of pain. A man whose childhood still tormented him as Addy's did her. Poverty and neglect had soiled the pure happiness of his boyhood. Enviable wealth and constant protection had taken the joy from her girlhood.

Nick deepened the kisses, devouring Addy with his passion. He gave his hands free rein, allowing them to roam over Addy's body at will. She was willowy thin and so delicately made that he could easily break her in two with his hands. He covered one breast with his palm, savoring the feel of her jutting nipple against his rough flesh. He wanted this woman—wanted her in a way he didn't understand. She was more than a body, more than the means of physical release. He wanted to absorb her, to bring her to him and make her his.

Nick lifted Addy onto his lap. She felt the hard, pressing throb of his arousal against her bottom. Her mind screamed that it was time to run. Her love-starved body silenced her mind by squirming against Nick while she thrust her tongue out to meet his.

He knew if he didn't stop now, it would be too late. Addy was responding to him, wild and hot and wanting. But she wasn't ready for him. He hadn't proven himself to her. When he took her, he wanted her to know what she was doing, to be sure of him and of herself. He wanted her to accept the fact that they were destined to become lovers, but he didn't dare risk letting her think there could ever be more to their mating. Addy had to come to him fully prepared to accept a short-term relationship.

He slowed the kiss, soothing her body with gently caressing strokes. Releasing her mouth, he leaned his forehead against hers. "I love the taste of you, Addy, and the feel of you. You've gotten me so excited I'm hurting."

"Nick?" She spoke in a hushed whimper, her arms still draped around him, her body still seeking closer contact with his.

He patted her face, tenderly, softly. "It's going to happen for us, but only when you're ready."

Pulling away, Addy stared at him. Her eyes were wide and round, her mouth open on a sigh. "You—you really do want me, don't you?"

"More than I've ever wanted another woman."

She slipped off his lap, then stood. Gazing down at him, she reached out with trembling fingers, then jerked her hand back before looking directly into his desire-filled eyes. "I want to believe you . . . I want to—"

"And you will, when I've proven myself to you."

"Nick?"

"When there are no more doubts in your mind or your heart, then you'll come to me and I'll give you more plea-

sure than you could ever imagine." He saw the startled look
cross her face, the sweet, pink flush that stained her cheeks.
"Don't worry about what happened in the past. You aren't
frigid or inadequate in any way. When you decide the time
is right, I'll show you just how good at sex you can be."

Addy couldn't breathe. Her lungs refused to function, so
heavy was the weight of emotions pressing down on her.
Nick's words set off an explosion of sensations inside her,
frightening her into action. Turning from him she fled,
running out into the hall.

Nick sat on the sofa, his body aching with unfulfilled desire. With any other woman, he'd have taken her body,
given her satisfaction and felt only mild affection for her the
following day. Addy McConnell was different. He knew that
once he'd experienced the ecstasy of being buried deep inside her hot, sweet depths, neither of them would ever be the
same again.

Damn, how had this happened? How had he allowed
himself to get so emotionally involved?

Addy stood in the foyer, gripping the staircase banister
with her damp hands. She could hear her heart beating,
drumming loudly in her ears. Her mind reeled from the sure
knowledge that she had come close, very close, to succumbing to Nick Romero's dangerous charm. Perspiration moist-
ened her aroused body.

He—not she—had called a halt to the passion that had
consumed them both. He could have taken advantage of
her, but he hadn't. That proved something, didn't it? Wasn't
his consideration of her feelings a sign that she could trust
him?

Slumping down on the bottom step, Addy propped her
elbows on her knees and cradled her chin and cheeks in her
hands. Dear Lord, how had her life gotten so far off course?
How had she, in one week's time, gone from a sensible, in-
dependent woman in control of her own life to a romantic

fool bound to an irresistible man, dependent upon him for protection and yearning for him to give her love?

The doorbell chimes echoed loudly in the foyer. Addy jerked, startled by the sound. Staring at the door, she hesitated momentarily, then made her way forward, peeking through the privacy viewer to see the mailman standing on her front porch. Without giving it another thought, she unlocked and opened the door.

"A package for you, Ms. McConnell." The tall, bearded mailman had been making the rounds in the Twickenham district ever since Addy had moved here five years ago. She didn't know his name, but recognized his friendly face.

"Thank you." She accepted the brown paper-wrapped box, then turned and stepped back into the foyer.

Nick grabbed the package out of her hands. "Why the hell did you open the front door? You should have called me!"

"It was the mailman, for heaven's sakes." Addy pulled on the package that Nick had slipped under his arm. "You don't think someone would send a bomb through the mail, do you?"

"It's been known to happen." He took the package into the den and set it down on the sofa. Addy followed closely behind him. "Get out of here. We have no idea what's inside and I don't want you anywhere around when I open this thing."

"We should call the police. Let them open it." She couldn't bear the thought of something happening to Nick. What if it were a bomb? What if he died keeping her safe?

"I won't take any chances, Red." He looked at her concerned face, that golden face with a smattering of freckles across her perky little nose. "I know what I'm doing. I'm highly trained, remember?"

Addy nodded, then walked out of the room, making her way down the hall and out onto the patio. Dingy clouds obscured the sun, casting a dreary glow over the gravel walkway leading to the wooden bench near the hedge that closed off the yard from the alley. The breeze picked up force, swirling minuscule particles of dirt and loose grass into the air.

Addy sat down on the backless bench, her nervous fingers idly picking at the profusion of flowers surrounding her. A dozen different questions whirled about in her mind, thoughts and images tormenting her with doubt, possibilities filling her with dread. She hadn't been expecting a package. She hadn't ordered anything, and the box was wrapped in plain brown paper and tied with string, childlike in its simplicity. Her name had been printed in bold black letters, the stick-on kind that could be purchased in any stationery shop.

Minutes ticked by, soundless except in her mind, where each second toned louder than a striking mantel clock. What would Nick find inside the mysterious package? Her feminine instincts told her that the contents weren't harmless, that they would, somehow, be connected to the man threatening her safety. Both she and her father were convinced that Gerald Carlton was the most likely suspect, but Nick hadn't allowed their certainty to sway his judgment. He'd told them that the only way to keep Addy safe was to keep an open mind, to suspect everyone, whether or not their motives were obvious.

The sound of distant thunder announced the possibility of rain. Glancing toward the west, Addy saw a dark horizon. With a great deal of anxious turning and twisting, she managed to stay seated, though she longed to rush back inside to be with Nick, to share whatever fate befell him. She didn't want him facing danger alone.

The moments dragged by like hours. The rumbling thunder grew close. The wind whipped around Addy, tousling her loosely confined hair and blowing dust into her eyes. No matter what, even if it started to rain, she wasn't going to move from this spot until Nick came for her. If she stayed right here and waited, everything would be all right. She would be all right. And Nick would be all right.

Sharp, bright lightning streaked the sky. Addy closed her eyes and prayed. The first tiny droplets of rain fell, hitting her bare arms and legs, sprinkling the bench and the gravel walkway. Thunder boomed loudly. Opening her eyes, Addy stared at the back of her house. Nick stood in the doorway, the open box in one hand, his black cane in the other. She gasped, relief spreading through her like syrupy sweet jelly over hot biscuits.

Jumping up, she ran to him. The dark sky exploded with lightning, the clouds bursting with rain. Nick wrapped his arm around Addy, holding the box behind her back as he pulled her close.

"Oh, Nick, I've been so worried!" Burying her face against his shoulder, she clung to him, whispering his name over and over again.

"I'm fine, Red." He didn't want her to see the contents of the box, but he knew he couldn't protect her from them. She would demand to see what lay inside and he had no right to refuse. She needed to know what type of lunatic they were dealing with and understand that they didn't dare narrow their list of suspects down to Gerald Carlton.

Nick pulled her with him into the kitchen, dropping the box on the countertop, then jerking Addy's trembling body against the solid strength of his own. He stroked her neck, her back, her hips, his big hand moving up and down slowly, caressingly. He threaded his fingers into her hair, pulling free the long titian strands from the thick bun.

She looked at him and knew that she loved him.

"Addy?" He had never seen an expression so serene on a woman's face. It was as if Addy had discovered some wondrous truth that erased all her pain and anger and fear.

"I was afraid . . . if there had been a bomb—"

"No bomb. Just pictures, and newspaper photos and articles." He circled her neck with his hand, soothing her damp flesh with the pad of his thumb. "You're not going to want to see those things, Red, so why don't you just let me tell you what they are."

She stared deeply into his dark eyes which were filled with tenderness and concern. "The package is from *him*, isn't it, the man who's determined to keep M.A.C. from bidding on the NASP project?"

"Yeah." Nick glided his thumb up and under Addy's chin. Right now he wanted to ease her fears, to caress her, to love her and keep her safe. "The guy's trying to play mind games with us, Red. Remember that. If he gets to you, then he's succeeded in what he set out to do."

"Let me have the box, Nick." She pulled away from him, turning toward the counter.

He released her, knowing that all he could do was stand by and watch her confront her past. "I'll have to call Rusty. He needs to know."

Addy's hand hovered over the box. Touching the lid, her fingers trembled. With haste born of fear, she slipped opened the box and stared at the contents. Nestled inside like brittle, golden autumn leaves, the old newspaper clippings lay scattered, mixed with snapshots of her brother. She reached out, but her fingers refused to cooperate. She couldn't touch the items. Tight, choking tears swelled in her chest and burned in her throat.

Nick stood behind her, his big, hard body a source of warmth and comfort. Slipping one arm around her waist, he whispered, "You don't have to do this."

A strangled cry escaped her throat. She balled her hands into snug fists. "This is going to kill Daddy. He never talks about Donnie. Never!"

Forging ahead with all the inner strength she could muster, Addy picked up a photograph of Donnie, dressed in his cowboy outfit and sitting atop his pony. Tears gathered in Addy's eyes. She blinked them away.

"Who would have access to pictures of your brother?" Nick asked.

It took Addy a couple of minutes to understand his question. "Oh, Lord, I don't know. Servants, friends, relatives. Anyone who's ever been at the house. Daddy boxed away all the old pictures years ago, but he kept them in the storage areas above the garage. He even kept all of Donnie's clothes—and all of Mama's things, too.''

"That narrows down the suspects somewhat, but still leaves all the major ones. Gerald. Ron. Brett.''

Addy picked up a fragile newspaper clipping. The headlines jumped out at her. It was the story of Donnie's murder. A photograph of his lifeless little body accompanied the article. "Oh, God, we can't show these to Daddy!'' She handled each article, each picture of her brother, her father, her mother and herself. Her parents' grief-stricken faces had been captured by some over-zealous photographer at Donnie's funeral. Stories of her mother's suicide four years later had made front page news.

The sour, sick feeling began in her stomach. Torturous pounding began in her temples. She swayed slightly and might have lost her balance had it not been for Nick's strong hold about her waist.

Suddenly she pulled away from him, running, running. She made it to the downstairs powder room a split second before her stomach emptied itself. Nick caught up with her in the powder room where she'd knelt on her knees in front of the commode. He grabbed a hand towel, wet it with cool water and bent by her side, laying his cane on the floor as he wiped perspiration from her pale face.

"It's okay, Red. I've seen grown men in the middle of battle react far worse.'' With tenderness and compassion, he cleaned her face and pushed back loose strands of damp, clinging hair.

"I don't want to relive those days.'' She accepted Nick's help as he eased her up and onto her feet.

"The person who sent the clippings and pictures knows that. He's counting on your pain and fear as well as Rusty's to get him what he wants.''

"Was there a note?'' She didn't hesitate to cling, to snuggle, to seek comfort in Nick's arms.

He held her, longing for the power to solve Addy's problems and ease her pain and sorrow. "Yes. I left it in the den."

"What did it say?"

"The same old stuff about bidding on the NASP contract."

"Daddy has to know." She laid her head on Nick's shoulder, closing her eyes, willing herself to be strong and brave. Her father would need her strength. "If only there were some way to keep Daddy from seeing the articles, the pictures of Donnie and Mama."

"Rusty is going to be able to handle all this old grief a lot easier than he's going to be able to deal with the continued threat on your life." Nick tightened his hold on her, silently cursing the demon whose sick mind was putting Addy in danger. He would not let anyone harm her. No matter what it took, he was going to keep her safe.

"What more can Daddy do? I'm under constant surveillance. You're with me night and day." She thanked the dear Lord in heaven for Nick. All the resentment, the distrust, the uncertainty vanished. Maybe she was a fool. She didn't know. She was certain of only one thing. She was falling in love with Nick Romero.

"Rusty can let me take you away from here. Out of Huntsville to some place no one knows about . . . where no one can find us." Nick had made that suggestion to Rusty a week ago. He'd told Nick that Addy would never agree. But now, the threat to her life had escalated. Things had changed. With or without her agreement, Addy would soon be going into hiding. He'd convince Rusty that it was the only foolproof way to keep her safe.

"I don't want to leave Huntsville, to run like some scared—"

Nick silenced her by placing his hand over her mouth. She glared up at him, her green eyes vivid with surprise. "You'll do whatever I tell you to do, woman. Understand?"

Addy nodded in agreement, remaining silent when Nick removed his hand. There was no point in arguing for the sake of arguing. Nick's background made him far more of an expert than either she or her father. If Nick said they had to go into hiding, then she'd go.

"You're awfully quiet, Red. Just what's going on in that sharp little brain of yours?"

"I was thinking how lucky I am to have you as my own personal bodyguard."

He stared at her, knowing there was more to her statement than met the eye. Strong emotions vibrated in the air, a pulsating tension between the two of them. She looked at him, her feelings written plainly on her face. Addy McConnell had fallen for him. It was what he'd wanted, wasn't it, for her to care enough to let him be her lover? Becoming Addy's lover could get complicated. Once he'd had her, would he ever be able to let her go?

"Well, I'll be damned," Nick said.

"We both may be damned," Addy said. "But I'm willing to take the risk."

Chapter 8

Nick opened the door and stepped back, avoiding a collision with Rusty McConnell. Addy's father barreled into the foyer like an out-of-control steamroller.

"Where is she?" A splattering of sweat dotted Rusty's ruddy cheeks. His deep baritone voice trembled with anger.

"She's in the den." Nick reached out a restraining hand, grasping the older man by the arm.

Rusty stopped, eyeing Nick with a harsh glare. "Is she all right?"

"Yeah, she's all right . . . now. But she won't be if you go storming in there and upset her." Gauging Rusty's reaction to his comment, Nick felt him relax slightly, his big, powerful body losing some of its rigidity. "Look, she's worried about you. She's more concerned by how this is affecting you than anything else." Nick released his tenacious grip on Rusty's arm.

"Where's the box?"

"She has it with her," Nick said.

"Dammit, man, why did you ever let her see it in the first place?"

"I didn't want her to see it, but I didn't have the right to keep it from her. She's not a child, and as much as you and I want to protect her, we're not doing her any favors by treating her like one."

"Hell, she is a child. My child! My only child . . ."

"Granted. But she's also a woman, an adult who's fought long and hard for the right to be treated as one." Nick nodded toward the living room. "We need to talk, just the two of us . . . alone, before you see Addy."

"Keeping secrets from her?" Rusty asked. "I thought you said we needed to treat her like an adult."

"Addy already knows what I'm going to say to you. I just didn't think it was necessary for her to have to hear it all over again while you and I thrash things out." Nick walked out of the foyer and into the living room, stopping briefly in the doorway to issue Rusty an invitation. "How about something to drink while we talk?"

Rusty grunted, then smiled. "Sure. Scotch. Neat." He joined Nick in the living room, watching while his daughter's bodyguard poured two glasses a third full, then handed one to him.

"Sit?" Nick asked, lifting the Scottish whiskey to his mouth, tasting it, savoring the smoky flavor.

"I know what you're trying to do, Romero." Sitting down, Rusty filled a blue brocade wingback chair with his big body.

Nick didn't respond. He simply stared at Rusty as if he didn't have any idea what he was talking about.

"You want to calm me down before I see Addy." D.B. McConnell took a hardy sip of his Scotch, allowing it to linger in his mouth before swallowing. "Seeing those pictures and newspaper clippings upset her more than she wants me to know. Right?" When Nick didn't reply, he continued. "You're trying to protect my daughter from me, aren't you?"

"Look, Rusty, I'm probably overstepping my bounds, but the last thing Addy needs right now is to see you coming apart at the seams."

"I agree." Rusty took another hefty taste of his drink. "I knew you were the man for Addy the night you threatened to castrate Gerald Carlton, the same night you saved her from a kidnapper."

"I admit that I care about Addy, that I'll do whatever it takes to protect her, but don't go ringing wedding bells and throwing rice. I've been a bachelor for forty-three years, and I plan on staying one another forty-three."

Rusty finished his Scotch, set the glass down on a nearby cherry table and stood. "I like that about you. You're honest with me, and I'll bet you're honest with Addy. That's good enough for me. Don't make her any promises you don't intend to keep."

Choosing to ignore Rusty's comments, Nick plunged right to the heart of the matter. "I need to get Addy out of this house, away from Huntsville." He set his unfinished drink down beside Rusty's. "It's the only way I can guarantee her safety."

"Has she agreed?"

"Yes, she has. Your daughter may be as stubborn as a mule, but she isn't stupid. We're dealing with an unknown quantity here, a guy who's making threats to kidnap— threats to kill—if you bid on the NASP project. If he doesn't know where Addy is, he can't hurt her."

"I've got a condo in Florida and an apartment outside Washington—"

"And everybody who knows you and Addy knows about the condo and the apartment."

Grunting, Rusty rubbed his chin as he considered other possibilities. "I've got friends and business associates all over, even in Europe. I can call in some favors and have the two of you on a plane to practically anywhere in the world within twelve hours."

"It'll be best if I take Addy someplace that even you don't know about." Nick waited for the lion's roar. He didn't have to wait long.

"What? You can't mean that you don't want me to know where my own daughter is? That won't wash with me, Romero! Wherever Addy goes, I want to stay in contact with her!"

"I've already called Sam Dundee," Nick said. "He's got a place lined up for us. No one except Sam will know our whereabouts. I'll check in daily with him, and he'll relay the message to you. If you need to contact us, then call Sam and he'll get in touch with us."

Rusty paced back and forth in front of the fireplace, his hands balled into fists as if he longed to smash something. "I don't like it... but you're right."

"Then you agree?"

"Yeah. Reluctantly, but I agree."

"Let's tell Addy."

The moment her father entered the den, Addy jumped off the couch and ran to him, throwing her arms around him.

Rusty soothed her, petting her like the child she was to him. "It's all right, baby girl."

"Oh, Daddy, please don't look at the pictures or the articles. It won't change anything. It'll just upset you." She gazed at him pleadingly.

He ran his fingers down her cheek, tenderly grasping her chin in his hand. "I don't need to see them. I'll just take a look at the note."

Addy sighed with relief. Going through the contents of the box had made her physically ill, and even now her mind could not erase the images of those long-ago newspaper articles—articles she'd never been allowed to see when they'd been fresh news. But her father would have seen them all, twenty-nine years ago when Donnie had been kidnapped and murdered, and twenty-five years ago when Madeline Delacourt McConnell had committed suicide.

"Ned Johnson is on his way over here," Nick said.

"You've already called the FBI?" Rusty shook his head. "Do you think there's any way they can trace the box, find out who sent it?"

"It's doubtful. I think we're dealing with a very intelligent person, one who's covering his tracks. I'd bet my life that our mystery man didn't leave any prints on the box or its contents. That's why I saw no reason not to take a look at everything before I called Johnson."

"Even intelligent people make mistakes," Addy said.

"That's what we're counting on." Nick pulled out a sheet of plain white paper from his pocket, handing it to Rusty. "Here's the note that was lying on top of the pictures and clippings."

Rusty released Addy, took the note and read it hastily. "M.A.C. doesn't have to bid on the NASP contract."

"Yes, we do," Addy said vehemently. "No matter who's behind this, Gerald or…or someone else, we can't let them get what they want. Not only will we lose millions, but it could cost hundreds of jobs."

"Your life is worth more than money or jobs," Rusty said.

"My life is safe." Addy turned to Nick, smiling. "Nick and I are leaving Huntsville before daybreak tomorrow, and we're not coming home until M.A.C. has won the NASP contract. Two more weeks and this will all be over."

"If only we knew for sure it was Carlton." Rusty clutched his hands in imitation of a stranglehold, crumpling the threatening letter. "I'd kill that bastard with my bare hands. I should have killed him years ago!"

"If Gerald is behind these threats, then the FBI will catch him." Addy hoped it was Gerald. She'd thought she was long over her hatred and bitterness, but she wasn't. Her ex-husband had put her through three years of agony and stripped her of her dignity as a woman. Death was too good for him!

"When I called Johnson to tell him about Addy's little package, he gave me some interesting information." Nick reached out, taking the badly crinkled letter from Rusty. "Information that possibly links the man who tried to kidnap Addy last Friday night to Gerald Carlton."

"What did Johnson tell you?" Rusty asked.

"The man who tried to kidnap me was named Linc Hites," Addy said. "He worked for a janitorial service that New Age Aerospace uses."

"Damn!" Rusty turned his attention to Nick. "Is there any evidence that Carlton and this Hites fellow actually knew each other?"

"None, but Johnson's keeping tabs on Carlton. If he's our man, then all we need is for him to make one little slip." Nick had gone over the list of suspects time and again. Unless the man behind the kidnap plot was someone unknown to the McConnells, then all the circumstantial evidence pointed to Gerald Carlton.

"Not much can be done without some hard evidence to back up our suspicions." Rusty slumped down on the sofa, his enormous body dwarfing the small couch. "All right. You and Addy go into hiding. When M.A.C. wins the NASP contract—" he smiled at Addy, and she smiled back "—you two come back to Huntsville. The threat will be over. He will have lost and we'll have won."

Nick wished things were that simple, and they just might be—if the person or persons behind the threats really did want to keep M.A.C. from acquiring the government job and this person or persons didn't seek revenge when things went sour. But what if they did seek revenge, or what if the contract bid was a smoke screen? It never paid to rule out any and all possibilities.

"Let's hope that's the scenario," Nick said. "We'll work under that assumption for the time being."

"Addy said you two were leaving in the morning." Rusty held out his hand and Addy accepted it, seating herself beside her father.

"Yeah. Before daylight." Nick picked up the infamous box. "I'll go wait for Ned Johnson and give you two some time alone."

"Thanks." Rusty put his arm around Addy. She rested against him, her head on his shoulder. "Oh, yeah, Nick, why don't I send some of Dundee's men with you? They could ride shotgun on your trip."

"Bad idea," Nick said. "An entourage will call attention to us. A man and woman traveling alone is commonplace. Trust me on this, Rusty."

Neither man said anything else, but they stared at each other for several silent moments, weighing each other, sizing up one another. Two strong men with the same singular purpose—protecting Addy from harm, no matter what the cost.

Nick turned, leaving the room. Addy had sensed the unspoken exchange between her father and her...her what? Her bodyguard. Her protector. Her defender.

"He told me he wasn't interested in getting married." Rusty leaned back so he could get a clear view of Addy's face.

"What?" Addy gasped, glaring at her father with startled green eyes.

"I asked him about his intentions," Rusty said with mock seriousness, without a hint of a smile.

"Oh, Lord, Daddy!"

"He said he intended staying a bachelor for another forty-three years."

Addy wondered what Nick had thought of her father's questioning. Had he resented Rusty's interference or had he simply found the notion that D.B. McConnell wanted him to marry Addy amusing? "He told me the same thing."

"The right woman could probably change his mind."

"You hadn't known the man twenty-four hours when you decided you wanted him for a son-in-law. How can you be so sure?" Addy pulled away, giving her father a questioning stare. "You liked Gerald when you first met him, too, remember?"

"Hell, don't remind me! That jerk had us both fooled. He was a charmer. Silver-tongued, smooth and—well, he was a man's man, or at least I thought he was."

"Nick Romero is all those things, too, you know."

"Nick's the genuine article. He's not pretending to be anything he isn't. And he's not pretending his interest in you, either. He knows that I'm aware of how much he wants you, and yet he told me honestly that he isn't interested in marriage."

"Are we both acting like fools again, Daddy, putting so much faith and trust in a man we hardly know, a man who came into our lives because of Dina?" Addy wanted to tell her father about Dina's real relationship with Nick, that the two had once been lovers, but she didn't want to add to the problems already plaguing him.

"You know about Nick and Dina, don't you?" Rusty's faded green eyes darkened, his gaze searching her face.

"She told you?"

"Nope. Dina didn't tell me anything, except how fond she's always been of Nick, but I read between the lines."

"Doesn't it bother you, knowing she slept with her husband's brother?" It certainly bothered Addy. Every time she thought about Nick and Dina, naked, hot and sweaty, in Nick's bed, she wanted to scratch out the other woman's eyes.

"Dina is very insecure. She thinks money is the answer to all of life's problems." Rusty took Addy's hand, patting it gently. "I know what Dina is, but I still want her. Hell, baby girl, I'm in love with the woman. Besides, I'm not lily-white pure myself. You know that."

"Then it doesn't bother you, knowing . . . knowing—"

"When Dina and I make love, I don't waste my energy thinking about who else she's been with." Rusty laughed, deepening the heavy lines around his eyes and mouth.

"Damn, this is hardly a subject a man should be discussing with his daughter!"

"If I were your son, you'd discuss it with me, wouldn't you?"

Rusty laughed louder. "You've got me there!"

Addy joined his laughter. He hugged her to him again. "Daddy, I think I'm falling in love with Nick."

"I'm not surprised. There's a chemistry between you two. I felt it the night you met. Romero doesn't know it yet, but I'd bet my last million that he's falling for you, too."

"I—I've decided to have an affair with him." Addy didn't look directly at her father, uncertain of his reaction.

"Good idea! Try him out and see how he performs." Rusty held back the hardy chuckle straining his lungs.

"Daddy!"

The chuckle burst loose from Rusty, filling the room with his good humor, releasing the tension that hung in the air like a dark rain cloud. "Don't think about the other women he's been with, not even Dina. Those women are a part of his past. You, Addy McConnell, could damn well be his future."

"I hope you're right, Daddy. I hope I have a future—" hastily she added "—with Nick."

He stood just outside the open door of Addy's bedroom, watching while she packed. She was very neat, every item folded and placed with precise care. On top of her slacks, blouses and sweaters lay her lingerie, skimpy little tidbits of silk and lace and sheer nylon in colors from the palest flesh tone to the most lush, vivid purple. He couldn't help but imagine what sort of frothy satin temptations she was wearing beneath her walking shorts and cotton pullover.

The antique grandfather clock in the hallway struck ten times. In less than seven hours he would take Addy away from her home, away from the familiar routine of her daily life. Only four people knew where they were going—the two of them, Sam Dundee and Elizabeth Mallory, the woman who owned the cottage where they'd stay for the next two weeks.

Nick wondered what would happen when they got to Sequana Falls, Georgia. How was he going to spend two weeks alone with a woman he desperately wanted, without seducing her into his bed? He'd never been in this predicament before, wanting a woman who needed more than temporary pleasure from him. Addy wanted him to prove himself to her, and the only way he could bed her and walk away without feelings of remorse and guilt was to give her what she wanted. Somehow, some way, he had to prove to Addy that she and she alone meant more to him than anything else on earth. Since he was fast coming to feel that way about her, he figured there had to be a way to prove it.

Addy's ex-husband had used her and abused her, emotionally if not physically. She was afraid to give herself to another man, unsure of his motives. Because of past experience, she'd come to the conclusion that men who showed an interest in her were after Rusty's money. Hell, he didn't give a hoot about her father's millions. If he'd wanted to marry for money, he could have done so more than once over the years. He bedded women who attracted him, women who turned him on. He had enough money to meet his needs. He neither wanted nor needed more. But he did want Addy McConnell, and he needed her, needed her in his arms, in his bed and in his life, as he had never needed another woman. Once he'd had her, it was going to take a lot of long, slow loving...a lot of hot, wild mating...to get enough of her to satisfy his craving.

"What are you doing lurking out there in the hall?" Addy closed the suitcase lid, zipped it, then set it on the floor beside her bed.

"I wasn't lurking." Nick stepped over the threshold and into her room, instantly feeling as if he'd entered a forbidden zone. "I was just watching you pack. Are you sure you got everything you need in one bag?"

"It's a big bag." She sat down on the edge of her pencil-post mahogany bed. "Besides, you said to pack light."

"I've never needed more than one suitcase." He glanced at her, noticing how at ease she seemed alone in her room with him.

"You've been traveling most of your life, haven't you?" She crossed her legs at the ankles.

Nick couldn't take his eyes off her legs, her long, slim legs that beckoned for his touch. "I don't own a house or even rent an apartment. I didn't need one when I was in the Navy, and when I was between DEA assignments, I'd either visit my grandmother in El Paso, get a hotel room or stay with my buddies Nate Hodges in St. Augustine and Sam Dundee in Atlanta."

"You've never mentioned Nate Hodges before. How long have you been friends?"

"Since SEAL training in Coronado." Nick's dark eyes glazed over with memory. "We were both a couple of eighteen-year-old half-breeds running from lives we hated, hoping to find something worthwhile. What we found was a living hell in Nam."

Addy wanted to run to Nick, to throw her arms around him and hold him close. She could tell by the tone of his voice, more than the words he spoke, that he was so alone, that he'd been alone all his life—a man always on the outside looking in. She longed to bring him inside, into the warmth and caring in her heart, to show him that he never had to be alone again.

"Daddy was in Korea. He never talks about it. He has this old-fashioned notion that women should be protected from life's harsher realities." Her father had tried, unsuccessfully to protect her mother. Sometimes she wondered if Rusty and Madeline had shared more of the agonizing pain and ugly reality of what had happened to their son would her mother have grown stronger instead of weaker in the years following Donnie's murder.

"Women experience most of life's harsh realities," Nick said, leaning against the colonial blue wall near the door. "No matter how much a man wants to protect his women, sometimes he's powerless. I think that's how your father feels now."

"He trusts you to keep me safe." Addy stood up, walking over to face Nick directly. "And I trust you."

Damn, how he wanted to pull her into his arms, to taste her sweet mouth, to feel the sleek leanness of her body. "No need to set your alarm clock. I'll wake you at three-thirty, and we'll hit the road by four." He didn't dare stay near her a minute longer, with those bewitching green cat-eyes of hers casting a spell over him.

When he turned to leave, Addy caught his hand, lacing her fingers through his. "Sleep tight then."

Bringing her hand to his lips, he brushed a feathery kiss across her knuckles. He could feel himself tightening, his whole body preparing for a feast to which he hadn't been invited. "Two weeks, Red, and if we're lucky, this will all be over."

"If we're lucky—" she whispered, then released his hand and stood back, watching him walk out of her room and close the door behind him.

Nick felt like beating his cane against the wall or smashing his fist through a window. He hadn't been this horny in years, and in the past, all it would have taken to ease his pain was a willing woman. This time nothing would give him relief except emptying himself into Addy McConnell's receptive body.

The grandfather clock struck midnight. Nick flipped on the bedside lamp, hauled himself out of bed and slipped into his faded jeans, forcing the zipper up over his arousal. He couldn't sleep. Hell, he couldn't even get any rest. Addy was in the room next to him, probably wearing one of her silky nightgowns and sleeping like a baby. She'd told him that she wasn't any good at sex. He didn't believe it. That bastard ex-husband undoubtedly didn't know the first thing about arousing a woman as sensitive and untried as Addy. If only she'd give him half a chance, he'd prove to her what a sensuous creature she really was; he'd give her unbearable pleasure and teach her how good it could be between them.

Retrieving his cane from where he'd propped it against the nightstand, Nick made his way across the room and out into the hall. Addy's door stood open. They both kept their doors open at night so he could hear every sound. Just in case.

Moonlight poured in through the Federalist-style fanlights above the double French doors that flanked each side of the fireplace in Addy's bedroom. The waxed pine floors glistened in the muted light, and the rich reds and blues in the scattered Oriental carpets gleamed like jewels.

Nick stepped inside. Addy lay in the middle of the big bed, shadows of the crocheted canopy drawing lines across her face. She had neatly folded back the white bedspread, laying it over the patchwork sampler quilt that graced the foot of her bed.

He didn't want to wake her, but he *had* to see her, to look at her. Despite the air-conditioned coolness in the house, Nick felt hot. Beads of perspiration dotted his upper lip and a trickle of sweat ran down his throat, getting lost in the mat of black hair that covered his upper chest.

Without warning, his foot banged into something in the semidarkness. He cursed the object, swearing softly under his breath. Looking down, he saw a brass pot filled with red geraniums near the window. If the damned pecking of his cane hadn't awakened Addy, then maybe his bumbling crash into the flower container hadn't, either.

"Nick?" She sat up in bed, throwing off the thin blue sheet that covered her.

"Sorry, Red. I didn't mean to awaken you. I—I thought I heard something," he lied. "I just wanted to check things out. Go back to sleep."

"I wasn't asleep." She slid her legs over the edge of the bed, allowing her feet to touch the floor. "I'm so restless that I can't sleep."

He took a good look at her then and wished he hadn't. She wore a teal-blue satin chemise that barely touched the top of her thighs. He sucked in his breath, calling on all his willpower not to reach out and grab her. Her curly red hair hung loosely about her shoulders and halfway down her back. Tousled and unkempt, it looked as if some man had been running his fingers through it. Dear God, that was exactly what he wanted to do. But he wouldn't stop with her hair—he wouldn't stop touching her until he had covered every inch of her body and counted every little copper freckle.

"I should go and let you try to get some rest. We've got a long drive ahead of us tomorrow."

Addy picked up her teal-blue lace kimono that she'd tossed across the nightstand. Easing into it, she stood. "Don't go." She took a tentative step toward him. "Stay."

"Bad idea, Red." Nick turned from her, starting toward the door.

"Please, don't go, Nick. Stay and...talk to me." She moved closer, her hand hovering over his back, almost touching him.

Keeping his back to her, he drew in a deep breath. "If I stay, Red, I'm going to do a lot more than talk."

"Oh." She trusted Nick with her life. She had even admitted to her father that she was falling in love with the man. But was she ready for them to make love?

"It's going to happen sooner or later, but there's no need for us to confront it tonight. There'll be time enough when we're alone in an isolated cabin in the middle of the Georgia mountains." He moved forward, taking a step out into the hall.

Addy followed him, touching his back with the palm of her hand. She felt him stiffen. His naked back was sleek and damp and warm. Her hand burned from the physical contact of flesh against flesh. "Don't leave me, Nick. Stay. Stay and prove to me that—"

"Prove to you that I want you more than I've ever wanted another woman? Prove to you that you're all that matters to me?" He turned around slowly, knowing that once he faced her there would be no turning back, knowing exactly what he was going to do and how he was going to prove himself to her. He prayed that he had the willpower to be the man Addy needed tonight.

She looked at him with big, hungry eyes, the expression on her face a mixture of longing and uncertainty. "I don't want to disappoint you."

He threaded his fingers through her hair, then gripped the back of her neck. "Don't you know that there's no way you can disappoint me? Just be yourself, Addy. Be the warm, loving and sensitive woman you are."

"What if—if—"

He moved his hand down her back to her waist, hauling her up against him. The sound of her indrawn breath when her soft body met his hard arousal fueled his hunger, increasing his determination to give this woman—his woman—unforgettable pleasure. "We're going to take things slow, Red. Slow and easy. I'm going to touch you and you're going to touch me, and we're going to make each other burn."

Gerald had always been in a hurry to find a quick release, never caring whether or not he gave her any pleasure. "But you're already aroused. You won't want to wait."

"That's where you're wrong." He touched her lips with his, but didn't actually kiss her. She sighed into his mouth. He drew in her sweet breath, running the tip of his tongue across her bottom lip. "I've never wanted anything the way I want you. Making love is best when it's not rushed, when you take your time and savor every delicious moment. Especially the first time."

"No one has ever *made love* to me before."

Gut-wrenching pain twisted his insides. He vowed that he would never hurt her, no matter how much he had to suffer. He would give Addy what no man had ever given her—*ecstasy.* "I'm going to make love to you, Red. And you're going to make love to me."

"But, Nick, I don't know how. What if—"

He kissed her, a gentle yet thorough kiss. Withdrawing his mouth from hers, he said, "Sometimes it's better not to talk so much. Stop talking, stop thinking and start feeling."

He walked her, backwards, toward the bed. His big hand never left her waist, his arousal stayed pressed against her belly and his lips kept brushing hers as the two of them moved slowly, inch by inch, making their way across the room.

Nick leaned his cane against the nightstand, then took Addy by the shoulders, carefully sliding her kimono down her arms and off her body. He tossed it to the floor. "I love the way your body is made, Red. All long and lean and sexy."

"I'm not—" She saw the look in his eyes, that look that said she'd better not disagree with him. "I've never thought of myself as sexy."

"You're the sexiest thing I've ever seen." He placed his hands on her upper arms, moving his fingers in gentle caresses downward, stopping at her fingertips. Slipping his fingers between hers, he stroked her.

She leaned into him, sighing at the unexpected pleasure his seemingly innocent touch created within her. "Nick?"

He ran his hands up and over her back, pausing briefly before cupping her buttocks. "You've got such a tiny waist and such a firm, tempting little butt."

He'd told her to stop talking and start feeling, but he hadn't stopped talking, and every word he said was driving her crazy. Did he know what he was doing to her? Was he aware of how arousing his words were?

Lowering his head, Nick took one tight, little nipple into his mouth while he continued kneading her derriere. Addy moaned when spirals of heated sensation darted outward and downward, pulling on her femininity, plucking the strings of a heretofore unknown passion. Instinctively, she raised her leg, brushing it against his, rubbing him intimately. He slipped his hand beneath her chemise, touching her stomach, then easing around to cup her naked behind.

For one heart-stopping moment, Nick thought he was going to lose it. All he could think about was ramming himself into her, seeking and finding the sheathing heat of her body, emptying himself and gaining relief for his unbearable ache. "I want to see you, all of you."

When he tugged her chemise upward, Addy placed her hands over his, momentarily halting him. "You'll think I'm skinny, that my breasts are too small, that my freckles are ugly."

"Damn!" Nick spit out.

Addy pulled away from him. He reached out, jerking her to him, taking her mouth with bruising force as he thrust his tongue inside her welcoming warmth. Heaven. That's what it was to be inside her. Sheer heaven. She didn't resist the fury of his kiss or the roughness of his hands as they skimmed her body, finally pulling her chemise up and over her head.

With his lips still touching hers, Nick gave her a gentle shove backward, tumbling her onto the bed. He came down with her, half on top of her, half beside her. "I'm not your ex-husband, Red. I'm no fool. I know that having a woman like you to care for me is worth ten times whatever money your daddy has in the bank."

Tears filled her eyes. She wiped them away with the tips of her fingers. She lay there totally naked, Nick's big, aroused body partially covering her. "Look at me, Nick, and tell me what you see. And, please, don't—don't pretend."

Raising himself on one elbow, he gazed down at her, then swallowed hard. Addy McConnell was as sleek and lean as the most prized thoroughbred. Her arms and legs were long and covered with a light dusting of copper freckles. Her hips flared slightly away from her minuscule waist. Her breasts were small, but high and firm, topped with golden coral nipples. And the hair between her legs was as fiery red as the curls framing her pretty face. "You're beautiful, Addy. I've never seen anything more beautiful."

"Oh, Nick." She reached out, opening her arms and her heart. She believed he meant what he said. He really did think she was beautiful.

"And your freckles are gorgeous. As a matter of fact, I've had more than one fantasy about kissing every freckle on your body." He kissed each one on her face. "You've got a lot of freckles, Addy. It could take me hours to taste all of them."

She didn't know how long it took Nick to accomplish the task. Eventually she lost track of time, giving herself over completely to the hedonistic upheaval going on in her body. She'd never known that a man could give so freely, titillating a woman with his hands and mouth as if he wanted nothing more than to please her.

Addy's breasts became so sensitized that even Nick's breath on them sent chills of agonized longing through her. When he took her into his mouth, she cried out, writhing beneath him, pushing herself upward, begging for relief from the excruciating pressure building in the core of her body. While he continued to suckle her, he slipped his hand between her thighs. She opened for him. He slid two fingers inside her, testing her. She bucked upward, crying and groaning, pleading with him.

"Easy, Red, easy. I'm going to take good care of you." His fingers sought and found the pleasure point hidden within her.

With a steady, gentle pressure, he massaged her, all the while his mouth tugged greedily on one of her breasts and his thumb and forefinger pinched at her other puckering nipple. He could feel her body tightening. "That's it, Red, let it happen. Don't hold back. Give in to what you're feeling.'' When the first spasm hit her, Nick increased the speed and pressure of his fingers, bringing her to the pinnacle, intensifying her pleasure. She screamed, her voice a ragged, tormented cry of release. He soothed her trembling body, kissing her closed eyelids, her nose, her open mouth.

When her heartbeat slowed and she was able to breath again, she opened her eyes and looked up at him. "I've never...you made me—oh, Nick."

He took her mouth as he longed to take her body. But it was too soon. She wasn't ready, despite the fact that he'd helped her achieve her first orgasm. He couldn't bury himself deep inside and take his own pleasure. That was not the way to prove himself to Addy. But, dammit all, he had to take just a little something for himself, enough to keep him from going totally insane.

Lifting himself up, he sat on the edge of the bed and pulled off his jeans. Beneath, he wore a pair of black briefs. Hesitating, he considered the consequences if he went ahead and stripped naked, if he disregarded the inner voice that warned him against such foolishness. With one quick jerk, he pulled the briefs down and off, then turned back to Addy.

She could see him in the moonlight, his big, bronze body poised over her. With more passion than knowledge, she touched him, circling his manhood with her fingers. He throbbed beneath her touch as she moved her hand up and down caressingly.

"Red, honey, you're going to have to stop that... sometime in the next few hours." His voice held a trace of humor.

"You like my touch?"

"Did you like mine?"

"You know I did."

He pulled away from her. She stared at him, puzzled. "If you don't stop, I'll lose it."

"I want you to lose it—inside me."

He thought he'd die. She was asking him to make love to her, completely, thoroughly. "Tonight's for you, Red. For your pleasure. If I take you the way you're asking, then I won't have proven anything to you."

She had to consider what he'd said for several minutes before she realized what he meant; then she smiled. "You've already proven everything you need to prove to me."

"I've got to prove something to myself." He kissed her savagely, then eased his tongue over her chin, down her throat and across her breasts to her stomach.

"Nick?" She felt the tremors of excitement building again, growing stronger with each swipe of his talented tongue.

"There's so many things I want to do to you, so many ways I want to make love to you." He lifted her hips in his big hands, bringing her body upward so that he could taste her. She tried to pull away. He held fast. "Let me, Red. Please, let me."

She gave in to his plea, never realizing the earth-shattering rapture that awaited her. She became lost in a fog of sensation where the world centered on Nick's mouth and her pulsating flesh. With uncontrollable convulsions Addy's body took the pleasure Nick gave her, rejoicing in each pounding quake of fulfillment.

Afterward she clung to him, weeping warm, salty tears of joy. When he pulled away from her, she reached out, grasping at air. He stood, then picked up his jeans and cane.

"Nick? What are you doing?"

"I'm going to take a shower, Red. I can't stay. If I do, I'm going to ram myself into you so hard, I'll rip you apart."

"Don't leave me. Stay. I want—I want us to really make love. I want you to—"

Nick turned and left the room. Addy lay there feeling satisfied and yet unfulfilled. Why had she ever told Nick that he'd have to prove himself to her? And why was he being so stubborn? The only thing she could figure out was that her father had been right. Nick Romero was falling in love with her and he didn't even know it. No man would put himself through such torment to prove himself worthy of a woman he didn't love.

Addy heard the shower running. She smiled. With a confidence born of her newly awakened feminine powers, she slipped out of bed and made her way down the hall to the bathroom. The door wasn't locked. Obviously, Nick didn't think she'd follow him. But he was wrong.

Moving as quietly as she possibly could, Addy crept toward the shower, eased open the glass door and stepped inside.

"What the hell? Addy?"

Without saying a word, she bent to her knees in front of him. The tepid water poured down over them. Nick reached out, taking her by her shoulders. "Get up, Red. You don't have to do this."

"I want to do this," she assured him, and proceeded to prove to him just how much.

Chapter 9

The hazy, muted light of dawn spread across the eastern horizon like distant candlelight seen through gauze curtains. The hum of the Bronco's motor kept time to the dull drone of the four-wheel drive's big tires as they moved over the asphalt roadway. Nick glanced in his rearview mirror. The nondescript brown sedan was still there. He had first noticed the car when they drove through Paint Rock, a wide-place-in-the-road town not too far outside of Huntsville. It was possible that the driver was simply headed in the same direction they were; it was also possible that he was following them.

Nick heard Addy sigh. Looking down at her head resting against his shoulder, he readjusted his arm that was draped around her. She'd been asleep for the past half hour. She needed rest. Neither of them had slept much last night.

When he thought about what had happened—and he hadn't been able to think of much else—he could hardly believe it. Not only had he made love to Addy more unselfishly than he'd ever made love to any other woman, but he experienced a kind of satisfaction he'd never known. He'd never felt so much like a man, never felt so strong as when he'd brought Addy to completion. Not once, but twice. Her cries of fulfillment had given him a precious pleasure. But when she had come to him in the shower, showing him how much she trusted him, how much she cared for him, he had been humbled and weakened by her generosity and love.

The very thought of her hands circling, her tongue tasting, her lips caressing, her mouth taking, hardened his manhood to an uncomfortable rigidity. Tonight... Tonight they would make love completely. He'd bury himself so deep inside her that he'd become a part of her, and then she would truly be his—his woman, in a way no other woman had ever been.

Just past the outskirts of South Pittsburg, Tennessee, Nick turned the Bronco onto the on-ramp of Interstate 24 and headed straight into the morning sun, which had just appeared, flashing its dazzling golden light like a wealthy woman displaying her array of diamond jewelry. Addy snuggled closer to his side; Nick ran his hand up and down her arm. God, he loved the feel of her. Lean and sleek, yet utterly soft and feminine.

He glanced in the rearview mirror. The brown sedan exited the on-ramp. Only a cherry-red Pinto separated the other car from the Bronco. Still a coincidence? Nick wondered. Maybe, maybe not. He'd wait and see. Before they went through Chattanooga, he'd have to find out one way or the other.

He didn't want to bother Addy with any undue worry, but if he had to make a hasty detour to discern the motive of the sedan driver, then he'd have to forewarn her. Although he'd found out just how strong and resilient Addy McConnell was, he knew that she had a breaking point. Everyone did. He wanted to get her to Georgia, to their private sanctuary deep in the mountains, where she would feel safe and secure... where they would have two weeks of undisturbed lovemaking.

Addy opened her eyes. Sunshine streamed through the Bronco's windows. She shut her eyes tightly, blocking out the blinding light. When she squirmed against Nick, he petted her, his big hand moving up and down her arm. She sighed, breathing in the clean, masculine scent that was Nick Romero—the man she loved.

Prizing her eyes open a second time, she squinted, then lowered her lids half closed and looked up at Nick, who was totally absorbed in driving. He was a man who concentrated on the task at hand, giving it his complete attention. Last night he had given her his thorough devotion, proving beyond a shadow of a doubt how much she meant to him. Recalling what he'd done to her—for her—sent tingling, reminiscent sensations spiraling through her body. He had made her feel everything, teaching her what a sensuous woman she was, proving to her how wrong Gerald had been about her. Nick made her feel needed...desired...beautiful.

If she lived to be two hundred, she would never forget going to him, slipping into the shower beside him and loving him as erotically as he had loved her. She had acted purely on instinct, driven by desire, prompted by love.

When Nick had reached fulfillment, his body had trembled with the force of his satisfaction. And she had gloried in the knowledge that she had given him pleasure. The experience had been raw, primitive, totally physical. The aftermath had been warm and tender and loving. Nick had dried them both, then walked her back to her bedroom and tucked her in, refusing to stay the few remaining hours of the night in her bed. She'd known he didn't trust himself not to make love to her again and again. It was what she'd wanted, but Nick wanted to wait. Tonight...ah, yes... tonight.

Closing her eyes, Addy slipped her arm around Nick's waist, giving him a gentle hug. "Where are we?"

Squeezing her arm, he glanced down at her, then returned his concentration to the interstate. "Crossing through the tip of Georgia. We aren't far from Chattanooga."

She raised up, moving slightly away from him. He removed his arm from around her and placed his hand on the steering wheel. Stretching, Addy yawned. "I didn't sleep very long then?"

"Less than an hour. You need more rest. You had a busy night last night." His lips curved into a smile as he remembered just what had kept them both so busy. Damn, how he would have liked to pull off the interstate, find a secluded stretch of road and take her hard and fast right there in the Bronco.

Addy saw him smile and felt a staining warmth in her cheeks. She punched him playfully on the arm. "Not as busy as it should have been." She couldn't believe she'd actually said that. What was happening to her? Loving Nick Romero, that was what was happening to her.

"Since we got some preliminaries out of the way last night, I'd say we were both ready to get down to some serious lovemaking tonight."

Addy laughed, the sound light, almost carefree. He'd done that for her, she thought. He was teaching her to enjoy herself, to trust her own instincts and give herself permission to play and have fun.

He hated the thought of having to tell her about the brown sedan, but he had no choice. They'd be in Chattanooga soon, and he couldn't allow the car to continue following them.

Noticing the pensive look on his face, Addy wondered what had caused it. "Are you worrying about your Jag? If you are, let me set your mind at rest. It's as safe as in Fort Knox in Daddy's garages along with his collection."

"Yeah, I'm sure it is."

"Daddy's still bothered by the fact that he doesn't know where we'll be," she said. "I could tell by the sound of his voice when we talked to him before we left."

"I'll call Sam every day, and he'll give your father a report."

"Daddy didn't like it when you suggested that it was best he didn't know too much, that way he couldn't accidentally slip up and tell Dina anything."

"I explained to Rusty why I felt that way." Nick glanced in the rearview mirror. Damn! He would have to make his move soon. "Dina might tell Brett Windsor, and I don't trust the guy. He might not be top on my list of suspects, but he's definitely still on the list."

"I think Brett is sweet—in a little-boy sort of way."

"Red, you don't need a sweet little boy, you need a hot-blooded man."

She ran the tips of her short, neatly manicured fingernails up the side of his neck, stopping to tease his earlobe. "And that's exactly what I have, isn't it, Mr. Romero?"

"Damn right." He clutched her knee, squeezing possessively, then slid his hand between her thighs. He wanted to find a way inside her tan slacks, inside her silk panties, to delve into the hot, moist depths of her body. But now wasn't the time or the place. Reluctantly, he returned his hand to the steering wheel.

"Look, Red, we're going to have to make a slight detour."

"Why?"

"A brown sedan has been following us ever since we went through Paint Rock. I've got to check him out. Understand?" He sneaked a quick glance in her direction. Her smile disappeared.

"Do you think...I mean, could it be...*him?*" Cold, numbing fear clutched her pounding heart and spread icy tendrils through her stomach.

"I don't know." Nick saw the sign that read Tiftonia exit. It would be one of the last exits before reaching downtown. Easing into the turning lane, he slowed the Bronco.

"What are you going to do?"

"See if he follows us."

"And if he does?"

"Confront him."

She sucked in a deep breath, then let out a long, slow sigh. "That could be dangerous."

"It would be even more dangerous to let this guy find out where we're going." Nick exited the interstate. The brown sedan did the same. Damnation!

"Did he follow us?" Addy started to turn her head.

"Don't look back. I can see him in the mirror. He's right behind us."

Nick saw a service station a few yards away. There were no cars around. The place looked deserted. He couldn't tell whether it hadn't opened for the day or if it had recently gone out of business.

Nick whipped the Bronco into the service station, then cut the motor. Opening the glove compartment, he reached inside and pulled out a .38 revolver. He saw the startled look in Addy's green eyes and wished to high heaven he didn't have to put the gun in her hands.

The brown sedan pulled in, parking on the other side of the station.

"Take this," he said, handing it to her.

Addy glared at the gun as if it were a live snake. With trembling hands she reached out, accepting the deadly weapon. "I don't know how to use this thing."

"Don't aim it unless you intend to use it. If your target is at close range, all you have to do is pull the trigger and you'll hit him somewhere. Just keep shooting until you empty the gun."

"Nick, you're frightening me. You're talking like you won't be coming back."

Leaning over, he kissed her forehead, then gave her shoulders a sound squeeze. "This is just a precautionary measure, Red. I'm coming back just as soon as I find out who this guy is and what he wants."

Turning, Nick opened the door. Addy grabbed the back of his shirt. He glanced over his shoulder. "Please be careful," she said.

"Stay in the Bronco and keep the doors locked."

Addy watched while Nick opened the back of the Bronco, pulled his battered suitcase toward him, unsnapped it and reached inside. He pulled out an automatic, and holding the gun in one hand and his cane in the other he approached the parked car. Addy held her breath. Seconds turned into minutes, minutes that seemed hours long.

She saw the car door open and a man emerge. From thirty yards away, Addy couldn't make out his features, but she could tell that he was shorter than Nick, with a stocky build. He hadn't pulled a weapon on Nick. That was a good sign. Then suddenly Nick punched the man in the chest with his cane. Addy's heart stopped. She gripped the heavy gun in her hands, her palms slippery with moisture.

"Dammit, man, I could have killed you!" Nick removed his cane from the man's chest. "Of all the stupid things for Rusty McConnell to do! I told him I didn't want any of Dundee's men following us."

"Mr. McConnell insisted. Hell, Nick, what was I supposed to do? The man is paying the bills, you know. Sam is working for McConnell, so that means I'm working for McConnell."

"Hugh, you should have checked in with Sam before you left. He would have counteracted Rusty's order."

"I'm sorry, Nick. I should have known you'd spot me." Hugh grinned, but Nick didn't. "As a matter of fact, I knew that you were on to me the minute you exited the interstate. That's why I pulled in here."

"There's a lady over there in that Bronco who's scared half out of her mind." Nick slipped the automatic into the back of his pants, anchoring it beneath his belt. "You get on your phone and call her daddy and tell him that his overprotective tactics didn't work, that all he accomplished was to frighten Addy. Then tuck tail and run back to Huntsville as fast as you can."

"Mr. McConnell is going to be madder than hell."

"I'm already madder than hell, Hugh. Who would you rather deal with, Rusty McConnell or me?" Nick spoke the words in a deep, even tone, yet each syllable dripped with menace.

"I get your point, Nick," Hugh said. "I'll call Mr. McConnell and tell him what happened. If he has any problems with my returning to Huntsville, he can call Sam."

"Good idea." Nick turned and walked away, leaving Hugh to jump back inside his brown sedan.

The moment she saw Nick walking toward the Bronco, Addy slid across the bench seat and unlocked the door. Nick bent down and got inside. Addy had a death grip on the revolver. Prying her hands loose from the .38, he placed it back inside the glove compartment, then pulled her into his arms.

"Oh, Nick—Nick—"

"Shh—shh— It's all right, Addy. Everything's fine."

"Who—who was he?"

"Hugh Talbot, one of Sam Dundee's men. Your father sent him to follow us."

She raised her head, her tear-filled eyes widening in surprise. "But you told Daddy that you didn't want anyone riding shotgun. Isn't that what you said?"

"Yeah, that's exactly what I said, but your old man had other ideas." Damn, he hated the way she was trembling, the way her voice quivered.

She clung to him, seeking comfort and reassurance. "I was so afraid something would happen to you, Nick. I—I couldn't bear it if anything happened to you."

"Nothing's going to happen to me, Red. And nothing is going to happen to you. We're going to the mountains for two weeks of seclusion." He tilted her chin, then gave her a quick, hard kiss. "And during those two weeks, we'll belong to each other, body and soul. I'm going to teach you to laugh and love and enjoy yourself."

"And what am I going to teach you?" Addy stared at him, her face filled with innocence, her eyes as starry bright as an adolescent girl's who'd fallen in love for the first time.

Nick pondered her question. A sharp, foreboding chill raced up his spine. What was Addy McConnell going to teach him? That all women weren't mercenary whores or party-girl blondes who'd slept with more men than they could count? That there were women in this world a man could trust with his heart and count on when the chips were down?

"You're going to teach me how to make you happy, Red, because that's what I want more than anything."

The late-afternoon sun blazed hot and bright, dancing off the hood of the navy blue Bronco. Inside, Nick and Addy remained cool. He watched the road signs while she dozed on and off, fitful in her uneasy sleep. He hadn't been to Sequana Falls in years, not since the summer Elizabeth Mallory had been eighteen, shortly after she'd graduated from college. Sam's young ward was brilliant. Her genius had become apparent at an early age, even before Sam's older brother had married Elizabeth's widowed mother. How old was Elizabeth now? Nick wondered. Twenty-two? Twenty-three? And did she still possess the clairvoyant powers that had driven Sam Dundee to the edge of madness?

Addy had fallen asleep again shortly after they'd exited the interstate and started making their way along the Georgia back roads leading to the mountains. The closer they came to their destination, the cooler the climate. But even at the higher altitude, the July sun proved a relentless adversary. Thank God for air-conditioning. But if he remembered correctly, Elizabeth's great-grandmother's cottage didn't have air-conditioning. Hell!

He saw the sign. Dover's Mill. It wouldn't be long now. Dover's Mill was the last incorporated town before reaching Sequana Falls, which wasn't located on any map. It had been a small settlement deep in the mountains, where a family of Scotch-Irish settlers named Ogilvie had put down roots. Their youngest daughter, Sequana, had married a half-breed Indian. Elizabeth Mallory was their descendant.

So in her veins flowed the blood of two ancient peoples—the Cherokees and the Celts.

Addy roused from her brief nap. Rubbing her eyes, she looked like a sleepy little girl. "I can't seem to stay awake."

"Traveling does that to some people," Nick said.

"How close are we to Sequana Falls?"

"Just a few miles."

"Sam must know this Elizabeth Mallory well to ask such a favor of her and to trust her implicitly." Addy rubbed the back of her neck and stretched her long legs out as far as she could in the confinement of the Bronco.

"She was his ward."

"From what I know about Sam Dundee, he doesn't seem the type to take on such a personal kind of responsibility."

"You're right about that." Nick grinned, thinking about his old DEA buddy. Sam Dundee didn't make friends easily. He was a brooding, cynical sonofabitch whose keen mind and sharp instincts had won him the respect of every man who knew him. Few liked Dundee; all feared him. Nick would match his own warrior's skills against anyone's, but in a fight he'd sure as hell want Sam Dundee and Nate Hodges on his side. Luckily for him, the two men were his best friends.

"Why did he?" Addy asked.

"Why did he what?"

"Why did Sam Dundee accept the responsibility of a ward?"

"His older brother, James, married Elizabeth's mother when Elizabeth was just a kid. James and Sandra died when Elizabeth was around twelve or thirteen." Up until his brother's death, Nick had seldom heard Sam talk about his family. But on occasion, usually after several drinks, Sam would mention Elizabeth. Nick wondered if Dundee had ever sorted out his feelings for the girl.

"How tragic, for all of them."

"Yeah." Nick maneuvered the four-wheel drive off the main highway and onto a stretch of gravel road. "Here's the turn-off to Sequana Falls."

"The road isn't even paved," Addy said, as she felt the jostling movements of the Bronco as it traveled over an uneven assortment of pebbles and rocks.

"This place is totally isolated. That's why it's perfect for our needs."

Addy stared at the towering trees, tall, majestic and ancient, that lined their pathway to Sequana Falls. Sunlight dappled down through the thick foliage, spattering shadows and shimmers across the road. The silence was eerie. After more than five miles, a clearing appeared. A cluster of small cabins lay on either side of them. They passed by, leaving the cabins behind. Another mile into the deep woods, a smaller clearing appeared. Set dead center was a circular driveway in front of an enormous, sprawling, two-story log cabin. A gigantic porch circled the house.

"This is Elizabeth's home." Nick pulled the Bronco up in front, directly behind an old, mud-splattered jeep.

"Where's our cabin?"

"Deeper in the woods, if you can believe it. And Elizabeth refers to her great-grandmother's house as a cottage, not a cabin."

"It's not a cabin?"

"The last time I saw the place it was painted white. It looked as out of place in these woods as we do."

Nick climbed down out of the Bronco. Addy didn't wait for him to make his way around to her side. Opening the door, she jumped down.

"Y'all made good time," a young woman standing on the front porch called out to them. "Welcome to Sequana Falls."

Addy shaded her eyes from the hazy afternoon sun. Looking toward the sound of the rich, melodious voice, she saw one of the most stunning women she'd ever seen in her life. Elizabeth Mallory's hourglass figure could not be disguised in the faded denim shorts and pale apricot cotton blouse. She was barefoot and braless. Her breasts swelled together like round, ripe melons.

Addy moved closer. Elizabeth descended the wooden stairs leading down from the wraparound porch.

"Elizabeth, let me introduce you to—" Nick said.

"Adeline McConnell," Elizabeth finished his sentence. "I'm so glad you're here, Addy. I hope Sequana Falls gives you the respite from worry and sorrow that you're seeking."

"Thank you." Addy couldn't stop staring at the other woman, whose beauty was almost ethereal. Her light, golden complexion was flawless, her eyes a deep, pure blue and her rich, coffee-brown hair had been French-braided and hung in one long plait to her waist.

"I know you'll want to go straight to the cottage so you can settle in and freshen up." Elizabeth approached Addy, a warm smile of greeting on her lovely face. "But I'm expecting you to share supper with me tonight."

"That's not necessary," Nick said. "We don't want to impose."

"It isn't an imposition." Elizabeth extended her hand to Addy. "It's so seldom we have visitors."

Addy felt the strength in the other woman's grasp as they exchanged a handshake. Elizabeth gazed into Addy's eyes, showing a depth of compassion and understanding that puzzled Addy. "We'd be honored to join you."

Elizabeth released her hand. "That's settled then." Reaching into her shorts pocket, she handed Nick an elaborately carved antique key. "There's only one path in and out to Granny's cottage. The only way you can reach it is on foot."

"No problem." Nick nodded toward the Bronco. "We packed light. One suitcase each."

"You won't need many clothes while you're here," Elizabeth said, a twinkle of mischief in her big blue eyes.

"I'll have to come down to your cabin once a day to phone Sam," Nick said. "I hope that won't pose a problem for you."

"I look forward to hearing from Sam on a daily basis. He seldom phones and hasn't been here since last Christmas." Elizabeth turned back toward her cabin. "If you'd like, I can have O'Grady bring your bags later."

"Is that old rascal still alive?" Nick asked, remembering the withered old man who must have been at least seventy the last time he'd seen him.

"Not only still alive, but still strong as an ox and stubborn as a mule." Elizabeth's smile created a radiance about her, an invisible but highly sensory light. "He and Mac-Datho have gone fishing this afternoon."

"Who the devil is MacDatho?" Nick opened the back of the Bronco, pulling forward his tattered leather suitcase and then Addy's expensive paisley-print bag.

"Oh, that's right, MacDatho wasn't born the last time you visited here." Elizabeth paused on the top step, just before reaching the porch. "You remember my German shepherd, Elspeth, don't you? Well, MacDatho is her son, born only a year before Elspeth died."

Nick handed Addy her suitcase, then returned to the Bronco for his own. "We'll head on over to the cottage. I think we can manage these two pieces of luggage. No need to bother O'Grady."

Elizabeth stood on the porch, backing slowly into the cool shadows. "Follow the path behind the cabin. It will lead you straight to the cottage." Opening the front door, she paused briefly. "I'll see you both tonight."

During the ten-minute trek through the woods, Addy and Nick spoke very little. Nick was busy surveying the area, apparently sizing up how inaccessible the cottage would be to any unwanted visitors. Addy spent the time absorbing the beauty surrounding her. She'd enjoyed so many happy hours of her childhood playing on the vast lawns of Elm

Hill, but she'd never been in the mountains before, in the middle of the woods.

Addy stopped in her tracks. Nick almost collided with her back. Wobbling slightly, he steadied himself with his cane.

"What's wrong?" he asked.

"Oh, Nick, look!"

He gazed off into the distance, at the small house that looked as if someone had dropped an A-frame Victorian dollhouse in the tiny clearing. The white paint was peeling slightly in spots, giving the structure an antique, weathered appearance. A rickety picket fence enclosed a neat little front yard.

"It's unbelievable," Addy said. "It's like something out of a fairy tale."

"Elizabeth calls it the honeymoon cottage because her great-grandfather had it built for her great-grandmother as a wedding gift, and they spent their honeymoon there and each anniversary for the next forty-some odd years of their lives."

Thoroughly enchanted, Addy walked toward the gate that hung open as if issuing an invitation. "There's something different about Elizabeth. I can't quite put my finger on it, but there's something—she's so serene . . . so . . ."

"Mystical?"

"Yes, mystical. You felt it, too, didn't you? What is it about her, do you suppose?"

"You mean you haven't guessed?" Nick followed Addy up the rock walk and onto the porch.

"Guessed what?" Addy paused, setting her suitcase down while she reached out for the key Nick held in his hand.

He gave her the key. "Elizabeth is a clairvoyant."

"You mean she can predict the future?" Addy grasped the key, half doubting, half believing Nick's assessment of Elizabeth Mallory.

"That's only one of her special powers," Nick said. "Just wait until tonight when you get the chance to know her better."

Addy inserted the key in the lock and turned the doorknob. She'd never known a clairvoyant and wasn't quite sure she believed in such a thing, but she knew one thing for certain. She definitely was looking forward to asking Elizabeth a few pertinent questions about the future.

Chapter 10

Cozy and old-fashioned, exuding homey warmth and
tranquillity, Elizabeth Mallory's kitchen smelled of cinna-
mon. Rustic wood blended with creamy beige paint on all
the walls, and worn, faded red bricks covered the floor. A
humid night breeze fluttered the aged lace curtains at the
open windows.

Addy spooned the last bite of apple cobbler into her
mouth, the melted vanilla ice cream coating the crust with
a milky sauce. "You really shouldn't have gone to so much
trouble for us."

"It wasn't any trouble," Elizabeth said, rising from the
round oak table, her ankle-length blue skirt swirling around
her legs. "Aunt Margaret made the cobbler this morning
before she left for Dover's Mill, and O'Grady caught and
cleaned the fish."

"I noticed that you still don't have any air-conditioning
at the cottage," Nick said, glancing out the window facing
the back porch. "You haven't put in any here at your house,
either, have you?"

"The cottage is seldom used." Elizabeth sighed, the sound barely discernible, but the dreamy, faraway look in her eyes was quite visible. "It's really a honeymoon cottage, you know. The last honeymooners who used it were my mother and James Dundee."

"I know it's a lot cooler up here in the mountains, but July is hot, even here." Nick wiped a fine sheen of perspiration from his forehead.

"Things will cool off later." Elizabeth began stacking their dinner plates. "It's going to rain sometime after midnight." Placing the dirty dishes by the sink, she turned on the faucet.

Addy stood, removing the used silverware from the dark-blue place mats. "Let me help you clean up. It's the least I can do after you served us such a feast."

Pushing back his chair, Nick stood and grasped his cane from where he'd propped it against the side of the table. "I think now would be the ideal time for me to call Sam and check in."

"Trying to get out of helping with the dishes?" Addy asked, smiling.

"The call should take a while." Nick grinned at both women, who were giving him pleasant but condemning looks. "I'll probably finish up just in time for another glass of iced tea." Not waiting for a response, he left the kitchen, the tapping of his cane as it hit the wooden floor reverberating in the silent hallway.

Addy pulled her cotton blouse away from her damp body, fanning the material against her chest. "I hope you're right about the rain cooling things off."

Elizabeth slipped the glasses and silver into the sudsy dish water. "Here in the mountains rain always brings relief from the heat. It's seldom this humid—only just before a storm."

"You're sure about the rain, aren't you?"

"I'm sure."

Addy pulled a glass from its watery bed, enclosing it in a soft, well-worn dish towel. "Nick said that you were... clairvoyant."

Elizabeth's laughter was warm and throaty, the utterly feminine sound mesmerizing. Addy stared at the beautiful woman standing beside her and saw the knowledge that lay in the depths of her pure blue eyes.

"Are you curious, Addy? Wondering what I know about you?"

"I'm being rude. Please, forgive me." A dim flush of embarrassment colored Addy's cheeks.

"You weren't being rude, just curious. And there's nothing to forgive." Elizabeth laid the clean cobbler dish on the drainboard. "We'll let the rest soak. Why don't we go sit on the back porch for a spell?"

Addy dried her hands and followed Elizabeth out onto the wide wooden back porch, which was simply an extension of the front and side porches. Several sturdy wooden rocking chairs were lined up against the south wall. Each woman sat, rocking her chair toward the center until they faced each other. Elizabeth reached out, taking both of Addy's hands into her own.

"You've come to Sequana Falls for two weeks, to wait out a danger that exists for you in Huntsville." Elizabeth smiled when Addy gasped. "I didn't gain this knowledge from second sight, my friend. Sam filled me in on the pertinent details."

"Oh."

"You'll leave here before two weeks," Elizabeth said, running the pad of her thumb over Addy's knuckles. "The reason is unclear...but...your father—your father will need you."

Addy felt her heartbeat accelerate, wondering if she dare believe this winsome young woman's prediction. "There's no way you could know who—I mean someone is plotting against us... my father and his company."

"I do not know the identity behind the threats." Elizabeth patted Addy's hand, then gave it a tight squeeze. "I have no control over the knowledge that comes to me and don't understand why some things are so clear in my mind and other things are obscured."

Addy pulled away, Elizabeth relinquished her hold. "It's a little cooler out here. If only the breeze wasn't so warm and humid."

"Do you like flowers, Addy? If you do, I'll show you my greenhouse one day while you're here. I grow my own herbs and spices, too, but my prize possessions are my roses."

"I love flowers, and I'd like very much to see your greenhouse. I'm sure Nick and I will get bored with all this peace and quiet after a few days."

A shuddering boom of distant thunder echoed in the moonlit stillness, followed by a sharp zigzag of lightning that dimmed the moon's pale glow. Addy looked up. Dark clouds ambled slowly across the sky.

Neither woman spoke. Only the vibrating resonance of the wooden rocker rounds mating with the wooden porch floor broke the hushed silence. Seconds became minutes and the moments floated away like dandelion fluff on a windy day.

Addy's mind drifted, absorbed with thoughts of the hours to come. Tonight she would be alone with Nick. She already knew that she would give herself to him, but what she didn't know was if they had a future together. She wondered if Elizabeth really could predict. Not moving a muscle in her face or neck, she glanced at the other woman.

"You don't have to be afraid of him." Elizabeth's soft voice carried on the nighttime air, like a soothing whippoorwill's song. "You're right about him, Addy. Nick Romero is your paladin—and you are and always will be his woman."

Addy felt the words surround her heart, freeing her doubts, but before she could reply, asking the questions that filled her mind, an enormous animal came bounding out of the darkness, leapt up the porch steps and made his way to Elizabeth's side. Addy cringed at the sight of the hairy creature, his keen amber eyes glowing, his sharp teeth visible as he panted heavily.

Elizabeth ran her fingers through the thick pelt of black fur, and the huge animal dropped to his haunches, apparently savoring her affectionate touch. "This is MacDatho. He won't hurt you. He knows you're my friend."

"What—what is he? I thought you said he was a dog."

"He's half German shepherd and half wolf." Elizabeth continued stroking her pet, speaking to him in a low, whispered voice. When MacDatho lowered his head to the floor and closed his eyes, Elizabeth turned to Addy. "You love Nick, but he has not yet put the proper name to his feelings for you. He will."

"Are you saying that Nick loves me?" Addy wished she could believe wholeheartedly in Elizabeth Mallory's power to foretell the future. But would she be a gullible fool if she did?

"It is destined." Closing her eyes, Elizabeth began rocking again. "You and Nick will share a life of deep love and commitment. I see—I see little girls."

"Little girls?" Addy scooted to the edge of her seat, completely ignoring MacDatho when he raised his head, his topaz gaze riveted to her face.

"Yes. Two little girls. Not twins, but very much alike . . . except— One has fiery hair and black eyes. The other has black hair and green eyes."

"Our children? Mine and Nick's?" Did she dare believe in this voodoo, this witchcraft? With all her heart and soul she longed to believe.

The back screen door opened. Loud, earsplitting thunder rumbled. Sitting up, MacDatho howled at the cloud-obscured moon.

"We'd better head back to the cottage, Red." Nick stepped outside. "I wouldn't want us to get caught in a downpour."

"It won't rain for hours," Elizabeth said. "How was Sam?"

"He's fine. You know Sam, a man of few words." Nick placed one hand on the back of Addy's chair. "He asked about you, Elizabeth."

Addy could actually feel the pleasure radiating from Elizabeth, like heat from a smoldering blaze. She could tell that Elizabeth cared deeply for Sam Dundee. Her certain knowledge of the other woman's feelings made her wonder how much Elizabeth's earlier comments had been based on natural instincts and how much on clairvoyance.

She saw my children, Addy reminded herself. Nick's children. Nick's little girls.

"Sam will call Rusty tonight and give him a report," Nick told Addy. "Daily reports should keep your father content."

Remembering Elizabeth's warning that they would return to Huntsville before the NASP contract was awarded because her father would need them, Addy said, "When you talk to Sam tomorrow, please find out if Daddy's all right. Ask him to tell Daddy to go for a checkup. I'm worried about his heart and his blood pressure."

"I'll relay your message." Nick circled her arm, urging her to stand. Addy looked up at him. Dark, hot passion blazed in the depths of his black eyes. Rising from the rocking chair, Addy accepted his extended arm, walking with him down the steps and out onto the pathway. Nick hesitated briefly, turning to say good-night to Elizabeth.

MacDatho howled again, his animal moan blending with the symphony of woodland night creatures. Thunder roared; lightning flashed. High atop the southern edge of the great Appalachian Mountains, Addy McConnell and Nick Romero moved toward their destiny. Tonight, the paladin would claim his woman.

The four-room cottage reeked with steamy heat, the humidity so high that Nick and Addy breathed in the heavy

moisture. When they stepped inside, a splintering flash of
lightning illuminated the living room. Nick took advantage
of the momentary light to visibly scout out the kerosene
lamp he knew was sitting on a round wicker table. Feeling
his way across to the expanse of windows facing the porch,
he found the book of matches lying atop the crocheted doily.
Removing the globe, he struck a match and lit the wick. A
soft, mellow radiance spread over the room with an ivory
luster, casting dancing shadows on the earthy-green, antique wicker furniture, the pale creamy walls and the flowered cushions.

Nick looked at Addy standing just inside the doorway.
Her topknot of thick red hair had begun to droop, fiery
tendrils curling about her face and neck. Dewdrops of perspiration dotted her face, more abundant than the smattering of freckles that covered her nose. Her cotton blouse
clung to her, outlining her tiny waist and high, firm breasts.
Her billowy tan slacks hung loosely about her hips.

Tall and slender as a reed, Addy moved gracefully across
the room. She possessed the very essence of nature—a fiery
warmth, an earthy allure. The amazing thing, Nick realized, was that she had no idea how unbearably beautiful she
was to him.

Tonight he would show her.

The wind picked up, swaying the treetops, pushing nearby
limbs against the windowpanes. Addy and Nick watched
each other, like two hungry animals preparing to attack.
Sweat trickled down the curve of Nick's spine, his shirt and
jeans absorbing part of the moisture.

Just thinking about Addy, just looking at her made him
hard. He'd become aroused on the walk from Elizabeth's
cabin. It would be so easy to take Addy quickly and ease his
throbbing ache. But he wouldn't—he couldn't. Tonight was
going to be a first for her, and he intended to make it a night
she'd never forget.

He could see the desire in her eyes, and the uncertainty.
She wanted him, but lacked the experience to give her

enough confidence to tell him so. Before this night ended, Addy would have confidence. He was going to give her that . . . and a lot more.

Slow and easy. That's how it was going to be—the first time. Addy needed the steady, progressive stimulation to prepare her for the pleasure to come. Even if it half killed him, he was not going to rush this sexual adventure. It meant too much to her, and to him.

Propping his cane against the table, Nick began unbuttoning his shirt. He watched Addy staring at him, her gaze following his fingers as they slipped each button from its hole. "It's so damned hot. This place could use a few fans."

Addy couldn't take her eyes off Nick, off the bare expanse of chest that lay between the two sides of his open shirt. She wanted to touch him. But he was all the way on the other side of the room, and her feet refused to move. "A fan in the bedroom would be good on a night like this."

"All we need tonight is that old wrought-iron bed. It looks pretty sturdy, don't you think? Big enough for two." He tugged his damp shirt off his shoulders and flung it on the wicker rocking chair on his left.

Addy's heart hammered in her chest. The thought of sharing that antique bed with Nick sent shivers of longing through her. "I wonder why Elizabeth has never run electricity out here to the cottage? If she did, she could put in air-conditioning."

"This house is meant for lovers. An isolated retreat used by people who neither want nor need lights or telephones or televisions or radios." Nick ran his hand down his throat, wiping away the perspiration.

Retrieving his cane, he took a tentative step toward Addy. Not moving, she watched and waited. When he was within arm's reach, he touched her, his finger pressing against her bottom lip. She opened her mouth on a sigh. He slid his finger over her chin, down her throat and ever so slowly slipped it inside her blouse. "You're hot, Addy. Hot and sweaty."

"Maybe—maybe I should take a bath. That should cool me off." She gasped when his finger slipped up and down between her breasts, popping open the top buttons on her blouse.

"Maybe you have on too many clothes." He undid the remaining three buttons, then tugged her blouse out of her slacks, easing it from her body and tossing it atop his shirt. "Isn't that better? Cooler?" Her sheer yellow lace bra did little to conceal her breasts, the dark areolae visible, the tight nipples straining against the flimsy material.

She wasn't cooler; she was hotter. Nick's smoldering gaze scorched her. Erratic tingling sensations tightened her breasts almost painfully. She wanted Nick to touch her there, to put his mouth on her, to suckle her. Memories of last night reminded her body of what it meant to be pleasured by a man who truly cared, a man whose only purpose was to give his woman pleasure.

Dropping his cane to the floor, Nick ran his hands up and down her naked arms. She trembled. "Do you have any idea how much I want you?"

"Oh, Nick." She swayed toward him, hoping he would kiss her.

Thunder shook the cottage. Nick jerked Addy into his arms, one big hand splayed against her back while the other sought and found her bra's catch. White, jagged lightning lit up the night sky. The wind's velocity increased, wailing and moaning as it ripped through the trees and whistled along the side of the house. Nick pulled her bra down her arms and off her body, then rubbed his hard chest against her thrusting breasts.

She flung her arms around his neck, savoring the feel of their nakedness as her nipples stabbed into his chest hair. "Oh, Nick, how can you make me feel like this?"

"Like what?" He kissed her neck, his tongue snaking out to taste her. Moving his fingers between them, he undid the front closure of her slacks, then slid his hands inside, scooting her zipper downward several inches. He grasped her hips, forcing her soft delta into his arousal.

"Like—like I'm going to... explode."

Cradling her naked buttocks in his palms, he petted her. "We're both going to explode... over and over again tonight."

Mimicking his actions, Addy loosened his jeans and slipped her hand inside, positioning it over his manhood, touching him through the thin barrier of his briefs. He pulsated with life. "I never knew I could feel like this. That I could want someone so desperately."

"Do you want me desperately, Addy?" His deep voice was as dark and mysterious as the man himself.

"You know I do." She closed her fingers around him.

"Then prove it." Issuing the command, he prayed she would have the courage to obey.

"I—" She started to say that she didn't know how. But she did. Releasing him and stepping away, yet still facing him, she moved backward, her feet edging slowly toward the open door of the bedroom. She stopped in the doorway.

Nick watched her intently, the shadowy darkness from behind her occasionally lit by lightning and silhouetting her tall, slender body. Gripping the elastic of her yellow lace bikini panties, she slid them down her legs, then kicked them aside. She stood before him, beautifully, irresistibly naked. Her willowy body called to him, the fiery curls hiding her femininity, tempting his touch. The look in her eyes promised him unbearable pleasure, and he knew that Addy would never lie to him.

Removing his jeans and briefs, Nick followed her, his gait a slow, heavy limp. Addy walked toward the mullioned door that led to the porch, opening it to stare through the screen door out into the raging night sky.

Nick came up behind her, putting his arms around her and pulling her naked back and buttocks up against his chest and manhood. His big hands splayed across her belly, his fingers inching downward, downward, until they discov-

ered the treasure hidden beneath her curls. His fingers petted her sensitive nub; her thighs opened and she moaned.

"You're wet and hot. You must want me. Do you, Addy?
Do you want me?" His fingers played her, strumming her
like an untried instrument on which he could make sweet
music.

"Yes," she groaned. "Yes, yes."

He bit her neck, then soothed her flesh with his tongue.
"Tell me how much you want me." While the fingers of one
hand stayed busy at their task below her waist, he raised his
other hand to cup her breast, his thumb flicking back and
forth over her distended nipple.

Her knees weakened. She leaned back, resting her slowly
dissolving body into his rock-hard frame. He throbbed
against her. With a strength born of her passion, she pulled
out of his embrace, turning slowly to face him. Her hand
hovered over his manhood. She looked up into his desire-hot
black eyes, knowing that he was hers, that she possessed as
much power over him as he did her. The thought exhila-
rated her, filling her with the glory of her womanhood. Pri-
meval, pagan urges flowed through her. She embodied the
strength and power of femininity. Creation and life were
hers.

Slowly, sensuously, Addy eased her hot, sweating body
away from Nick. Opening the screen door, she walked onto
the porch. A fierce, humid wind whipped her hair loose,
flipping it around her naked shoulders like flames from a
flickering torch. Nick stood in the doorway and watched
her, totally mesmerized by her wild abandon.

She beckoned him to come to her. He obeyed. Bright
lightning flashed. Sweat dripped from his big body like
moisture from an icy glass on a hot summer day. His bare,
bronze chest glistened, his small male nipples pebble-hard.
Addy watched a trickle of perspiration clinging to his left
nipple. She longed to put her lips on him, to curl her tongue
around him and lick away that tiny wet droplet.

The moment he was within arm's length, she lowered her head, moving toward his chest. Her tongue flicked out, capturing the drop of sweat from his nipple. Nick moaned, then grabbed her, his mouth covering hers, his tongue thrusting into her in a parody of a more intimate act. She returned the kiss with all the passion, all the untamed longing she felt. Mouths captured, tongues ravaged, teeth titillated.

Nick dropped to his knees, burying his face in the delta between her thighs. He barely felt the warm, hard surface of the wooden porch beneath him. He was surrounded by the smell and taste of his mate—his woman. Running his hands from her hips to her thighs, he spread her legs apart. She swayed. Adjusting his head at an angle, he delved his tongue, seeking out her sweet nectar. He gripped her buttocks to steady her as her legs began to buckle. When she braced herself on his shoulders, he moved his hands around and up to her breasts, taking their soft, smooth weight. The constant pressure on her femininity and her nipples quickly drove Addy over the brink into a shivering, groaning climax. Nick soothed her as he brought her down to her knees in front of him.

She fell into his arms. The hot, damp air did little to cool their heated bodies. Their hands became wet as they touched each other, exploring one another's bodies as if they were new and uncharted territory. Tender kisses turned wild. Lips sought out every inch of slick, fiery flesh.

"I want it all, Nick," she moaned into his mouth. "I need you inside me."

Knowing he could never make it to the bedroom, let alone to the bed, Nick lay back on the porch floor, pulling Addy on top of him. Bracing her hands above his shoulders, she rubbed her body against his. He grabbed her hips, stopping her.

"Open up for me, Addy."

She spread her legs, pressing against his arousal.

"Now take me, Red. Take me!"

She raised her body, positioning herself. Nick grabbed her by the waist, then waited for her agreement.

"Nick?"

"Together, Red. Let's do it together."

And they did. In one swift, synchronized move they became one. Addy flung her head back, her long red hair cascading down her back, feathering across Nick's legs. He thrust up and into her again and again with a savage urgency that almost sent him tumbling over the edge. He slowed the pace, then stopped, allowing her to take over while he reached for her breasts.

The sensations were so intense that Addy couldn't stop herself from increasing the pace, riding him harder and harder until fulfillment burst inside her like a giant balloon of red-hot pleasure. She screamed out, her throaty voice echoing in the darkness, rivaling the resounding booms of thunder. Spasms of ecstasy shook her body; then she collapsed on top of Nick.

He gave her the time she needed to recover from the series of aftershocks that rocked her. She covered his face with kisses. He ached with his need, nearing the breaking point. With three hard, animalistic surges he found his own satisfaction. He spilled his seed into her with powerful, jetting release.

Addy clung to him, crying for joy at the sounds of his loud groans. She was Nick's woman; he was her man. Tonight they had come together, mating like beasts, unable to control their baser instincts. It had been savagely glorious and gloriously spiritual. Despite the very carnality of their lovemaking, their union had created an eternal bond. Addy knew, as surely as she knew her name, that she would never let Nick Romero go.

Easing Addy to his side, Nick raised up, gazing into the black sky, listening to the sounds of impending rain. "We'd better get inside, Red, before the bottom falls out."

They helped each other to their feet. Nick regretted that he couldn't carry Addy inside. With his bad leg and in his weakened condition, he might drop her.

Sensing his feelings of regret over not being able to carry her to their bed, Addy dashed toward the door. "Catch me!" she teased.

He laughed, realizing that she'd known how much he wanted to lift her into his arms and carry her. He followed her inside. She was bent over, pulling the quilt and top sheet down the antique iron bed that had been painted a dark moss green. Coming up behind her, he rubbed against her, then gave her a playful shove. She tumbled onto the bed and turned over quickly, spreading open her arms. "How long will it be before we can do it again?"

Lowering one knee on the bed, he leaned over her. She stared into his eyes. "I don't think it'll be too long. You wore me out, Red, but parts of my body are still raring to go."

She glanced down at that part of his body and smiled. "Someone told me that men past forty couldn't do it two times in a row."

He came down on top of her, sliding into her wet, tight sheath. "Someone told you wrong."

Chapter 11

Addy awoke to the sound of drizzling rain. Opening her eyes, she looked across the room to the unclosed door leading to the porch. Pellets of moisture had sprayed through the screen, dotting the wooden floor with raindrops. Reaching out for Nick, she found an empty space on the other side of the bed. She rolled over onto Nick's pillow, burying her face in the softness as she breathed in his unique scent that clung to the hand-embroidered case. She cherished every element that made Nick Romero who and what he was, even the lingering smell of his manliness mixed with her feminine fragrance.

Last night had been—magic! There was no other word to describe what had happened or how it had made her feel. Despite the fact that Nick hadn't proclaimed his love for her, not even in the throes of passion, Addy knew in her heart that he loved her. He might not be able to admit it to himself quite yet, but sooner or later he would face the truth. They were meant for each other, destined to be lovers. He was her champion, her paladin, the man she had waited a lifetime to love. And she was his woman, the *only* woman for him.

Addy wondered where he was. When she got out of bed, she remembered that she was stark naked. Smiling, she thought about her clothes and Nick's strewn about in the living room. Glancing across the bedroom to where Nick had placed her suitcase on the small French sofa, Addy debated whether to wrap herself in the lightweight quilt on the bed or to seek out her satin robe. She decided on the robe, quickly making her way across the room to her suitcase. Slipping into the floor-length, sea-foam green robe, Addy began searching for Nick. After a thorough check of the four rooms and bath, she returned to the bedroom and opened the door to the porch. Stepping outside, she felt the cool, misty spray of summer rain.

Nick stood at the edge of the porch, wearing only his jeans, unbuttoned and riding low on his lean hips. His body was coated with a fine sheen of moisture, his thick black hair curling around his neck and ears. He held a large ceramic mug in his right hand as he leaned against the banister railing with the other. He seemed totally absorbed in watching the rain.

When Addy approached him, he turned. The smile that lit his face quickened Addy's pulse. His eyes glistened with the look of beckoning temptation.

"Good morning, beautiful," he said. "You've slept half the day away."

She stood several feet from him, simply staring at him, thoroughly enjoying the sight of his big, bronze body—remembering every word, every touch, every sensation the two of them had shared. "I feel beautiful. You've made me beautiful."

"You were always beautiful, Addy." He put the mug to his lips, downing a swig of black coffee.

"Have I really slept half the day away? What time is it?"

"Almost eleven." He grinned, then nodded to his cup. "I've made coffee. Want some?"

"How did you make coffee? I didn't see anything in the kitchen except an old wood stove."

"Former SEALS and DEA agents are very capable. We're used to surviving under primitive conditions."

"You built a fire in the stove?"

Setting his mug on top of the banister, Nick walked toward her, limping heavily. Every nerve in her body alerted itself to his approach, sending tingles of excitement racing through her.

"I'm good at building fires." Leaning down, he took her lips in a good-morning kiss as passionately sweet and moist as the rainy Georgia day.

He threaded his fingers through the long, silky mane of her hair, cradling her head in his hand, drawing her closer and closer, deeper into his kiss. She skimmed the side of his face, letting her fingers caress his jaw. Gradually, he slowed the kiss, then rested his forehead against hers.

She traced his ear with her fingertips, circling the diamond stud sparkling in his lobe. "When did you get your ear pierced?"

He bit her playfully on the neck as he wrapped her in his arms. "While I was in the hospital. After I nearly lost my leg."

"What made you want to have your ear pierced?" She tongued his ear, then nuzzled the side of his neck.

"My hair got long and my beard and mustache grew, so I looked pretty scruffy there for a while. One of my nurses said I looked like a pirate, that all I needed was a gold hoop in my ear."

"You're very susceptible to suggestion, aren't you?" She gasped softly when Nick loosened the tie belt on her robe and slipped his hands inside, cupping her behind.

"Very. How about you, Red? Are you open to a suggestion?"

When he pulled her against his arousal, she sighed. "Was she pretty?"

"Was who pretty?"

"The nurse who talked you into having your ear pierced?"

Nick chuckled, sensing Addy's teasing remark displayed a certain amount of jealousy. "She was very pretty. Bosomy and blonde. And she didn't just talk me into having my ear pierced, she actually pierced it herself and supplied the gold hoop." He felt Addy stiffen. She tried to pull back, but he held her tightly. "You asked, Addy, and I told you the truth. I'll never lie to you."

"What—what happened to the gold hoop?" Addy hated the blond nurse and every other blonde who'd ever been a part of Nick's life.

He kissed Addy on the nose. "I gave the hoop back to her when I left the hospital."

"You've known a lot of women, haven't you Nick?" Addy felt a growing sense of uncertainty, wondering if she was a fool to believe that Nick loved her.

"I've never known anyone like you, Adeline McConnell."

"Is that good or bad?"

"Ah, Red, that's good—very, very good." He captured her reply, silencing her as he made love to her mouth with a thoroughness that left her breathless.

Through a hazy fog of passion, Addy realized that Nick was an expert at changing the subject to suit himself. She pulled out of his arms so quickly that his grab for her missed the mark, allowing her to escape into the bedroom.

Nick watched her disappear into the house, knowing that she was feeling a little insecure. She was new to this business of being a man's lover, new to the joys of sexual pleasure. Addy was the type who'd fancy herself in love, and a woman in love could be less than accepting of a man's past relationships.

He'd give her some time alone, but not too much time. If she started thinking too much, she'd start doubting herself again, and she'd doubt him, too. Finding his cane and their hastily shed clothing on the living-room floor, Nick retrieved his cane and gathered the assorted items. His shirt and briefs. Her blouse and slacks, bra and panties.

A few minutes later, he found her seated at the small kitchen table, a mug of steaming black coffee in front of her. When he entered the room, she glanced up at him.

"I suppose we should try to fix some breakfast." She glanced at the wood stove, which had already heated the room to a toasty warmth.

Leaning on his cane, he stood beside her. "How about a bear claw? There's a fresh pack in the cupboard."

"Fine. They'll taste great with coffee."

Nick pulled the package of danishes from the second shelf, ripping open the plastic and pulling out two of the sticky buns ladened with almond slices. They ate and drank in silence, each sneaking glances at the other.

"What would you like to do today?" he asked.

"What is there to do?"

"Oh, I don't know. A swim in the creek. A hike in the woods."

Addy nodded toward the window. "Have you forgotten that it's raining?"

"I guess we'll have to find something to do inside."

"I suppose so."

Nick pointed his cane at Addy. She stared down at the gold-tipped walking stick. He tapped her on the chest, between her breasts. She swallowed, her heartbeat accelerating rapidly. He ran the tip of the cane down her body, sliding it under her belt, loosening it until the front of her satin robe fell open.

Addy sucked in her breath. The gold tip felt damp and cool against her warm body. Moving the shiny lacquer rod slowly downward, across her stomach, hesitating momentarily at her navel, he positioned it between her thighs, rubbing it against her fiery curls.

"Nick..." Her voice vibrated with the urgency of her emotions.

"This cane was a gift from my friend, Nate Hodges."
Nick continued stimulating her with the walking stick. "We
were in the SEALS together for ten years."

Addy squirmed in the wooden chair, wanting to run from
Nick, from the tormenting rod he'd positioned between her
thighs, but she felt trapped by her own sensuality, her own
wild desire. "Nick...please—"

"What is it, Red? What do you want?"

Moaning when he increased the tempo with which he was
rotating the cane, Addy reached out, grabbing the stick,
clutching it in her fist. "I want to take this cane and knock
you senseless! You—you know what you're doing to me.
You're doing it on purpose."

Jerking the cane away and out of her grasp, Nick smiled,
then stood. He held out his hand. "Come on, Red. Let's go
back to bed. You can knock me senseless without ever
touching this walking stick."

"You're so damned sure of yourself, aren't you?" Addy
glared at him, knowing that she wanted a repeat performance of last night as much as he did.

"I'm sure you want exactly what I want." He took her
hand, tugging until she stood.

"And what do you want?" She refused to budge when he
tried to pull her toward him.

"I want to take you back to bed, drag you beneath me
and bury myself deep inside of you. I want to—" With one
powerful jerk, he brought her into his arms and whispered
into her ear, using hot, raw words to describe his needs,
telling her in the most basic words a man can use precisely
what he wanted.

Addy clung to him, her lips accepting his marauding
mouth. Slowly, steadily, they made their way to the bedroom. By the time they reached the bed, both were flaming
fierce and bright, both more than ready to burn themselves
out quickly.

He lowered her to the bed, taking her with a swift, savage lunge that made her cry out from the intensity. Clutch-

ing his buttocks, matching him thrusting move for thrusting move, Addy gave herself to Nick, taking from him every-thing he had to give. The moment ended almost before it began, each hurled into the spiraling whirlwind of fulfill-ment. Breathless, sweaty and totally spent, they lay side by side in each other's arms, uncaring of the time, the weather or their whereabouts.

Days passed in a sensual blur of pleasure and happiness, unlike anything Addy had ever known. She didn't want her private time with Nick to ever end. Daytime melted into nighttime, each twenty-four-hour period losing its distinc-tion as one week ended and another began. Life took on new meaning, each moment a joy to be shared. They learned to use the old wood stove together, preparing basic meals, not once sharing another feast with Elizabeth, although they visited her daily so Nick could check in with Sam Dundee.

They swam in the creek and played under the waterfall. They took long walks in the woods and spent endless hours talking, each totally fascinated by the other, yearning to learn every little detail. At night they sat on the porch, watching the fireflies and listening to the woodland crea-tures' nocturnal songs.

And they made love—morning, noon and night.

The only reminder of the outside world came when they visited with Elizabeth and made their mandatory phone call. All was well in Huntsville. Rusty's doctor had given him a thorough checkup, proclaiming him as fit as he could be for a man of seventy with a bad heart and high blood pressure. In four days the NASP contract would be awarded. Nick and Addy would leave Sequana Falls. And, hopefully, all danger would have passed.

A pleasant evening breeze rustled through the trees. Addy sat in the small porch swing; Nick sat on the floor, bracing his back against the banister. Twilight descended, painting the sky in various shades of purples, pinks and oranges. As far as the eye could see, vast woodland spread across the mountain, the smell of pine heavy in the air.

"Okay, you left the SEALS after ten years and started back to school." Sitting on one leg, Addy used the toe of her other foot to put the swing in motion.

"Yeah, I was a twenty-eight-year-old college kid." Nick propped his hands behind his head. "I'd decided I wanted to be a DEA agent and I needed more education. That's how I met Sam. He'd done a stint in the marines."

"So you and Sam went to school together, became friends and joined the DEA."

"That's about it. We both fit the bill, had most of the qualifications. Except Sam didn't speak a second language, so I taught him Spanish. Knowing a second language, especially Spanish, is a plus. And we'd both been in the service and already had some combat training, some knowledge of weapons. That sort of thing."

"Do you miss being an agent?" Addy wondered if Nick was the kind of man who simply couldn't settle down, who would always need danger and excitement in his life.

"Sometimes. It's a demanding, stressful job." He edged his way closer to the swing, shifting himself slowly across the porch. "They weed out the guys who haven't got what it takes in a fifteen-week training program at Quantico, Virginia."

"You had what it took, didn't you, Nick? You were physically and mentally a tough guy."

Rubbing his bad leg, Nick stared at Addy. "Well, that Uzi proved I wasn't as physically tough as I thought I was."

"Having a crippled leg doesn't make you any less of a man," Addy said, tempted to throw her arms around him and kiss away the pain she saw in his eyes. "I've never known anyone who's more a man than you."

Reaching out, he tickled the bottom of her bare foot. "You're prejudiced, Red. You're only saying that because I'm such a fantastic lover."

She giggled. "You are so conceited."

Holding her heel with one hand, he traced the veins atop her foot with his fingers. "You've made me conceited, panting after me all the time, dragging me off to bed all hours of the day and night, groaning and moaning and crying out when you come. What's a man to think, other than that he's a stud?"

Addy twisted her leg when Nick ran his fingers higher, caressing her calf. "All right, I'll grant that you're a stud—but..."

"But what?" He kissed her ankle, then ran his tongue all the way up her leg to her knee. Brushing aside her billowy cotton skirt, he slid his hand up her inner thigh.

"But you should give me some of the credit. After all, not just any woman could keep a forty-three-year-old man primed and ready all the time."

With both of them laughing, Nick pulled Addy out of the swing and down onto the floor and into his arms. "I think I've created a beautiful, insatiable monster."

"Am I your creation, Nick?" She unbuttoned his shirt and placed her lips on his chest.

Yes, by God, she was his creation. With his patience and tenderness and loving administrations, he'd given Addy the confidence in her own sexuality that she needed to become the woman who'd been buried inside her all her life. With each word of encouragement, with each reassuring, inspiring touch, he'd brought her out of the darkness to which her ex-husband had doomed her. She was his now. His woman...his heart, his soul...his very life.

When the time came, how the hell was he going to be able to take her back to Huntsville and leave her? He'd never been a man for commitments, always moving on when things got too serious. He wasn't the marrying kind, and Addy deserved no less. She'd want marriage and kids, if she could have them, and the kind of love that lasted forever. He didn't know if he was capable of that kind of love, of that kind of lifetime pledge. There was one thing she knew for sure—he hadn't had his fill of Addy, not by a long shot. He was nowhere near ready to give up what they'd found together. Nothing in his life had ever been this good.

"Nick? Nick, what's wrong?" She took his face in her hands, forcing him to look at her.

"Nothing's wrong, Red. Not a damned thing." He buried his face against her breasts, nuzzling her nipples with his nose. "You're my woman, you know that, don't you?"

She sighed, clinging to him, savoring the sheer physical pleasure of being so near the man she loved. "I remember the morning after you rescued me from my kidnapper, you told me that someday I'd become one of your women. Looks like you were right."

"I was wrong," he said, then covered her face with a dozen tiny kisses. "There's never been another woman like you, and there never will be again. You're unique. What I feel for you is different. You're mine—my woman—and I never want you to belong to anyone else."

"Oh, Nick—I love you so much. You must know that. Surely you've guessed." She could feel the rat-a-tat-tat of her heart drumming within her chest. She longed to hear him repeat the words, to vow his undying love for her, but she knew he wasn't ready, that she'd confessed her love too soon.

"Ah, Red. You mean the world to me. I—"

She covered his lips with her index finger, silencing him. "I'm not asking for anything you can't give. You've been honest with me. That's all I ask now and in the future. Don't ever lie to me, don't ever pretend something you don't feel."

"When I'm with you, I don't have to pretend anything. What I feel for you is real. I just don't know if it's love or not because I've never been in love." He kissed the tip of her finger, then drew it into his mouth.

"What about Dina?" Addy hadn't given Dina a thought in days, but she couldn't forget what the woman had once meant to Nick.

"I didn't love Dina, not the way you mean. My teenage male hormones loved her lush, little body."

"I've learned just how powerful sexual attraction can be. Do you think— I mean, is that what you feel for me?"

He pulled her close, pressing her head to his chest. "I've never felt such a strong physical attraction to a woman, but—there's more. A lot more. I enjoy being with you, Red. In and out of bed. I like you. I admire you. And I trust you more than I've ever trusted a woman."

Lying in his arms, Addy smiled. Even if he didn't know it, even if he couldn't bring himself to consider the possibility, Nick Romero *was* falling in love with her. "I trust you, too. Not only with my life, but with my heart."

"If I could ever love a woman, it would be you."

"Is that a promise?"

"That's a fact, Red."

Tender touches and sweet kisses gradually turned to frantic groping and wild, tongue-thrusting lunges. Clothes disappeared and naked bodies appeared. Entangled limbs and damp, moist flesh mated in a savage, mindless dance of pleasure. Man and woman joined. Giving and taking. Finding release. Claiming ownership. Silently professing love in its most elemental form.

Nick heard the loud rapping on the door. Before Addy became fully awake, he'd already leapt out of bed and was feeling around on the floor for his jeans.

"What is it?" Addy asked.

"Somebody's at the front door."

They both heard the voice. "Nick? Addy? It's Elizabeth." Then a mournful wolf howl erupted from Mac-Datho.

"Oh, Nick, something's wrong!" Addy slid out of bed and pulled on her satin robe.

He wrangled with his rumpled jeans, finally getting them zipped. Picking up his cane, he walked over to the door, Addy right behind him. When he opened the door, Elizabeth ordered MacDatho to *stay,* then stepped inside, her flashlight casting a steady stream of light into the bedroom.

"I'm sorry to disturb you so late, but Sam called. He said to call him back immediately. It's urgent."

"Did he say what's wrong?" Addy asked.

"No, he didn't say." Elizabeth reached out, touching Addy's arm, giving her a reassuring squeeze.

"We'll get dressed and come on up to the cabin." Nick held the door for Elizabeth, who stepped back out onto the porch.

"Wait!" Addy cried. Elizabeth stopped. "Do you know what's wrong? Have you felt anything?"

"Your father needs you. That's all I know." Elizabeth turned and left, disappearing back into the woods, the everfaithful MacDatho at her side.

In frenzied haste, Addy dressed in black slacks and a turquoise cotton sweater. She waited while Nick laced his shoes. "Elizabeth told me the day we arrived that we wouldn't stay here the full two weeks. She said then that Daddy would need me. Oh, Nick, do you suppose Daddy's had a heart attack or a stroke?"

"Don't jump to conclusions. We'll know what's going on as soon as I talk to Sam." Holding his cane in one hand, he offered her the other. "Ready?"

Fifteen minutes later, Addy clutched the cup of hot tea that Elizabeth had handed her the moment she and Nick entered her cabin. Nick had just gotten through to Sam. Three people and one half-wolf dog stood in Elizabeth's living room, waiting for news.

Elizabeth placed her arm around Addy's shoulder. "Drink your tea. It will help soothe your nerves."

"Did you put something in it?"

"It's herbal tea, that's all."

With trembling fingers, Addy put the cup to her lips, sipping slowly. The tea was hot and sweet and soothing.

"Yeah, I understand. When did it happen?" Nick asked Sam Dundee.

Addy handed her cup to Elizabeth, then approached Nick, tugging on his shirtsleeve. "Tell me, what happened?"

Nick slipped his arm around her shoulders, drawing her to his side. "There's no way I'll be able to keep her here," he told Sam Dundee. "We'll head back to Huntsville tonight."

"Nick?" Fear shook her like the impact of a high-powered rifle.

He held her tightly as he continued his conversation. "How's Hester?"

"Is something wrong with Jim?" Addy squeezed Nick's arm.

"I suppose Johnson is at the hospital," Nick said.

"Nick!"

"I'll be in touch as soon as we get there." Nick hung up the phone, turned to Addy, and pulled her completely into his arms. Tilting her chin, she stared up at him. "It's bad, Red. You're going to have to be strong for me and for yourself, but mostly for Rusty."

"Tell me, dammit, just tell me!"

"Your father and Jim Hester had a late dinner meeting tonight. When they returned to the M.A.C. executive offices, they were ambushed."

"Ambushed?"

"Your father's chauffeur-bodyguard was shot. He's dead."

"Alton's dead? My God, he's been with Daddy for years!"

"Jim Hester was shot, too." Addy tensed in his arms. "He's still alive. He's in surgery."

"What about Tiffany? Who's taking care of her?"

"Hester's sister-in-law has Hester's little girl with her."

Addy swayed, her legs buckling under her. Nick steadied her, then helped her to a nearby chair. Bending down on his knees in front of her, Nick prayed she was strong enough to handle the worst news. "The person or persons who shot Alton and Hester kidnapped your father."

"No! Oh, Daddy!" Slouching over, her shoulders drooping, Addy covered her face with her hands. "I was the target! They threatened me, not Daddy! I don't understand this. Why kidnap Daddy?"

"Dina received a call from the kidnapper," Nick said, pulling Addy's clenched fists into his hands, stroking her knuckles, trying to soothe her. "He wants you to withdraw the NASP bid."

"The NASP bid really is what he's after, isn't it? It's not a red herring like you thought." Addy stared at Nick, her eyes overly bright, glazed with anxiety. "It's Gerald. It has to be. But—but he'd know—he'd know I don't have the authority to withdraw the bid."

"Calm down, Red. If Carlton is behind Rusty's kidnapping, we'll nail him. I promise you." Nick couldn't bring himself to tell her that he still doubted the validity of the NASP bid threat, that his gut instincts told him that Rusty's kidnapping had another motive. Someone wanted Addy McConnell back in Huntsville, and they'd used the only conceivable method to ensure her return.

"What if he's already killed Daddy? They killed Donnie. Daddy paid the ransom and they still killed him."

Nick felt her panic. Grabbing her by the shoulders, he shook her soundly. "Don't do this, Red! Don't fall apart on me now."

Elizabeth stepped forward, her clear blue eyes focusing on Addy. "Your father isn't dead." Standing beside Addy's chair, Elizabeth touched her cheek. "Your father won't be killed. You will return to Huntsville and save him."

Nick swung around, glaring at Elizabeth. "She doesn't need to hear this."

"Yes, I do." Shoving Nick aside, Addy stood. "I've got to go back. We need to leave as soon as possible."

Grasping his cane, Nick followed her to the door, but couldn't keep up with her when she broke into a run once she'd entered the yard.

"Addy, stop!" Nick flung open the front door. "Dammit, woman, will you slow down!"

Elizabeth caught Nick by the wrist, halting him. "Keep her guarded, every moment. She's in danger."

"Don't you think I know that!"

"Her enemy is someone she knows."

Nick could hear the deafening roar of his heartbeat throbbing in his ears. "What else? You know more, don't you?"

"He means to kill her." Elizabeth's grip on Nick's arm tightened. "A woman has been helping him, but she doesn't want Addy harmed."

Elizabeth released Nick. They stood for several long moments, staring at each other, Nick uncertain whether or not to believe this woman's soothsaying abilities. Sam had once told him that she possessed unearthly powers, that he'd seen Elizabeth Mallory turn barren soil into flowering life and call the animals out of the forest to come to her and they obeyed. Sam had said that his ward, his brother's stepchild had the ability to see inside a person and predict their future. Sam Dundee had never lied to Nick.

"That's all I know," Elizabeth said. "Hurry and go after her. Now, more than ever, Addy will need her paladin."

"Her what?"

"You, Nick, she will need you, her knight in shining armor. No one else can save her. Only you."

Chapter 12

Nick had broken all the posted speed limits on the trip to Atlanta where a private plane awaited them. They arrived in Huntsville at seven-thirty in the morning, both of them were bleary-eyed and exhausted from worry and lack of sleep. Taking a cab from the airport, they went directly to the hospital. Hot and humid early morning sunshine greeted them the moment they stepped onto the pavement, and one of Ned Johnson's FBI agents, Alan Sturges, met them at the lobby entrance.

"Any word on my father?" Addy asked as the agent whisked them through the lobby and into an elevator.

"Sorry, ma'am, there's no news to report." The young, slender investigator punched in the correct floor, then turned to Nick. "Ms. Lunden is upstairs. We've had quite a time with her. Even Brett Windsor can't do anything with her."

Hell, that's all they needed, Nick thought, an overwrought, hysterical Dina. Addy was close to the breaking point herself; she didn't need Dina's theatrical show of concern sending her over the edge. "What's Dina doing here?"

"She refuses to leave until she sees Ms. McConnell," Agent Sturges said. "She and Windsor have been here since about five this morning."

"Has Jim come out of surgery yet?" Addy asked.

The elevator stopped. The doors opened. The three stepped into the hallway.

"No, ma'am. He's been in surgery for hours. It doesn't look good. He was shot up pretty bad, I'm afraid."

Nick gave the young agent a deadly look, silently reprimanding him for being so blunt with Addy about Hester's condition. "Come on, Red, think positive thoughts."

The minute they rounded the corner that led to the surgery waiting area, Dina Lunden came running toward Addy, tears flowing down her rosy cheeks, her arms spread wide. At the touch of Dina's arm around her, Addy cringed, then chastised herself for being so insensitive to the other woman's feelings. Maybe Dina really did care about her father. If she didn't, she certainly was putting on an award-winning performance.

"Oh, Addy, it's just awful! This shouldn't have happened. If only you had stayed in Huntsville, instead of running off to God knows where and going into hiding." Releasing her tenacious hold on Addy, Dina faced Nick. "It's all your fault. I had no idea when I invited you to my engagement party that you would wind up making such a mess of things."

Brett Windsor came forward, placing a comforting arm around Dina. "Now, Dina, stop talking nonsense. Neither Nick nor Addy could have prevented Rusty's kidnapping."

Dina glared at Brett, her eyes bright and wild. "You know I'm right, dammit!" Flinging off Brett's arm, she walked away from him.

Turning to Addy, Brett gave her a gentle hug. "I'm so sorry about all this. Dina's been hysterical ever since she heard Rusty had been kidnapped."

Addy accepted Brett's comfort, thankful that he was around to help keep Dina in check. "You were with Dina when she was told about Daddy?"

"No, as a matter of fact, I wasn't." Brett glanced over at Nick whose dark, pensive stare issued a warning. "I've found my own apartment. I moved out of the mansion three days ago."

"Addy! Oh, Addy!" Janice Dixon ran down the corridor, her blond ponytail flip-flopping up and down on her back.

Pulling out of Brett's embrace, Addy put her arms around Janice. "Oh, Janice, you didn't have to come down here, but I'm so glad you did."

"I've been checking with Dina. She told me what time they were expecting you and Nick to arrive." Teary-eyed, Janice forced a smile. "I—I thought you might need me."

"Of course I need you." Addy hugged Janice with the fierce protectiveness of an earth-mother defending her child. "You're my best friend and favorite cousin."

"Has there been any word on Uncle Rusty's whereabouts? A ransom demand or anything?"

"Nothing new," Addy said. "We're waiting to hear, and praying that Daddy's all right and that Jim survives his surgery."

While the endless minutes turned to an hour and then two, Dina continued to rant and rave, ceasing only when Brett or Nick soothed her. Addy sat with Janice, and Agent Sturges watched over them all.

Ned Johnson appeared in the doorway. Nick rose from his seat directly across from Addy. He said a silent prayer that Hester was still alive. He might well be their only chance of finding Rusty—if he'd seen the kidnapper's face and could identify him. "Ned?"

"Hester made it."

Addy sighed with relief, tears glistening in the corners of her eyes. When she stood, walking toward Nick, Janice rose and followed her. Nick, who stood in the doorway talking quietly with Ned Johnson, reached out and pulled Addy to his side.

"Look, Red. I'm going in with Ned to question Hester just as soon as he comes around. The doctors say it could be another hour, maybe longer."

"You think he can identify the kidnapper?" Addy asked.

"We're hoping he can," Johnson replied.

"Agent Sturges will stay with you when I go in to question Hester." Nick's big hand splayed across her back. He titled her chin upward, his dark eyes demanding her compliance. "Don't even go to the bathroom unless he's waiting right outside the door. Understand?"

"I understand." She caressed his cheek with her fingertips. "Don't worry about me."

"Brett is taking me home," Dina announced. "I'm simply exhausted." Stopping in front of Addy and Nick, she gave them a heated look. "You will call me the moment you get word on Rusty, won't you?"

"Of course we will," Addy said.

"He's all right, you know." Dina glanced over at Brett, who held her by the arm. "Isn't he?"

"I'll drive her home and stay with her until she calms down. I think a couple of Valium should do the trick," Brett said.

Addy felt a surge of relief once Dina had left. Her father's overwrought fiancée had gotten on everyone's nerves with her moans and sighs, her constant flood of tears and her irrational babbling. Thank the Lord that Brett had been able to persuade her to go home. The FBI was doing everything possible, but Addy knew that a great deal depended on what Jim Hester would be able to tell them about the shooting and her father's kidnapping.

Nick led her back inside the waiting area, sitting down beside her on a vinyl sofa and pulling her into his arms. She rested there, reassured by his comforting strength.

Nick stood inside the ICU cubicle where Jim Hester had just regained consciousness. Ned Johnson, an RN at his side, leaned over Hester's bed and spoke his name.

"Mr. Hester, I'm Ned Johnson. I'm with the FBI. I need to ask you a few questions."

Jim tried to speak, but his voice broke in an awkward squeak when he said Addy's name. He looked up at Agent Johnson pleadingly.

"Ms. McConnell is fine. She's waiting outside, very concerned and eager to see you."

"Alton?" Jim Hester's voice was only a choked whisper.

"He didn't make it," Johnson said. "But the doctors say you're going to be all right. What we need to know in order to find the man who did this to you and kidnapped D.B. McConnell is if you can identify the assailant."

"Mask," Jim gasped. "He wore a mask."

The stocky nurse nudged Ned Johnson out of the way and checked her patient's oxygen supply. Turning back to the FBI agent, she said, "Only a few more questions."

Nick moved to the the foot of the bed. Seeing Nick, Jim reached out. His hand, strapped with an IV needle, trembled. "Romero."

"Good to see you alive, Hester. Addy's been worried sick about you."

"We didn't know...what...hit us," Jim said in a weak, quivering voice. "We drove into the parking lot." He stopped talking, giving himself a much-needed respite. "Before we...knew...what was happening, he opened fire. Shot Alton first...then me. I was on the pavement... couldn't—couldn't get to Rusty."

"I'm afraid that's all," the nurse said. "You'll both have to leave now."

"Just one more question." Ignoring the protective RN, Nick walked around to the side of the bed, reaching down to take Jim Hester's hand. "Can you tell us anything about the man who attacked you, anything that might help us?"

"Mask and hat." Jim squeezed Nick's hand with what little strength he could muster. "Didn't see his face...or hair. Tall. Well-built. I'd say fairly young... by the way he moved."

"Was he driving or on foot? Did you see any kind of vehicle?" Ned Johnson asked.

"That's two questions," the nurse scolded.

"Didn't see a car. Sorry," Jim said.

Nick gave Jim's hand a strong, reassuring squeeze. "Thanks, Jim. You get some rest, and I'll bring Addy in to see you later."

Nick hated hospitals with a passion, especially ICU units. They were an all-too-vivid reminder of his own close call with death, of the endless days and nights he'd lain, helpless and alone. His only link with life had been the pain, which he'd used to push him forward into each new day.

He'd never be the same man he was before Ian Ryker had gunned him down with an Uzi. The doctors had told him that he was lucky to be alive, and he knew they were right. But he'd lost a lot, the proper use of his leg, his job as a DEA agent, his ability to carry his woman in his arms.

Outside the ICU, Ned Johnson gripped Nick's shoulder. "Not much to go on, is it? Whoever we're dealing with isn't taking any chances."

"He's cunning and shrewd, all right, but my bet is he isn't completely sane. He's kidnapped Rusty McConnell and is demanding that Addy withdraw the bid on the NASP contract. Obviously, he hasn't done his homework or he'd know that Addy doesn't have the authority to withdraw that bid."

"He's making mistakes then, isn't he?"

"Let's just hope he makes enough for us to catch him before somebody else gets hurt."

"Ms. Addy McConnell?" A plump, middle-aged woman in a bright-orange sweat suit held the waiting-room phone in her hand.

Standing, Addy replied. "I'm Addy McConnell."

"Telephone call for you."

Addy took the phone from the woman's meaty little hand. "Hello."

"Ms. McConnell?" The man's voice was muffled, sounding similar to the caller who'd threatened her at the day-care center over two weeks ago.

"Yes." Addy's heart seemed lodged in her throat. Her ears throbbed with pressure.

"I know who kidnapped your father."

"Who is this? What do you want?"

Janice rushed to Addy's side, pulling on her arm. "What's wrong? Should I get Agent Sturges?"

Addy glanced out in the hallway where the FBI agent guarding her waited patiently by the door. With a shake of her head, Addy placed her index finger over Janice's mouth.

"I can help you find your father," the caller said.

Addy knew this was the same voice, the same man who'd threatened her before. "Do you have him? Is he all right?"

"I know where he is, and I'll tell you if you'll meet me."

"Meet you?"

Janice grabbed Addy's wrist, shaking her head and silently mouthing the word no. Addy jerked away from her cousin.

"If you'll come to the coffee shop right now, I'll meet you there and tell you who kidnapped your father and where you can find him."

"How do I know I can trust you?"

"I'm your only chance of keeping your father alive. They're going to kill him. It's up to you whether he lives or dies."

Addy swallowed, wishing she could calm the erratic, deafening rhythm of her heart. Clutching the phone, she breathed deeply. "I—I have an FBI agent guarding me. He'll never let me leave the floor without him."

"If you ever want to see your father alive again, you'll find a way. If anyone, and I mean anyone, comes with you, then Rusty McConnell is a dead man."

"How—how will I recognize you?"

"I'll be wearing a Huntsville Stars T-shirt and cap. I'll wait ten minutes."

The dial tone hummed in Addy's ear. "No! Wait—"

Janice whirled Addy around to face her, grabbing her by the shoulders. "What the hell was that all about?"

Addy led Janice to the far side of the room, away from the curious stares of other ICU patients' family members. "The man on the phone says that he knows who kidnapped Daddy and he knows where Daddy is."

"You've got to tell the FBI and Nick," Janice said.

"I can't do that. He wants me to meet him in the coffee shop. Right now. If anyone comes with me, they'll kill Daddy."

"He's bluffing. If he's in the coffee shop, he can't kill Uncle Rusty."

"He may not be the kidnapper. I think he may just be working for them."

"It isn't safe for you to go down there and meet him alone. He could do anything. He could shoot you right there in the coffee shop." Janice nodded toward the open door. "Besides, Agent Sturges isn't going to let you go anywhere without him. If he did, Nick would kill him."

Addy's instincts warned her that Janice was right. It wasn't safe for her to meet this telephone caller, but if there was even the slightest chance that he was on the level, that he could lead them to Rusty, she had to take the chance, didn't she? If her actions meant the difference between saving her father's life and his death, then she had no choice.

"You can help me," Addy said. "I want you to distract Agent Sturges long enough for me to get to the elevators."

"No, Addy, I won't do it. I don't want anything to happen to you."

Addy took her cousin's face in her hands. Forcing a smile, she tried to sound reassuring. "Look, I won't take any unnecessary chances. The coffee shop will be full of people. And, if I'm not back in a few minutes, then you can tell Agent Sturges where I went. Okay?"

"Addy, are you sure?"

"No, I'm not sure, but I do know that this may be our only chance to save Daddy."

Addy watched while Janice sauntered over to the FBI agent. No man could resist her cousin's feminine charms. The woman was lethal. Within minutes, Janice had maneuvered Alan Sturges inside the waiting area and over to the coffee table, set up and replenished by hospital volunteers for the convenience of the ICU visitors. While Janice poured two cups of coffee, handing one to Sturges, Addy slipped into the hallway. Taking one last glance backward, she saw that Janice had her arm laced through the agent's and was smiling up at him, her hip resting seductively against his thigh.

Addy punched the elevator down button. While waiting, she kept checking to make sure no one was aware of her escape. The elevator doors swung open. Three people disembarked. Rushing inside, Addy punched the lobby button, drew in a deep, courage-seeking breath and said a prayer when the doors closed and the elevator descended.

Despite the air-conditioned cool of the elevator, drops of perspiration trickled down Addy's neck. Her palms were coated with sweat. Her pulse beat rapidly. Her mouth felt as dry and parched as desert sand.

She knew she shouldn't be doing this. Nick would be furious when he came out of ICU and found her missing. God, what had gotten into her, thinking she could rescue her father, that she could confront a man who could well be one of the kidnappers? She wasn't thinking straight. If the man in the coffee shop chose to kidnap her or even kill her, what help could she be to her father?

Just as Addy made the monumental decision that she was going to go back upstairs and tell Nick about the phone call, the elevator doors opened at the lobby level. Quickly, she punched the ICU floor button. Before the doors closed, a man entered. With fear racing through her like molten lava down a mountainside, Addy looked up to see who was sharing the elevator with her. Recognizing the man, she sagged with relief.

"Oh, thank God, it's you!"

"What's wrong, Addy? You seem frightened."

"I'm all right now. I wasn't expecting to see you." The man reached around Addy, pressing the open button.

"What are you doing? I was on my way back upstairs."

"I'm surprised Nick Romero let you out of his sight."

When Addy tried to press the ICU floor button again, her companion placed his hand over hers, pulling her away from the control panel. Addy glared at him.

"I have a gun in my coat pocket, Addy, and I'm quite prepared to use it."

"You?"

"We'll walk outside together, like old friends, and go to my car. Once we reach our destination, I'll tell you everything you want to know about Rusty's kidnapper."

Addy followed his instructions, cursing herself for being such a fool. Not only had she acted impulsively but she had doomed herself and her father. Icy chills of fear racked her body as her kidnapper opened his car door and gave her a gentle shove. Once trapped inside the moving vehicle, Addy turned her head slightly, watching the hospital until it faded out of sight. The car soon blended in with the afternoon traffic, its two occupants escaping any undue notice as they left behind Addy's protection—Nick Romero and the FBI.

Addy knew her only hope now lay with Nick being able to somehow figure out who had taken her. But would he be able to piece the puzzle together in time to save her and her father? Would he, unlike she and her father, ignore all the circumstantial evidence and go with his gut instincts? Dear Lord, please help him. If ever she had needed her paladin to come to her rescue, it was now.

Scanning the ICU waiting area, Nick didn't see Addy. Alan Sturges stood by the windows, drinking a cup of coffee and flirting with an overly attentive Janice Dixon. Where the hell was Addy? Was she in the rest room? If so, why wasn't Sturges standing guard outside the door?

Nick marched over to the FBI agent, gripping his shoulder in a vise-like hold. "Where's Addy?"

"Right over—" Sturges's face turned pale, his eyes widening in surprise and fear. "She's got to be in here! I just saw her a few minutes ago."

"Well, she sure as hell isn't here now, is she?" Nick swung the younger man around to face him. "If anything has happened to her, your life isn't worth—"

"It's not Alan's fault," Janice interrupted. "I've been deliberately distracting him. He—he didn't see Addy leave."

Nick released Sturges, then reached out and grabbed Janice by the shoulders. "What do you mean 'leave'? Where did she go?"

"Down to the coffee shop." Tears filled Janice's big blue eyes.

"How the hell did this happen?" Nick's gut tightened into a painful knot. His heart drummed like a roaring tornado. His big hands trembled on Janice's shoulders. "Why would she slip away to go to the coffee shop?"

"A man called."

Hot, acrid bitterness rose in his throat, the physical evidence of a fear too great to be born. "What man?"

"I don't know," Janice cried as Nick tightened his hold on her. "He—he told Addy that he knew where Uncle Rusty was, and he knew—knew who'd kidnapped him."

"Is she meeting this man in the coffee shop?" Perspiration broke out on Nick's face, dotting his forehead and upper lip. He felt the sticky, moist drops of sweat dripping down his back.

"Yes!" Janice's cries grew louder; tears streamed down her face. "I tried to stop her!"

He shook Janice so forcefully that Agent Sturges clamped his hands over Nick's, trying to free the woman from Nick's wrath. Realizing that he was hurting Janice, Nick released her. "Dammit, how could she have done something so stupid?"

Janice sought comfort in Alan Sturges's arms. "She said to tell Alan—Agent Sturges—what she'd done if she didn't come back in a few minutes."

"How long has she been gone?" Nick's voice was a low, deadly growl.

Swatting away a torrent of tears, Janice glanced up at the wall clock. "About—about five minutes."

"Sturges," Nick yelled, "go find Johnson! Tell him what's happened. I'm going down to the coffee shop, and you'd better pray that I'm not too late."

Nick spent the rest of the day in a living hell, fearing the worst and hating himself for leaving Addy in another man's care, even for the few minutes it had taken to question Jim Hester. Someone had timed that phone call just right. Someone had known the minute he'd left Addy. Sturges and Johnson had known, and so had Janice Dixon. Had she been able to contact Ron Glover? Were they the man and woman behind all the threats, behind Addy's attempted kidnapping, the recent shootings and Rusty's abduction? It made perfect sense, didn't it? Glover had been on Nick's list of suspects since the very beginning.

The FBI had set up headquarters at Rusty's mansion, waiting for any kind of instructions from the kidnapper. Thankfully, Dina had slept through the afternoon and evening. Nick had been the one to tell her what had happened to Addy. He'd never seen such sheer horror on Dina's face. Did she really love Rusty McConnell enough to care about his daughter? She sure as hell acted as if she did, as if her own life depended upon Rusty's and Addy's safety.

Mrs. Hargett had been the one to take charge, to prepare sandwiches and coffee for the agents who swarmed over the house like a cluster of drone bees. The housekeeper had also been the one to keep Dina out of the way, soothing her with words and pats and occasional cups of tea that Nick suspected were laced with liquor. By nightfall, Dina was quiet and unobtrusive.

Nick sat in Rusty's huge den, his vision clouded over with memories of the past eight days he'd spent with Addy in Sequana Falls. He heard the agents' voices and saw them moving about the room, but his private thoughts blocked out the reality.

Nothing could happen to Addy. His life wouldn't be worth living without her. If he ever got his hands on the man who'd done this to her, he'd kill him. Slowly. Painfully.

The telephone rang. Every man in the room froze. After an agonizing moment of suspended time, Ned Johnson picked up the receiver.

"McConnell residence."

Nick held his breath, waiting. Silence so profound that they could almost hear one another's heartbeats encompassed the den. Then Johnson said, "What? Is he all right? Where was he found?"

Nick rushed over to Johnson, grabbing him by the arm. "Who's been found?"

Ned replaced the receiver, then turned to Nick. "Rusty McConnell has been found. He's alive and unharmed."

"When? Where?"

"The Huntsville police found him wandering around on the side of the interstate. They thought he was drunk." Ned motioned to two of his agents. "Hankins, you and Murphy go down to the police station and bring Mr. McConnell home. He'll be a little groggy and disoriented. He's been drugged."

"Drugged," Nick said. "If he's been drugged the whole damned time, then he's probably not going to be able to tell us who kidnapped him."

"If the kidnapper let McConnell go, then you can bet your life he didn't reveal his identity."

Within an hour, D.B. McConnell had been brought home, and he'd showered, shaved, eaten and smoked a cigar. No one had told him that Addy was missing, not even Dina, whose tearful reunion with her fiancé had just about convinced Nick of her sincerity.

Nick had stayed out of sight, watching Rusty's homecoming from inside the house while Dina, Mrs. Hargett and half a dozen agents surrounded Rusty on the veranda. If Rusty saw him, he'd ask about Addy. As far as her father knew, Addy was still in hiding, safe and sound.

Ned Johnson approached Nick, who'd found himself a peaceful spot out in the backyard. "McConnell has to be told. I thought you might want to be the one to tell him."

"Yeah, thanks. She was my responsibility, and I let some maniac get to her. If anything happens to Addy—"

"Don't talk like that to her father."

"If anything happens to her, I hope Rusty breaks my damned neck."

"Mrs. Hargett is keeping Ms. Lunden occupied. We've got McConnell in the den." Ned placed his hand on Nick's shoulder. "He can't identify the kidnapper. He didn't see much more than Hester saw, except he saw the gun. A 10 mm., but we would have know that soon, anyway, from the ballistics report on the bullets the doctors dug out of Hester and Alton."

"Anything else?"

"Yeah. His attacker was driving a dark blue Buick. Rusty got a glimpse of the license plate. He remembered the first four digits. We're running a check now, but don't get your hopes up. You know as well as I do the car was probably stolen."

"Can you give me a few minutes alone with Rusty?" Nick asked.

"Sure thing."

As it turned out, Nick didn't get more than three minutes alone with Addy's father after explaining to him what had happened at the hospital. The telephone rang, stunning everyone into silence.

Ned Johnson motioned an angry and outraged Rusty McConnell toward the phone. "This could be our boy calling."

Clinching the receiver so tightly that his knuckles whitened, Rusty answered, "D.B. McConnell."

"You had your chance, McConnell." The muffled voice held an edge of sadistic pleasure. "All you had to do was not bid on the NASP contract and Addy would have been safe."

"Who the hell is this? If you've done anything to harm my daughter, I'll—"

"You'll what?" The man laughed. "You should have followed instructions."

"I can still cancel the bid," Rusty said. "Is that what you want?"

"It's too late, much too late for Addy."

"No, no it isn't. Tell me what you want and I'll do it. Just don't hurt Addy."

"She won't be in any pain. It's going to happen so quickly, she won't feel a thing. One big boom and she'll be joining her illustrious Delacourt ancestors. Of course, you won't find enough of her to bury in the old family cemetery."

The line went dead. Rusty cursed loudly, using a string of profanities that would have put the foulest-mouthed hoodlum to shame.

Ned Johnson and Nick jumped on Rusty the minute he replaced the receiver, asking him question after question. Rusty went over the conversation again and again.

Nick knew there had to be a clue in the kidnapper's words, if only he could figure out what it was. As minutes ticked by, slowly but surely counting down the last moments of Addy's life, Nick kept making Rusty repeat every word the caller had said. Finally, Rusty broke under the pressure, turning on Nick. Rusty's big, hard fist made contact with Nick's jaw, knocking the younger man to the floor. Nick decided right then and there that he was glad he hadn't been on the receiving end of Rusty McConnell's wrath when the old man had been a little younger and in his prime.

Dina, who entered the room just as Nick picked himself up off the floor, ran to her fiancé, encircling his thick waist with her slender arms. "You can't go on this way, Rusty, darling! You must get some rest."

"How the hell can I rest when some lunatic has my daughter and is planning to...blow...her...up." Forceful, manly tears streamed down Rusty's ruddy cheeks and rocked his robust frame. He clung to Dina, who cooed soothing words to him as she stroked his back.

Once again Nick went over the kidnapper's messages, praying that something would click in his mind. *It's too late for Addy. She won't be in any pain. One big boom and she'll be joining her illustrious Delacourt ancestors. You won't find enough of her to bury in the old family cemetery.*

Nick paced the floor, ruffling his already mussed hair with restless fingers. Again, Romero, again. *One big boom. Delacourt ancestors. Old family cemetery.*

Wherever the kidnapper had taken Addy, he'd planted a bomb. But where had he taken her? And how long before the bomb exploded?

Delacourt ancestors. Old family cemetery. Elm Hill! God, it was a long shot, but what if Addy's kidnapper knew about her mother's ancestral home? Addy had told him that no one had lived there since she and her father had moved out twenty-five years ago.

Nick found Rusty and Dina sitting together on the living-room sofa. Rusty gazed up at him with tear-filled eyes. Addy's father looked every day of his seventy years.

"Where's Elm Hill?" Nick asked. "How do I get there?"

"Elm Hill?" Rusty sat up straight, his tired expression growing alert. "You think he took her to Elm Hill?"

"It's possible. He mentioned her Delacourt ancestors and the old family cemetery."

"The cemetery is on the estate." Rusty jumped up. "I'll go with you and show you the way."

"No," Nick said. "I'm playing a hunch. Addy could be anywhere. You need to stay here by the phone in case the kidnapper tries to get in touch with you again."

"Then take one of Johnson's boys with you."

"If the kidnapper is still there with her when I arrive, I don't want to scare him off. I'll have to go in alone."

Rusty pulled Nick into his bear-like hug, stunning Nick with his affection. "You save our girl."

Nick couldn't reply. He hoped Addy's father knew that he'd do anything for Addy, even die if it was necessary.

Rusty gave Nick instructions on the quickest route out of Huntsville to Elm Hill. Dina, Rusty and Ned Johnson followed Nick outside to his silver Jag.

"Keep in touch by car phone," Johnson said. "I don't like you going out there alone. Anything could happen."

"If I'm wrong about Elm Hill, it won't matter." Nick got behind the wheel, revved the motor and drove down the driveway.

He wasn't a very religious man. Hell, he hadn't been inside a church since his grandmother used to drag him off to Sunday mass. But he sought out God's ear, hoping that The Man Upstairs was listening. He needed a big favor, and he was willing to make any kind of deal necessary. Could he make a deal with God? If he could, he'd promise Him anything in exchange for Addy's life.

Chapter 13

He had stripped Addy down to her black teddy. For a while she'd been afraid he was going to rape her. He had touched her intimately and called her sweet Addy.

Why had she never seen this side of him? Obviously he was a very sick man—a man so obsessed with her father's money that he had already killed two men and was plotting two more murders.

She didn't know how long she'd been alone in the front parlor at Elm Hill. It could have been hours since he'd left. She didn't know.

Straining to see the digital timer attached to the heavy canvas belt he had strapped around her waist, Addy toppled over. Biting down, clamping her teeth to keep from crying, she tumbled around on the dusty floor until she righted herself again, sitting up on her knees. The rope that tied her hands behind her was attached to her ankles.

Even though he had been on Nick's list of suspects, she had never once actually considered him. How could she have been so blind? She and her father had opened their home to him, had accepted him as a part of the family because he was Dina's stepson.

Alone and frightened, Addy went over in her mind everything that happened since Brett Windsor had driven her to Elm Hill.

He had forced her inside the house at gunpoint, made her remove her clothes, and then had run his hands over her with rough, sadistic, sexual pleasure. Closing her eyes, she shut out the dawn light that crept through the tall, bare windows. She couldn't stop herself from reliving those terrifying moments she'd spent with Brett before he'd left her alone to die.

Outside a night owl hooted and a thousand katydids sang in unison.

Brett forced her to her knees, almost knocking her over in his attempt to subdue her. With unnatural strength, he jerked her hands behind her back, binding them securely with nylon cord, then draping the rope over her ankles, effectively hog-tying her.

"Don't do this, Brett." She wasn't too proud to beg; the threat of dying had quickly put her priorities in the proper order.

"Oh, sweet Addy, I had hoped we'd have more time together. I was so looking forward to making love to you." Brett traced the lines of her face with his fingertips. "But that was before Nick Romero had you. I don't want his leavings. Not a second time."

"Are you talking about Dina?" Addy tugged on her wrists. The cord was tight, with very little slack, allowing no chance for escape.

"Did you suspect that we were lovers? Or did Romero tell you?"

"Brett, if it's the money, Daddy will pay you whatever you want if you'll just let both of us go. You and Dina can fly out of the country with millions." She hoped that she could reason with him, despite his apparent madness.

"I don't want a few measly millions." He carried the battery-operated lantern with him when he moved toward the door. "I plan to have it all. Everything that belongs to D.B. McConnell will be mine and Dina's in just a few months."

"If you kill Daddy and me, Dina won't inherit anything. She—she's not even named in Daddy's will."

"Not yet, but she will be. Once she and Rusty are married."

"Then...you...you haven't hurt Daddy?" An instant surge of relief rushed through Addy. Somewhere in all this craziness there just might be a note of sanity, a ray of hope in the darkness. "Where is Daddy, Brett? What have you done with him?"

"I set your father free only moments before I returned to the hospital and met you at the elevator." Brett smiled at her, his stunning, boyish smile that disguised a sick mind. "I had to kidnap Rusty. You left me no other choice when you allowed Romero to take you into hiding. It was the only way to get you back to Huntsville."

"Why did you have to get me back to Huntsville? I don't understand."

"You're the one I had to kidnap in order for my plan to work. You, Addy, you. Not your father. Rusty's probably at home now, all safe and sound."

Addy sighed with relief. If her father was free, he'd be able to tell Nick and the FBI that Brett was behind all the threats. Suddenly the reality of the situation hit her. Surely Brett wasn't so insane that he would have released a man capable of identifying him. "Does Daddy know that you—that you're—"

"I kept Rusty drugged the whole time. He has no idea who kidnapped him."

"Nick will figure it out. He'll find me, and when he does, he'll kill you. Do you hear me, Brett? Nick will kill you."

Addy called after him, but he didn't reply. She heard his footsteps as he walked out into the foyer and opened the front door. He returned quickly, carrying the lantern and a nylon duffel bag. Bending over beside her, he dropped the bag to the floor.

"Brett, I thought you liked me." Addy had no idea if she could get through to him, but she had to try. What other alternative did she have?

"Addy, sweet, I do like you. I would have made you my wife, if only you'd shown the least bit of interest in me." He unzipped the duffel bag. "I would have allowed you to live another year or so, until I'd disposed of your father and you'd made me your only beneficiary."

"How is killing me now going to get you all of Daddy's money?"

"Once you're dead and Rusty marries Dina, she will, of course, become his only beneficiary." Pulling out a heavy canvas belt, Brett laid it out carefully on the floor. "He will be so overwrought after losing you that Dina will fear for his sanity, but loving him the way she does, she'll be able to persuade him to marry her as soon as possible."

Suddenly Addy realized Brett's diabolical plan. Oh, dear Lord, why had her father fallen victim to Dina's seductive charm? If that woman hadn't wormed her way into their lives, none of this would be happening. And she would never have met Nick Romero, her one hope of survival. "You're going to kill Daddy, too, aren't you?"

"Kill Rusty?" Brett's maniacal laughter echoed in the stillness of the empty parlor. "No, no. Rusty will be so distraught over your death that he'll go into a steady decline— aided by Dina, naturally. After a few months, the memory of how you died will completely destroy your father. He'll probably die suddenly with a heart attack. Of course, if he doesn't oblige us by dying, we'll give him a little assistance. Who knows? Rusty might lose his sanity and put a gun to his head and pull the trigger."

"Daddy would never kill himself!" Addy screamed, unable to control the rage burning inside her. "Anyone who

knows Daddy would never, ever believe his death was suicide.''

''That's where you're wrong, sweet Addy.'' Brett removed something that looked like a small, digital clock from
the nylon bag. ''You're going to die such a horrible death
that—well, there won't be any body to bury, no funeral, no
chance to say farewell.'' Brett dug out a spool of wire, then
lifted up a metal box and placed both items on the floor beside the canvas belt.

Sour, salty bile burned a trail up Addy's chest and into her
mouth. She thought she was going to throw up. What was
Brett going to do to her? *There won't be any body to bury.*
''If you were after Daddy's money, why did you demand
that he not bid on the NASP contract when you knew it
would mean millions in profits for M.A.C.?''

''The NASP contract proved to be an effective smoke
screen, didn't it? No one will suspect me in the kidnappings
or murders because I would have nothing to gain from
M.A.C. losing out on the NASP contract.''

''You wanted us to suspect Gerald, didn't you?'' Addy
glared at her kidnapper, longing for the freedom to attack
him, to kick and scratch and hit. Anger welled up inside of
her, bubbling like boiling liquid ready to overflow.

''You and Rusty jumped at the chance to condemn Carlton.'' Brett shook his head, grunting in a mock show of
sadness. ''Don't you think hiring Linc Hites was a stroke of
genius on my part? His only connection to anyone who
knew you was to your ex-husband.''

''How did you meet Linc Hites?'' She wondered how long
she could keep Brett talking. She needed time—enough time
for Nick to fit all the pieces together.

''Linc and I owed the same man, a rather unsavory busi-
nessman, some money. Isn't coincidence a wonderful thing?
It brought me together with Linc Hites and brought you together with Nick Romero.''

''And it brought Daddy and Dina together.''

"Oh, that wasn't coincidence, sweet Addy. That was planned." Brett flipped open the metal box. "I've mapped out everything from the very beginning. When you didn't succumb to my charm, I had to do a little replotting. Simple enough, really—until Romero showed up and thwarted the first kidnapping attempt, then hung around causing trouble."

"Nick's gut instincts kept telling him that something was wrong about the kidnapper's demand. All the while Daddy and I suspected Gerald, Nick wouldn't rule out other possibilities. Sooner or later, he'll figure it out, Brett. You won't get away with this."

"Later won't help you, Addy." Brett's steady, knowledgeable hands worked quickly, removing a small wad of some kind of rubbery substance from the metal box. The glob reminded her of the Silly Putty the children played with at the day-care center. "Romero may think he's a real tough guy, but he's not so smart. Not nearly as smart as I am. And, if by some miracle, he does figure out that Dina and I planned this whole thing, then I'll just have to dispose of one unwanted and unneeded old Latin lover."

"Dina would never let you kill Nick. She loves him."

"I can handle Dina. She may love Romero, but she loves money even more. Besides, she's as deep in this mess as I am."

"Does she love money enough to kill for it? To risk the death penalty if she's caught?"

"Dina does what I tell her to do. Ever since my father died, she's depended on me."

Addy watched while Brett turned and came toward her. She wanted to run, but she was hog-tied and could barely move. Cringing when Brett slipped the canvas belt around her, easing it beneath the cord that bound her wrists and ankles, she willed herself to be strong. Now was not the time to panic. She was still alive. Things weren't hopeless. Not yet.

"I admit that I don't especially like Dina, but I can't believe she's capable of murder," Addy said.

"She isn't. Dina hasn't murdered anyone."

Brett clipped the digital timer to the canvas belt, then attached the thin wiring to the fuse he'd fastened to the dab of putty-like substance he'd molded across the belt's metal buckles.

"I had to promise not to hurt you before Dina would agree to help me with the kidnapping attempt," Brett said. "I convinced her that all I wanted was to hold you for ransom. She knows how badly I need money. She's such a sentimental creature. She's really become quite fond of Rusty, you know."

Addy realized that she'd just been wired with a bomb of some sort. She knew very little about such things, but the evidence was there before her, an undeniable fact. Brett Windsor intended to blow her to kingdom come. A surge of pure fear-driven bile filled Addy's mouth. Turning sideways, she threw up, retching until her stomach emptied itself.

Brett took a linen handkerchief out of his pocket and wiped Addy's mouth, then grabbed the cord that bound her and dragged her into the corner of the room.

"As soon as I set the timer, I'll have to leave to call your father and Romero and give them the sad news." Reaching down, he activated the digital timer. Silently the deadly device began ticking away the last minutes of Addy's life.

Outside a night owl hooted and a thousand katydids sang in unison.

Huddled on her knees, wearing nothing but a black teddy, Addy McConnell awaited her rescue. While time raced by quickly, she consoled herself with one thought. *Nick Romero.*

Nick would find her before the bomb exploded. He had to find her. He was her paladin, her champion. He would never allow anything to harm her.

She knew with a certainty born of her love for Nick and her hopes for the future that she couldn't die. Not now. Elizabeth Mallory had prophesied that Addy would give Nick children. Two little girls. She could picture Nick's daughters. The two perfect angels, one with her flame-red hair, the other with his midnight black. One with her green eyes, the other with his dark brown.

They would name the eldest, the green-eyed brunette, Maria, after Nick's grandmother. And the younger, the brown-eyed redhead, would be called Madeline, after her own mother.

While the digital timing device blinked away the minutes, Addy kept her sanity by planning her future with Nick, by thinking about Maria and Madeline and about what a proud papa Nick Romero would be.

Nick pulled into the weed- and grass-infested circular drive at Elm Hill. The first, tentative rays of sunshine peeked from behind the far horizon. The dawn of a new day was breaking. He prayed that Addy was still alive to greet the morning.

The old antebellum mansion stood as a regal, if somewhat decaying, reminder of a South that had ceased to exist years ago. Like a Southern belle long past her prime, the house sagged with the ravages of time and abandonment.

Nick felt in his pocket for the key Rusty had given him, but when he tried the door it swung open. His heart accelerated at the thought that someone had been there before him. Examining the lock more carefully, he found that it had been jimmied. Addy was here. He could feel her presence.

There had been no other car in the drive and he hadn't run into any traffic on the lonely stretch of road leading to the turn-off. If Addy's kidnapper was still here, he was on foot. Taking no chances, Nick pulled out his 9 mm. automatic. Damn his noisy cane! But if the kidnapper was inside, he would have already heard Nick's car when he arrived. Time was of the essence if a bomb was involved. He hadn't dared waste precious minutes parking farther away and walking.

Making his way into the foyer, Nick waited a few seconds, allowing his vision to adjust to the shadowy darkness inside the mansion. He checked the parlor on the right side. Empty. He turned left. Then he saw her.

Damn! She was half naked, hog-tied and huddled in the corner of the room. Thank God, he'd found her still alive. He wouldn't allow himself to think about what her kidnapper might have done to her. Walking as fast as his slow stride would allow, he crossed the room.

Addy saw the dark figure approaching her. When she'd heard the car, she'd wondered if Brett had returned. Now she knew that Nick had come to rescue her.

"Nick!" she cried. "I knew you'd come."

Kneeling in front of her, he laid his gun and cane on the floor, then ran his hands over her face, cupping her chin in his palm. "Damn, Red, I've been out of my mind!"

He surveyed the situation quickly, able to see the canvas belt attached to her waist. Early morning sunlight illuminated the room with a hazy, topaz glow. Nick recognized the C-4 plastic explosive immediately. God knew he'd seen enough of it in Nam. Although the stuff was deadly, even in tiny pieces, it was one of the most stable explosives around. So damned stable that he and his SEAL comrades had occasionally set it on fire and used it to cook their food. C-4 created an instant hot flame.

And the damned stuff was readily available on the black market, especially in a military town. And Huntsville was a military town. The right person could easily have done the wrong thing, using his position to confiscate C-4 and make himself a nice little profit.

Nick released the catch on his cane. The sharp stiletto blade popped out. With careful manipulation, he removed the knife and immediately began slicing away at the heavy canvas belt. "We've got to get this off."

"How much time do we have?" She stared at him, her gaze locking with his.

He glanced down at the digital timing device. Only minutes remained, but it would be more than enough time for him to cut through the belt, remove it from Addy's waist and get her out of the house. "Plenty of time, Red. Just sit still and I'll have this thing off you in a few minutes."

"Brett Windsor kidnapped me."

"Dammit, why didn't I follow my instincts?" Nick kept his eyes focused on his knife and his hands, on the task of cutting through the belt. He tried not to think about Windsor or what he would do to the man once he'd been caught.

"Brett's insane. He—he planned to kill Daddy, too. Once Daddy and Dina were married, Brett was going to kill Daddy and make it look like either a heart attack or a—a suicide."

Nick cursed the strength of the canvas. His sharp knife had cut through less than halfway. "As soon as I get you out of here, I'll call Ned Johnson. They'll pick up Windsor, and if he's not in jail by the time I get to him—" He heard the floorboards in the foyer creak. Someone else was inside the house. But he didn't dare waste time checking out the intruder's identity. With every beat of Addy's heart, the blinking red timer clicked off another second of her life.

"Nick, it's Brett. He's come back!" Addy cried.

Too late, Nick swung around. His gun lay beside him. Brett Windsor stood in the doorway, the morning sunlight silhouetting his muscular frame.

"Move away from Addy nice and slow," Brett said. "I have no problem with shooting both of you and then letting the bomb take care of the rest."

"Don't risk your life," Addy whispered to Nick, seeing him eye his gun lying a few inches from his knee. "I'd rather die than—"

"Don't talk nonsense," Nick said, his voice so low she barely heard him. "I don't have a life without you, Red."

"Stop whispering and get the hell away from her!" Brett walked into the parlor and pointed his gun directly at Nick's head.

Nick obeyed, standing slowly and walking away from Addy, limping badly without the aid of his cane. He hoped he could find a way to buy them a little time. "Pretty ingenious plan you worked out, Windsor. Get rid of Addy. Make it look like someone who wanted the NASP contract was the murderer, then once Dina married Rusty and became his primary beneficiary, see that he has a heart attack."

"Gerald Carlton had better hope he has an alibi for the past few hours." Brett laughed, then nudged Nick in the stomach with his gun.

"Where did you park, Windsor?" Nick asked. "I didn't hear you drive up."

"I parked far enough away so you couldn't hear me." Brett grinned, showing his straight, white teeth. "I haven't got time to tie you up, Romero, so I'm going to have to shoot you."

"Yeah, that would be the only smart thing to do. But before you shoot me, tell me how you knew I'd found Addy."

"Dina called me, the minute you left." Brett shook his head and grunted several times. "I hope she doesn't freak out on me. She's upset about all the killing. Dina's such a delicate little thing. I don't know how she would have survived all these years without me."

"Haven't you got that backwards, Windsor?" Nick taunted, wondering if he could rile the other man enough so he'd make a mistake, one that might give Nick the chance to jump him.

"What do you mean by that?"

"You've been living off Dina ever since you went through your share of your father's estate. For months now, Rusty McConnell has been paying your bills."

"He's damned rich enough to pay my bills. He knows I keep Dina happy, and that old fool is so hung up on our Dina that he'd do just about anything for her."

"I doubt he would have welcomed you so cordially if he'd known you and Dina were lovers."

Addy sucked in her breath so loudly that Nick heard her, and knew that Brett had, too.

Brett laughed, his toothy grin sinister in a way that made Addy wonder why she'd never noticed the neurotic glint in his eyes. "Oh, we've all loved her, haven't we, Nicky? That's what she calls him, you know." Brett turned toward Addy, giving her a hasty glance. Nick took a step in his direction. He turned back quickly. "No, you don't!"

"I've known Dina a lot longer than you have," Nick said. "She won't be able to live with herself if you go through with this. She'll break under the pressure."

"That won't be your problem."

All three occupants of the parlor heard the cars drive up, doors slam and footsteps pound on the veranda. Wild-eyed and clearly frightened, Brett grabbed Nick, twisting his arm behind his back and sticking the 10 mm. against his waist.

Dina Lunden ran into the parlor, then stopped dead still when she saw Brett and Nick. "Please, Brett...darling, you mustn't do this."

"What the hell are you doing here, Dina?" Brett asked, his voice shrill.

Rusty McConnell bounded into the room, stopping at Dina's side. "My God!"

"You brought Rusty with you!" Brett screeched. "What were you thinking of? This wasn't part of my plan. None of this was. Everything's going wrong."

"Brett, don't kill anyone else. If you let Nick and Addy go, then Rusty won't file charges, will you, Rusty?"

When Dina turned to him, D.B. McConnell glared at her, then at Brett Windsor. "That's right. I'll see that you're set up with as much money as you think you'll need, and I'll hire a private plane to take you anywhere you want to go."

"I want it all," Brett said, releasing Nick and walking toward Dina, whose arms were outstretched in a pleading, come-to-me gesture. "Dina and I can't live on a paltry six million dollars. I killed once for such a small amount. This time, it'll have to be more."

"Brett?" Dina dropped her open arms. "You didn't kill your father. He—he—Ashley had a heart attack."

"There are ways to fake a heart attack," Brett said.

Nick knew he had a slight chance of catching Windsor off guard as long as Dina kept talking to him. He had to risk it. Now!

Nick jumped Brett. The 10 mm. flew out of Brett's hand and slid across the floor. The two men locked in a struggle of brute strength, fists pounding, knuckles crunching. Brett Windsor was no match for his bigger, stronger opponent. Nick landed one final blow, knocking Brett to the floor.

"Nick, the gun!" Dina yelled.

Then Addy screamed when she saw Brett's bloody hand reach out and grab the 10 mm. from where it had landed on the parlor floor. As if in slow motion, the scene reeled off in front of Addy. Still lying on the floor, Brett turned over, aimed the gun and fired at Nick. Dina ran across the room, her voluptuous body separating the two men. The bullet entered her neck. She fell forward, face down on the floor.

Another gunshot sounded. Ned Johnson stood in the doorway, his automatic in his hand. Brett Windsor lay lifeless, his blank stare facing the ceiling.

Rusty McConnell rushed over, cradling Dina in his arms. Blood gushed from her wound. Nick took a moment to check her condition. Brett's bullet had hit an artery.

"Johnson, get over here quick," Nick said, then rushed to Addy.

While he busied himself cutting through the canvas belt, Nick heard Dina's dying words. "Oh, Rusty, darling, forgive me. I—I never meant for—"

"Nick, are you all right?" Tears streamed down Addy's flushed cheeks.

"I'm fine, Red." He kept sawing away at the belt. "Johnson, you'd better get Rusty and Dina out of here. Fast."

"We don't have much time, do we?" Addy asked.

"Enough," Nick lied. Two minutes and counting down. The red numerals flashed a warning signal. Sweat coated the palms of Nick's hands.

Ned Johnson picked up Dina's lifeless body. "Come on, Mr. McConnell. Let's get Dina outside and let Nick take care of things in here."

"But Addy—" Rusty said.

"Nick's got everything under control," Johnson assured D.B. McConnell.

"I can't leave Addy." Rusty refused to budge.

Ned carried Dina's body outside, returning momentarily with two young agents who forcefully dragged an enraged D.B. McConnell out of the house.

Only another inch to cut through. Sweat poured off Nick's face. One minute. Fifty-nine seconds. Fifty-eight.

Addy knew time was running out. She said a silent prayer. God wouldn't let them die. Not now when they'd just found each other. "Nick, I love you."

Forty-six seconds. Cut. Forty-five. Cut. Forty-four. Cut. "I love you, too, Red. I love you so damned much." Forty seconds. Cut. Thirty-nine. Cut.

The last thread broke. The belt fell free. Twenty. Nineteen. Eighteen. Grabbing the deadly canvas strap, Nick ran as fast as his bad leg would permit, praying with each faulty step that he'd make it outside in time. If Addy hadn't been hog-tied, he would have left the belt in the house and told her to run. Ten. Nine. Eight.

Reaching the veranda, he raised the belt high in the sky. Five. Four. With all the strength in his arm, he flung the bomb out into the wooded area, away from the house and away from the parked cars. He made it into the foyer when the explosion rocked the house, shattering several windowpanes.

"Nick! Nick!" Addy screamed his name over and over again.

Picking himself up off the floor, Nick hurried into the parlor, rushing to Addy's side. He bent down, cutting through the nylon cord that bound her. Pulling loose from the severed rope, Addy fell into Nick's open arms. She cried tears of happiness while Nick covered her face with frantic kisses.

"If anything had happened to you... if I'd lost you." Nick's voice quivered with the strength of his feelings.

Addy reached out, covering his cheek with her hand. She felt the damp stickiness of his sweat, and then she felt something else. Running her fingers upward, she looked at Nick. Tears filled his eyes.

"I'm all right. You saved me." She kissed him and hugged him and kept right on crying.

He held her in his arms, refusing to release her, even when Ned Johnson and Rusty McConnell came into the parlor. He wouldn't even let Rusty touch Addy. He couldn't bear the thought of letting her go. He'd never known what it was like to value someone else's life more than his own, to know that if she died, he didn't want to live, either. Addy McConnell was his whole world, and he was never going to let her out of his sight again. Not for the rest of their lives.

Guilt riddled his insides like a spray of buckshot. He blamed himself for the nightmare Addy had endured at Brett Windsor's hands. He had suspected the guy was capable of doing practically anything for money, but he'd allowed his past relationship with Dina to blind him to the possibility that she was an accomplice. Damn, he felt like a fool and could only imagine how Rusty McConnell felt. Addy's father had fallen in love with Dina and brought her into their lives. He had to feel guilty as hell.

Nick kept reliving the evening at the hospital when he'd left Addy in Alan Sturges's care. He'd had no idea he was risking Addy's life by trusting someone else to keep her safe. As long as he lived, he would hear Elizabeth Mallory's warning just before he and Addy had left Sequana Falls. *Keep her guarded every moment.* If only he had listened to that warning, Brett Windsor would never have gotten to Addy, would never have put her through a living hell.

When Addy had needed him most, he had let her down. It was his fault that she'd almost died—that she'd come so close to being blown into a zillion pieces. Just the thought of it gave him cold sweats. He should have realized the NASP contract was nothing more than a red herring, which would have ruled out Gerald Carlton. And he should have realized sooner that Ron Glover might be devious enough to plot Addy's kidnapping, but he wasn't smart enough to plan it. If he'd known Janice Dixon better, he would have known she loved her cousin and uncle far too much to have done anything to harm them.

Dina. Damn the woman! And bless her, too. He had to give her credit. When it came right down to it, she hadn't been able to turn a blind eye and let Brett kill Addy. If Dina hadn't finally admitted the truth to Rusty, then Nick had no idea what would have happened. Rusty and Dina's arrival at Elm Hill, along with Ned Johnson and his FBI agents, had put an end to Brett's evil plans.

And there was one thing Nick knew for sure—he owed his life to Dina. She'd taken the bullet that had been meant for him. Maybe it had been her way of trying to make amends, her final chance for forgiveness. It seemed wrong, somehow, that a woman as vibrantly alive as Dina should have died so tragically. But if she had lived, what would the future have held for her? Prison? After all, she'd been an accomplice to two kidnappings and two murders.

"Almost everybody's gone." Addy stood in the doorway of her father's den. "Janice and Ron are still here, and as usual he's moody and surly."

"How's Rusty? He seemed to hold up all right during the funeral."

"I haven't seen him so unhappy and sad since—since Mother died. It'll take him quite a while to get over Dina, especially her betrayal."

"Rusty's tough. He'll bounce back eventually. Who knows, he might even fall in love again."

"Ginger's with him now. She's fixed him a plate, and they're sitting in the kitchen eating. She cares about Daddy, and—and I think she's good for him." Addy entered the den, hesitating slightly before moving to Nick's side. "Don't you want something to eat?" She slipped her arm through his.

He stiffened. He didn't deserve her love. His stupidity had almost cost her her life. "I'll eat later."

"I know the funeral was as difficult for you as it was for Daddy." Addy ran the tips of her fingers down Nick's arm until she reached his hand. She laced her fingers through his. "Dina was the first woman you ever loved."

He squeezed her hand with such force that she cried out. "I'm sorry." Loosening his grip, he tried to pull away, but Addy wouldn't let go of his hand.

"It's all right that you loved her, Nick. Stop hating yourself because you cared about Dina, because you didn't think she was capable of the things she and Brett did. Daddy loved her. He trusted her. Even I never once considered Dina a suspect." Knowing that Nick was eaten alive with guilt,

Addy longed to help him forgive himself for being human enough to make mistakes.

"You'll never be able to forget what happened, and neither will I," Nick said, refusing to look at her, afraid he wouldn't be able to resist the love and understanding he'd see in her green eyes.

"No, we'll never forget, but in time—"

Nick brought Addy's hand to his lips, brushing tender kisses across her knuckles. "I let you down, Red. It was my fault that Windsor got to you. If I had done my job, you would have been safe."

She reached out, covering his cheek with her open palm. "Stop beating yourself up. If anyone is to blame, it's me for being foolish enough to sneak away to the elevator. I realized my mistake on the way down to the lobby, but by then it was too late. Brett was there waiting for me."

Nick jerked her into his arms, his dark eyes searching her face. "When I think about what could have happened."

"It didn't happen." Addy spread her arms around his waist, holding him tight. "You figured out where Brett had taken me. You rescued me, saved me, just as I knew you would. Haven't you figured it out, yet, Nick Romero? You're my knight in shining armor."

"Some knight! I'm afraid my armor is tarnished, Red. You've built me up into something I'm not. You think I'm so wonderful, such a damned hero, when all I am is an over-the-hill ex-SEAL and ex-DEA agent. A guy who's been everywhere, done everything and seen too much of the sick, evil, dark side of life."

"Why are you doing this? Why are you trying so hard to convince me what a bad guy you are?"

"Because I am a bad guy, Red." Shoving her out of his arms, he turned his back on her. "I can't possibly live up to the image you have of me." He walked toward the windows, stopping to stare sightlessly out onto the lawn. "Remember the man you met at Rusty and Dina's engagement party? You didn't like that man, Addy. You weren't impressed with him at all. Well, I'm still that same man."

"Yes, I suppose you are." Addy couldn't bear to think that she would lose him, but she could feel him slipping away from her. "I was wrong about you, though. There's a lot more to Nick Romero than his Latin lover-boy charm."

"Is there?" Nick had to make her realize that he wasn't in her league. She was head and shoulders above him, a woman who deserved only the best, and he didn't even come close. "You know what my SEAL buddies called me? Romeo. And believe me, I lived up to my nickname."

"I suppose I should be jealous of all those women, and I guess I am a little, but I'm also grateful to them." Smiling, Addy touched him on the shoulder. He cocked his head sideways so he could see her. "All that practice has made you a wonderful lover."

How the hell could she joke about it? He'd thought that reminding her of his past would make her see what poor husband material he'd make. "You just plain refuse to see me as I really am. You've created some fantasy man." He walked away from her. "I'll disappoint you, Red. I'll let you down. I'm no good at this commitment business."

"What are you so afraid of, Nick? Why are trying to put up walls between us?"

"I'm afraid of hurting you. I'm afraid that one day you'll wake up and realize what a mistake you made, that I'm not the man you thought I was."

Addy didn't go after him. She let him walk away, knowing that nothing she could say or do could make him feel any different about himself. Nick loved her as much as she loved him, but he thought she didn't really know him, that she saw him only as her rescuer, only as a lover. How could she prove to him that she knew exactly who he was?

Nick Romero, a flawed and imperfect man with a colorful and slightly unsavory past, was destined to be the father of her children. Somehow she'd just have to convince him that a reformed Romeo would make a faithful husband and an adoring father.

Three days after Dina's funeral, Addy McConnell went home, back to her house in the Twickenham district. Her father and Nick Romero accompanied her.

July had become viciously hot and humid, with heat indexes topping the hundred-degree mark daily. Tempers were short, moods constantly changing. She and Nick had spent little time together. His decision, not hers. He was trying to distance himself from her, to prepare her for his departure.

Addy suspected that today was the day Nick would make an attempt to leave her. But if he thought for one minute he'd ever get away from her, he'd better think again. She wasn't about to lose the best thing that had ever happened to her.

Addy served iced tea in the den. Rusty and Nick sat opposite each other, the older man inspecting the younger, eyeing him critically.

"You'll be settling down here in Huntsville, won't you?" Rusty asked. "Long-distance romances seldom work."

"Sam Dundee has offered me a job in Atlanta," Nick said.

"Hell, stay on here. Take over as security chief at M.A.C. Tandy McHenry will be retiring in a few months." Rusty puffed on his cigar, then blew smoke rings into the air.

Addy sat down beside Nick on the small sofa. She knew what game her father was playing. It was called "Running Addy's Life."

"Thanks for the offer, Rusty, but—"

"Damnation, boy, quit hem-hawing around." Rusty got to his feet, his ruddy, freckled face flushed with agitation. "You're staying here in Huntsville and marrying Addy, and that's final!"

"Daddy!"

"I hardly think it's your place to decide who Addy marries," Nick said.

"I'm her father, aren't I? Who better to pick out the right man for her?"

"I think Addy should have a say in this. After all, it's her life. If she's as smart as I think she is, she won't saddle herself with a guy like me for the rest of her life."

"You're perfect for her, and you know it," Rusty said.

"That's where you're wrong." Nick stood, facing Addy's father. "I'd wind up disappointing her. I don't know the first thing about love and commitment. Hell, I'm a forty-three-year-old bachelor."

"Boy, do you know how much Addy will be worth when I kick the bucket? She'll be one of the richest women in the United States."

"I don't give a damn about your money, about how rich Addy is. If I married Addy, I'd sign a prenuptial agreement. Addy, without one red cent, is worth a king's ransom. She's the kind of woman who's priceless."

Rusty grinned, his smile lighting his face. "I agree. A man would be a fool to run out on a woman like that, wouldn't he? Especially if the two of them are in love with each other and create red-hot sparks when they're in bed together."

"Daddy!" Addy jumped up, placing herself between the two bickering men. "I think this has gone far enough. You two are discussing me as if I'm not in the same room, as if I'm not perfectly capable of talking for myself."

Rusty glanced from his furious daughter to a dark and brooding Nick. Flashing them a brilliant smile, Rusty walked over to the door. "Well, girl, start talking before your man starts walking."

Addy stared at Nick. He stared back at her. They heard the front door slam and then Rusty's limousine pull out of the driveway. They continued staring at each other.

"I'll go upstairs and get my suitcase. I think that's where your father's new chauffeur put it." Nick turned to leave.

Addy grabbed his arm. "I want an autumn wedding. October or early November. It'll take that long to plan the kind of wedding we should have."

Nick glared at her, disbelief in his eyes. Had he heard her right? Had she said *wedding?* "What are you talking about?"

"I don't want an engagement ring. I'm not much on wearing a lot of jewelry. A simple, wide gold band will be fine."

"Addy?" He turned completely around, looking her directly in the eye.

"We should go back to Sequana Falls for the honeymoon and stay in our cottage. That's where you fell in love with me, wasn't it?"

"I haven't asked you . . . we haven't discussed—"

"Nick Romero, if you think I'm going to let you run out on me, then you don't know me very well. I've waited my whole life to love a man the way I love you. I didn't think it was possible. I thought people only felt this way in romance books or in the movies."

"I'm not much of a bargain, Red. I don't know the first thing about being the kind of husband you need."

Addy smiled. "If you run, I'll follow you. There's not a place on this earth where you can hide. You're going to marry me, Nick, and that's final."

How could he respond to a statement like that? Addy was one determined woman. Did he have the guts to take the risk? If he married her, could he keep her happy? "You'll be taking a mighty big chance on me, Red."

"Do you love me, Nick?"

"Do I— Yes, I love you!"

"Have you ever loved another woman the way you love me?"

"No, never."

"Then I'm not taking such a big risk, am I?"

Grinning, Nick lifted his cane, placing it across Addy's back. Taking the ends of the cane in each hand, he pulled her toward him, pressing her against his chest, fitting her body snugly to his. "As long as you know what you're getting."

"I know exactly what I'm getting." She slipped her arms around his neck. "I'm getting the man I love."

Nick and Addy lay in the middle of her antique bed, their naked arms and legs entwined. Damp with their mingled sweat and the sweet essence of sex, they kissed and stroked and whispered love words.

"Aren't you glad you decided to stay and marry me?" Addy licked the perspiration from his tiny male nipples.

He grabbed her hip in his big hand, pressing her closer to his side. "You're a very persuasive woman, Mrs. Romero-to-be."

"Mmm—hmm. I like the sound of that. Mrs. Romero. Addy Romero." She snuggled against him.

"I suppose you know that you've accomplished an impossible task," he said.

"What's that, taming a wild man?"

Nick laughed, playfully swatting her behind. "No. Capturing the most sought-after Latin lover in the world."

Moving quickly, Addy straddled his hips, tossing her long, flaming hair over her shoulder. "You've accomplished a task just as difficult. You've taught me what real love is all about."

Taking her hips in his hands, he moved her up and down, groaning when he felt a resurgence of passion tightening his body. "And I've also turned a Plain-Jane, frustrated old maid into a beautiful, sex-crazed hussy."

"Why, Nick, what a thing to say! I was never a frustrated old maid, just an unfulfilled woman."

"Woman, I'd like to fulfill you, and soon." He surged up against her, showing her he meant what he said.

"I think we should fulfill each other." She slid down his legs to his ankles, then lowered her body until her breasts touched his thighs. She ran her hands over his calves, caressing him.

"You've never said anything about my scarred leg." Nick threaded his fingers through her hair while she spread kisses over the top of his hairy thighs. "You've kissed it and caressed it, and you act as if it doesn't look any different from my good leg."

Addy's tongue touched him intimately. He groaned. "The scars on your leg are a part of you. When we make love, when I see you naked, I don't think about your crippled leg, except to regret all the pain you must have endured."

"I'm not quite the man I used to be because of—"

"Nick Romero, you're more man with a crippled leg than any man I know with two strong legs. I've told you that before. Weren't you listening?"

She stroked him, pleasuring him with her wanton tongue. "Ah, Addy, you're good for my ego."

"I'm good for *you*, Nick."

He didn't disagree. She moved up his body, straddling his hips again. He thrust himself up and into her, grasping her waist as his mouth sought her breasts. She rode him wild and hard. He gave her a thorough loving, losing control the minute he felt her tighten around him and cry out her release.

In the aftermath of a second heated mating, they lay in each other's arms, listening to the sound of their breathing. Sated and spent, they touched each other with tender weakness.

"I—I lost two babies when I was married to Gerald." Addy's voice sounded loud in the hushed stillness of her bedroom.

"I know." He kissed her forehead. "Your father told me all about it."

"The doctors said I might not be able to carry a baby full term." She took a deep breath.

Nick pulled her close, kissing her with gentle sweetness. "I love you, Addy. You." He kissed her again. "Whether or not we ever have a child won't change the way I feel about you. We're so damned lucky to have found each other. What more could we want?"

"I want to give you children."

"Addy, sweetheart—"

"Elizabeth said that I would have children. Your children." She smiled at him when he stared at her in confusion.

"Elizabeth saw children in our future?" God, he hoped Sam Dundee's little soothsayer knew what she was talking about. If ever a woman wanted and needed children, it was Addy.

"Two little girls, Nick. Maria will be the eldest. She'll be our little green-eyed brunette."

Nick raised up, bracing himself with his hand as he leaned over Addy. "Maria, huh? After my grandmother."

"And Maria's little sister will have my red hair and your black eyes. I want to name her Madeline after my mother."

The conviction in Addy's words made him believe these little girls would be a part of their future. Their finding each other and falling in love had been a miracle. Who was to say that God wouldn't grant them two more miracles? "You know what, Red? I can't think of anything I'd like better than to be surrounded by adoring females for the rest of my life."

"And I can't think of anything I'd like better than being one of those adoring females." She cuddled against him. "I love you, Red."

"I love you, too." Silently she added, I'll love you forever, *my paladin.*

*   *   *   *   *

HE'S AN
AMERICAN HERO

A cop, a fire fighter or even just a fearless drifter who gets the job done when ordinary men have given up. And you'll find one American Hero every month only in Intimate Moments—created by some of your favorite authors. This summer, Silhouette has lined up some of the hottest American heroes you'll ever find:

July: HELL ON WHEELS by Naomi Horton—Truck driver Shay McKittrick heads down a long, bumpy road when he discovers a scared stowaway in his rig....

August: DRAGONSLAYER by Emilie Richards—In a dangerous part of town, a man finds himself fighting a street gang—and his feelings for a beautiful woman....

September: ONE LAST CHANCE by Justine Davis—A tough-as-nails cop walks a fine line between devotion to duty and devotion to the only woman who could heal his broken heart....

AMERICAN HEROES: Men who give all they've got for their country, their work—the women they love.

IMHERO5

INTIMATE MOMENTS®
Silhouette®

Take 4 bestselling love stories FREE

Plus get a FREE surprise gift!

Special Limited-time Offer

Mail to Silhouette Reader Service™

P.O. Box 609
Fort Erie, Ontario
L2A 5X3

YES! Please send me 4 free Silhouette Intimate Moments® novels and my free surprise gift. Then send me 6 brand-new novels every month, which I will receive months before they appear in bookstores. Bill me at the low price of $2.96 each plus 25¢ delivery and GST*. That's the complete price and—compared to the cover prices of $3.50 each—quite a bargain! I understand that accepting the books and gift places me under no obligation ever to buy any books. I can always return a shipment and cancel at any time. Even if I never buy another book from Silhouette, the 4 free books and the surprise gift are mine to keep forever.

345 BPA AJJY

Name	(PLEASE PRINT)	
Address	Apt. No.	
City	Province	Postal Code

This offer is limited to one order per household and not valid to present Silhouette Intimate Moments® subscribers. *Terms and prices are subject to change without notice.
Canadian residents will be charged applicable provincial taxes and GST.

CMOM-93RR   ©1990 Harlequin Enterprises Limited

Silhouette Books has done it again!

Opening night in October has never been as exciting! Come watch as the curtain rises and romance flourishes when the stars of tomorrow make their debuts today!

Revel in Jodi O'Donnell's STILL SWEET ON HIM—
Silhouette Romance #969
...as Callie Farrell's renovation of the family homestead leads her straight into the arms of teenage crush Drew Barnett!

Tingle with Carol Devine's BEAUTY AND THE BEASTMASTER—
Silhouette Desire #816
...as legal eagle Amanda Tarkington is carried off by wrestler Bram Masterson!

Thrill to Elyn Day's A BED OF ROSES—
Silhouette Special Edition #846
...as Dana Whitaker's body and soul are healed by sexy physical therapist Michael Gordon!

Believe when Kylie Brant's McLAIN'S LAW —
Silhouette Intimate Moments #528
...takes you into detective Connor McLain's life as he falls for psychic—and suspect—Michele Easton!

Catch the classics of tomorrow—*premiering* today—
only from ▼ *Silhouette*

If you've been looking for something a little bit different and a little bit spooky, let Silhouette Books take you on a journey to the dark side of love with

V SILHOUETTE *Shadows*™

Every month, Silhouette will bring you two romantic, spine-tingling Shadows novels, written by some of your favorite authors, such as *New York Times* bestselling author Heather Graham Pozzessere, Anne Stuart, Helen R. Myers and Rachel Lee—to name just a few.

In July, look for:
HEART OF THE BEAST by Carla Cassidy
DARK ENCHANTMENT by Jane Toombs

In August, look for:
A SILENCE OF DREAMS by Barbara Faith
THE SEVENTH NIGHT by Amanda Stevens

In September, look for:
FOOTSTEPS IN THE NIGHT by Lee Karr
WHAT WAITS BELOW by Jane Toombs

*Come into the world of Shadows and prepare
to tremble with fear—and passion....*

Fifty red-blooded, white-hot, true-blue hunks from every
State in the Union!

Beginning in May, look for MEN MADE IN AMERICA!
Written by some of our most popular authors, these
stories feature fifty of the strongest, sexiest men, each
from a different state in the union!

Two titles available every other month at your favorite
retail outlet.

In September, look for:

DECEPTIONS by Annette Broadrick (California)
STORMWALKER by Dallas Schulze (Colorado)

In November, look for:

STRAIGHT FROM THE HEART by Barbara Delinsky
(Connecticut)
AUTHOR'S CHOICE by Elizabeth August (Delaware)

You won't be able to resist MEN MADE IN AMERICA!

What a year for romance!

Silhouette has five fabulous romance collections coming your way in 1993. Written by popular Silhouette authors, each story is a sensuous tale of love and life—as only Silhouette can give you!

SPRING FANCY
Three bachelors are footloose and fancy-free...until now.
(March)

Mother with Love
Heartwarming stories that celebrate the joy of motherhood.
(May)

SILHOUETTE SUMMER Sizzlers
Put some sizzle into your summer reading with three of Silhouette's hottest authors.
(June)

SILHOUETTE Shadows
Take a walk on the dark side of love—with tales just perfect for those misty autumn nights.
(October)

Silhouette CHRISTMAS Stories
Share in the joy of yuletide romance with four award-winning Silhouette authors.
(November)

Silhouette®

A romance for all seasons—it's always time for romance with Silhouette!

Silhouette Books
is proud to present
our best authors,
their best books...
and the best in
your reading pleasure!

Throughout 1993, look for exciting
books by these top names in
contemporary romance:

DIANA PALMER—
Fire and Ice in June

ELIZABETH LOWELL—
Fever in July

CATHERINE COULTER—
Afterglow in August

LINDA HOWARD—
Come Lie With Me in September

When it comes to passion,
we wrote the book.

BOBT2

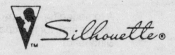